UPSY-DAISY

JACK BARRATT

Matador
9 Priory Business Park,
Wistow Road, Kibworth Beauchamp,
Leicestershire. LE8 0RX
Tel: 0116 279 2299
Email: books@troubador.co.uk
Web: www.troubador.co.uk/matador
Twitter: @matadorbooks

ISBN 978 1838593 223

British Library Cataloguing in Publication Data.
A catalogue record for this book is available from the British Library.

Printed and bound in Great Britain by 4edge Limited
Typeset in 12pt Minion Pro by Troubador Publishing Ltd, Leicester, UK

Matador is an imprint of Troubador Publishing Ltd

UPSY-DAISY

I dedicate this novel to Edward Reece: actor and writer, who read his own stories on the BBC.

Sadly, by the time *Upsy-Daisy* was published, Ted had passed away.

ONE

Wally Watson stood to attention as though he were still a squaddie. He stood tall, exuding confidence. Before him, behind the grill, sat a contrasting species, Mr Julius Grimshaw – thick lenses, overweight, unfit. To Wally, used to vigour and vitality, his interlocutor seemed insipid like cheap beer.

'I'm sitting in for Mr Gregory who's unwell.' Julius twirled a pencil between his fat fingers.

Wally nodded understandingly, seriously. In fact he almost saluted, then quickly realised he was in the council offices, and not a military mess.

'So I'll deal with your application,' continued Mr Grimshaw, who then coughed, and phlegm rattled round his throat like in a pinball machine. 'What job have you done during the last few years, Mr... erm...?' He glanced at the application form.

'Watson. Walter Watson. Most of the time I was in the army.'

'Really. Well, that's interesting.' Julius chanced a little quip. 'Nobody will try it on with you, will they?'

'Yes, they will. But only once. Have you served, might I ask?' ventured Wally.

Julius looked up at him. 'Still serving, Mr Watson.'

Surprised, Wally stood even taller. 'Which outfit?'

'The Lord's.'

A frown creased Wally's brow; his eyebrows met like dark wool on knitting needles. 'The Lord's…? The cricket pitch?'

'No. Higher than that.' He tapped a silver cross on his lapel.

Wally smiled out of respect. 'Ah, the Sally.'

'No,' said Grimshaw. 'Superb though the Salvation Army are, my mob is higher.'

Again Wally frowned, an elongated twitch. 'Er… on the roof?'

Julius Grimshaw looked quickly about him, as though eavesdroppers might be lurking. 'No. Higher! The sky.'

Then the working man's wisdom of Wally clicked in: *This chap's a religious nutcase.* But he didn't want to offend, so he said, 'The sky! Well, you can't climb higher than that.'

A change visited Mr Grimshaw's jowls like sparse mist settling on tiny hillocks and his eyes became dreamy. 'You could climb with us on Sunday mornings at The Sanctuary in Daisy Hill.'

Wally swallowed and thought quickly. 'Ah, on the Sabbath I try to help others. I often visit my mother in Yorkshire.' This, in fact, was quite true. He was due to go. 'But I'll think about your offer. Now, about this grass-cutting job.'

Mr Grimshaw reluctantly abandoned the unknown vague future for the council's active present. 'Ah yes. Clock on at the old gas works, eight o'clock sharp, Monday morning.'

Not relishing recruitment for anything else, Wally presented a neat soldier's dismissal and marched from the council offices, rolling his eyes as he passed a young waiting couple.

❦

Dick and Josephine sat in the council offices, in the housing department, waiting for Mr Grimshaw, the housing officer. They seemed to have been waiting for two long weeks, perhaps three, and were fidgeting like bored children with impatience. Eventually he arrived just as Dick hummed, 'Here Comes the Bride'. Jo elbowed him.

Mr Grimshaw was a roly-poly, and carried a cup of hot coffee and biscuits.

'Sorry I kept you waiting.' His double chin wobbled in time with his half-truth. He raised his coffee cup as if to propose a toast but sat down instead and nibbled on a custard cream. 'Got to keep the pecker up, eh!'

Jo was fascinated by the double chin, which had a life of its own. 'Well, we all need our caffeine shot at times.'

'What can I help you with?' He gulped his coffee; the chin wobbled, syncopating with the words.

'We'd like a council house,' Dick said. Jo tapped him with her foot. 'Please,' he added.

'I'll bet you would.' Mr Grimshaw's voice was grimmer than his name. 'So would hundreds round these parts. It's a problem for us all,' he added, fondly stroking his stomach. 'I'm afraid we haven't enough houses to go round. However, I'll put you on the list.'

Dick, rather partial to Gilbert and Sullivan, whistled a strain of 'I've Got a Little List'. Once again Jo kicked him.

Mr Grimshaw stretched out a burly arm, dipped into a box and extracted a form. 'Where are you living at present?'

'At hers.'

'But we are overcrowded since my brother returned from Afghanistan.'

'We've been kipping in his bedroom, but now we're back on the sofa.'

'What, all three of you?'

'No!' *You old fool*, thought Dick, but said, 'Me and the wife.'

'It's only a two-bedroom terrace,' Jo explained, 'and my parents sleep in the front bedroom.'

'Well, at least you're not on the street,' observed the housing officer.

'That's true,' Dick agreed. 'But I've got my eye on a covered alleyway if that happens.' He felt suddenly cheesed off and wanted to shout, 'You dozy, bloated bleeder.' But feared a red card from Fatty and a kick from his wife, so he just sighed.

Mr Grimshaw nibbled another custard cream, slurped his coffee and his chin wobbled with ecstasy. 'State your current address, and if anything turns up I'll inform you.' He scribbled away, the biro ran dry and Dick's patience expired.

'What a bloody clown.'

'Pardon?' Mr Grimshaw peered over his glasses.

Jo kicked Dick. 'Get some... muddy brown... paint... for my dad's shed. We're painting it. Thank you. We'll be off.' She manhandled Dick from the building, and whispered, '*You're* the clown. We depend on berks, er, clerks like him to help us.' During their brief interview, a client in the adjacent cubicle had heard all that ensued and laughed lightly at some of it. He'd merely called to pay out an employee's fire claim. He rose and followed the housing hopefuls into the car park and watched as they climbed into a white van. Before the ignition had been turned, the stranger caught them up and tapped on the driver's window.

✤

In the council offices car park, Wally cocked a long leg over an ancient sit-up-and-beg bike and pedalled smartly away. He loved his cycle, which was cheap – free in fact – to use and kept him healthy. Head down he pedalled towards Daisy Hill, Down Daisy and Upsy-Daisy. He pedalled at a steady fifteen miles an hour and arrived at the crossroads, where a pleasant briny smell told him he was almost home.

He was about to turn left and head for the caravan park when he noticed a young woman leaning over her cycle with frustration written all over her. He dismounted and walked across.

'Hiya… Problems?'

'Yes, but I don't know exactly what.'

Wally leaned his own wheelie against a wall then took hers and stooped over it.

'The chain keeps coming off,' she explained.

He walked back to his own mount, and from the carrier bag under the saddle took out a rolled leather sheathing which he spread on the ground, and unrolled it, displaying an array of implements and gadgets. He selected a small spanner.

'See this bolt going through the centre of the back wheel?' He tapped it with the spanner. 'Well, the nuts on either side have to be kept tight, otherwise the wheel moves towards the front of the bike and the chain becomes slack.' He pulled back the chain and tightened the nuts. 'There y' are. Job done.'

'Oh, you are kind.'

'I know that, love. It's my weakness. Well, that and lovely lasses. Any road, it'll take you home.' He gazed at her. She had green eyes. She was lovely. *Oh yes. I fancy her*, he told himself.

'Thank you. I've just got to go as far as the church in Daisy Hill,' she said.

He grabbed his own bike and bounced away, calling, 'Don't do anything I wouldn't do.'

Dick wound down the window and glowered at the person interrupting his irritation.

'Sorry to accost you, sir, but I couldn't help but overhear what the fat fellow said.' He thumbed back over his shoulder towards the ostentatious council offices. 'If they had spent less on that buildings they could have built more council houses. However, I might be able to help.'

'With a house?' asked Jo.

He nodded and smiled.

'What's the catch?' demanded Dick.

'No catch. Just step outside so's we can talk.'

Jo was out and round the back of the van in a flash. Dick, weary of it all, clambered out slowly.

'My name is Vic Venables. I'm a freelance insurance broker and I come into contact with various folk, sometimes putting one person in touch with another. Apparently you young people are living with this young lady's parents.'

'Only until we can get, well, afford a place of our own,' put in Jo, hastily.

'And when do you think that will be?' asked Victor, but not unkindly.

The young couple eyed each other, shuffled; Dick gazed at his shoes, noticed they needed repairing.

'Would you be willing to live in a two-berth caravan?'

'You bet,' she said.

'Yeah,' agreed Dick. 'But I repeat: what's the catch?'

Vic smiled, showing a gold incisor. 'There is none. Unless you regard doing an easy part-time job a snag? A job where the money's not bad. A caravan where the rent is cheap. Before you ask, the job is collecting insurance premiums that I can't get round to myself. Reminding customers their insurance is due. Selling a policy when you can, for which you receive commission. And you get a retainer for collecting premiums and expenses for petrol. Not a bad number, eh?'

'I thought collecting insurance money had been done away with?'

'No, young sir. Not quite. You are referring to life policies and endowments. I am talking about general branch: motor, fire, accident, and so forth. We sell goods on tick as well. And you need transport, which I see you have.' He raised apprehensive eyebrows at Dick's van.

'Yeah! I know it's a bit tatty,' Dick admitted.

'Collecting insurance money does not require a Rolls-Royce… Interested?'

Together they sang, 'Yes.'

'Right. I'll be in touch. Meanwhile, here's the address.' He wrote it neatly on a page from an accounts book and handed it over. 'Ask for Mrs Marks. Tell her Victor has sent you. I believe the van is still available.'

With that, Victor Venables walked to his small but flashy saloon car, revved it up and sped away.

The young couple, stunned, looked at each other and smiled then threw their arms about each other.

'Break,' shouted Dick. 'I need air.'

'What are we waiting for?' said Jo, with a smile as wide as her face.

Dick jumped back in the van. 'You navigate and I'll drive.' He glanced at the address. 'Upsy-Daisy, here we come.'

❀

Wally dismounted and looked round at the caravan site. 'It's tatty, but it grows on you,' he muttered. They'd have to manage without him this weekend, he'd promised to visit his parents.

TWO

On the third try Dick managed to start the van. He then zoomed away with a plume of celebratory smoke from the exhaust, and followed directions towards the North Norfolk coast.

He proclaimed his current happiness by humming, 'Onward, Christian Soldiers'. Then he stopped, mid-refrain. 'It has a funny name, hasn't it, this caravan site? Upsy-Daisy!'

'I think it sounds sweet.'

'Sweet or sour, we need it.'

The van travelled at a steady thirty-five as Jo watched the scenery slide leisurely by. Built-up areas gave way to countryside; fat-fleeced sheep grazed on green stubble, eating a decapitated crop from the previous harvest. In the next field, early shoots of winter wheat – harvested in April – poked exploratory fingers through rich, black soil.

'Jo, keep your eyes peeled for a signpost.'

Three sleek, frisky foals gambolled round a shady paddock and the following field was an estate of pig huts, and the residents rolled around in glorious mud. Dick and Jo came to a crossroads displaying a signpost. 'Daisy Hill straight on,' Dick said. 'Down Daisy to the left.'

'And Upsy-Daisy to the right,' said Jo, and her eyes smiled as she pointed, obviously glad to be getting a home of their own.

Dick steered the vehicle harshly into a narrow lane; it protested with squealing wheels. On either side, clipped hedges bristled with short back and sides and they bumped along to another sign.

'Upsy-Daisy,' sang Jo. Then her face dropped, matching her complaint. 'I thought it was a caravan site!'

'Well, it's, erm, a mixture,' he explained by way of assurance. 'Part site, part… er, village.'

A dozen caravans were on display and they all had one thing in common: they were all tatty.

'But, it seems, it's a dump.' Dismay coloured his voice like one who's lost a football match. 'All I can hope for is that the van Venables suggested is habitable.'

'Or inhabited,' she giggled.

Dick caught on and they chuckled together. 'Then we can continue our search.'

'Look at that,' she exclaimed. 'Really! Thomas the Tank Engine country.'

Two 1930s railway coaches stood, looking forlorn, as though all the best bits had been purloined by railway enthusiasts. But the coaches still boasted their maroon exteriors. Almost opposite, a short way along, stood an old caravan with a sign: 'Site Shop'.

Dick brought his van to a halt underneath the sign, and in front of the shop.

'I'll enquire here.' He swung from his driving seat and entered the shop, to be met by a rotund proprietor. 'Hello,' he said brightly. 'I'm looking for Mrs Marks.'

'You're looking at her.' She rolled a cigarette along badly drawn vermillion lips. Behind her a sign proclaimed: 'Smoking Is Dangerous'.

'Ah! Good afternoon. My name is Richard Coningsby. A Mr Victor Venables suggested I should contact you.'

'Right.' She puffed smoke signals. 'Contact me about what?'

'About, er, renting a caravan.'

'Got your passport?' She grinned, displaying coloured teeth: brown and grey. 'Don't fret, son. Just my little joke. But are you going to collect for him – for Vic?' She walked round her counter, feeling the texture of a white wrapped loaf. 'Y' see, collectors get a cheaper rent. Vic will sort that out when he gets here.'

Dick made a mental note not to buy any bread from here.

'Well, how do we gain access? To the caravan? Me and my wife?'

Mrs Marks took a key from a hook. The key had a

label on it. 'Here y' are. Further along. Blue and white van… Have you any kids?'

'Er, no. We've not been married long.'

Her pencilled eyebrows showed some surprise by springing up to her hairline. 'Since when did that matter? Only I have lots of nice toffees.' She wiggled a fat finger, topped with a green nail, at a row of coloured sweets in large glass jars.

Dick smiled, thanked her and backed out of the shop, as though guarding his back pocket. Back in his white van he said, 'Never buy anything edible from that dump. Right, blue and white caravan, further along.' He turned on the ignition, and, being warm, it responded, so they were able to jerk, kangaroo style, to their new home. When they stopped, Jo observed, 'Not very big, is it?' Her top lip went up at one corner.

Desperate for everything to go well, he said, 'Well, it's not bad. OK, it only has two berths, but there's only two of us. And it's better than your mother's sofa.' Before he inserted the key he read the label stuck to the door – 'For Victor's collectors' – and as they let themselves in, he mused that it must be an important job – or at least Venables must be an important person.

'It's not very warm,' remarked Jo.

'It will be when we get steamed up.' He flicked a switch and an electric fire sprang to life, offering them a ruddy welcome. They tried various switches, all of which responded. 'Oh, great, everything's working.'

Jo entered the tiny kitchen and spied a kettle. 'I'll make some tea.'

'You have to fill that plastic container with clean water first. Look, somebody outside has just filled their container with fresh water from a tap. I'll fill ours.'

An elderly resident was filling his water container as Dick approached the tap. The man stopped the tap, changed hands and turned the water on again. 'These containers get heavy. You have to be ambidextrous.'

'Oh, that leaves me out,' Dick said. 'I'm Sagittarius.'

The elderly gent wrinkled a puzzled brow, then staggered off, weighed down with his container.

'I'm only jok… Oh, what's the point.' Dick filled his container then returned to his caravan. 'I wouldn't say they are all highly intelligent here, Jo.'

'We should fit in then. You'll need to buy some milk.'

'Oh no! Not from the site shop. It's tatty.'

'What about dried milk, so's she'll only handle the packet?'

'OK. Let's both go. I'll introduce you,' he laughed.

They left the van, walked along and reluctantly entered the site shop. 'Hello, Mrs Marks. It's me again. This is my wife, Jo.'

'Joe! Joseph?'

'No, no. Josephine, as in…'

'Not tonight, eh.' And Mrs Marks wobbled with her own mirth.

Dick's eyes wandered for the second more painstaking time round the grubby emporium. In front of the chipped counter a sack of spuds vaunting green shoots crouched like a dropout in a side street. The cellophane-wrapped white loaf, earlier fondled by Mrs Marks, had gone, to provide the staff of life for some innocent site dweller's high tea. His thoughts were interrupted by his wife's voice.

'I was wondering if you had any dried milk.'

'Better than that. I stock the fresh stuff. The real McCoy.'

'No thanks, it has to be dried. Y' know, in a packet.'

Mrs Marks stooped under the counter. A sliding door slid and the retailer produced the requested packet, which was surprisingly clean. The price was displayed on the packet and Jo was able to present the correct money.

'Thank you, ducky. It's cash only here. I don't do cards.' Then she produced another key. 'This is for the privy. Your own private privy. Obviously you've not used it yet. Every van has its own. All mod cons here, y' know – well, mostly. You're new to this?'

'New to an organised site,' said Dick.

Mrs Marks seemed to swell with importance. 'You'll learn. But there are rules. No livestock. Empty your own Elsan. Patronise the site shop.'

Dick took in the mess. 'But…'

'And no buts.'

At that point the phone rang. She extricated it from under a pile of knitting wool on the counter and wedged the instrument under her ample chin. The customers heard a voice but not the meaning. Then she smirked, grimaced and shrieked.

'And make sure you bloody well do. If you catch the last train again, you'll catch my fist. I read your cup after you'd gone, and it don't half give you away, not half it don't.'

She rummaged in a large box of wool, as though to produce knitting needles, but instead brought out a stained teacup which she passed to Dick who held it betwixt finger and thumb.

'Plain as daylight, it is,' she shouted down the phone. Dick winced. 'A brazen bitch a-swiggin' a Guinness.' The voice on the phone protested, but she shouted it down. 'And she's half naked. I know your game, Markie. But I've got the proof. It's in the bleedin' cup. Isn't it?' she said to Dick, who peered apprehensively into it.

'Well, I'm not sure…'

'There you are. He can see it… Who? Mr thingy here, a new tenant. Our new arrival. Course he's clean. And he's a witness. Ain't you?' she said to Dick, and rapped his knuckles with a pencil.

'Oho. Yes, of course.'

'There y' are. He can see her as bold as brass. Well, think on you do.' And she slammed the phone down.

'You men are all the same… I'll tell *your* fortune sometime.'

'Oh, thank you. Well, I think we'll go.'

'Half price, if you pay in advance,' she said.

'Oh, thanks. That's decent. We've never had a rent reduction before.'

'Rent?' She glared at him. 'I'm talking about reading tea leaves.'

Dick took two steps back, and held his right hand limply, the hand with which he'd held the cup. 'By the way, darling, we need a Dettol spray.'

Mrs Marks stooped beneath her counter and produced one. 'There y' are, borrow mine, but bring it back.'

'Thank you so much,' Dick said and began to retreat from the shop, jerking his head at Jo to follow as though he had a twitch. Outside, he breathed deeply. 'Thank God for that.' They walked towards their van.

'I don't remember saying we needed a Dettol spray,' Jo said.

He began to spray his right hand. 'After holding that dreadful cup, I need delousing.'

The elderly gentleman who had filled his water container earlier walked by them. 'Ah, we meet again.' He held out his hand; Dick shook it. 'Major Merryweather. At your service.' He turned and bowed to Jo.

'Pleased to meet you,' she said.

'New arrivals, eh! Have you reported to the guard room?' He thumbed over his shoulder.

'Oh, you mean the shop,' she said. 'Yes, we've just been in.'

'But you managed to escape.'

They both laughed. 'Yes, it's a bit topsy-turvy, eh!' said Dick.

'As well as Upsy-Daisy,' the Major added, and, chuckling, walked away whistling 'Colonel Bogey'.

They went into their caravan and brewed two

mugs of tea, adding dried milk diluted with cold water. 'Oh, not a bad drink after all,' Dick said.

'Quite nice. My mum reckons dried milk came into its own during the war, with the rationing, when she was a girl.'

'Did you know, if Nazi Germany had invaded, this area is one of the places they would have landed?'

Jo opened a packet of coconut biscuits and offered one to Dick.

'I trust you didn't buy these from the site shop?'

'No fear,' she said. 'I already had them. Anyway, these are protected in a packet. But how do you know about that?'

He took a final swig of his tea and placed the empty mug on the hinged table top. He frowned. 'Know about what?'

'About the war? About that invasion which didn't happen?'

'I read about it, of course. It's our history. I like history. If I'd been a bit brighter, I could have been a history teacher.'

'So what,' she said. 'If I'd been a bit brighter, I could have been an accountant or even a politician.'

'If I'd been a *lot* brighter, I could have been a genius… Ney, ney, ney ney ney,' he sang nasally.

She reached over and pulled his hair. 'Big baby. Well, instead of history, let's study geography.'

'Ow. That's too hard. So… what do you want to know?'

'I want to know about this sight for sore eyes.

This site. This dump. Let's go out and do a bit of geographying.'

It was now late afternoon and the weather itself had developed a chill. So the new residents each donned an anorak, stepped outside and locked the door. No sooner were they on the footpath than they heard music in the distance. They headed eastwards, towards the sea.

'Sounds like Classic FM,' Dick said, cupping an ear.

'Could be Radio Norfolk, but it's too far away to tell.'

They walked up the incline, a turf of coarse grass which gave way to sand at the top of the rise. The hummock stood about 300 yards away from their caravan. They paused on the summit and looked out towards the sea.

'It's beautiful,' she breathed. 'What a lovely view.'

'Right! So, *we* can boast a sea view from our house.'

'House? Caravan. Ugh!'

'Your mum's sofa didn't have a sea view.'

'Sorry, love. I'll try not to be so despondent. We're actually lucky compared to some folk.'

'Well, this morning, grumbling Mr Fat Arse didn't or wouldn't offer us…'

'Who?'

'Grimshaw, council offices. He did bugger all for us. Now he doesn't need to bother. We have our own place.'

'Listen! That music is a bit clearer.' They stopped, looked about them but couldn't see anyone. 'It's a Strauss waltz,' she said.

'Yeah, like I said, Classic FM.'

'Oh, look, a boat.' She almost skipped on the spot. 'They're waving to us.'

'Be polite. Wave back.'

As Jo enthusiastically returned the greeting, the music sounded slightly nearer. A small man, who'd been curled up by a comfortable sand dune, emerged from behind his bolthole and approached them from behind, a transistor radio slung round his neck. As Jo, preoccupied, raised her arms to wave, the man took it as an invitation to dance. He cupped her left hand in his right, placed his left arm round her waist (but not too close) and took a step. Jo, a dancer since her teenage years, though momentarily surprised, went with the rhythm and waltzed a few steps. After eight bars, the music stopped – and Dick applauded.

'Well done. You wouldn't get that in a council house!'

'Ah! I take it you are new here.' He shook Dick's hand. 'Sparrow. Septimus Sparrow. At your service.'

It was years since Dick had been greeted thus. 'And your service is indeed welcome. And this lovely lady is my wife, Josephine. Shortened to Jo. Well, *she's* not shortened, just the name.'

'A lovely lady with a snappy name,' he said quickly. 'Any time you feel the urge…'

'Urge?' she echoed, slightly alarmed.

'To dance. The urge to dance.' His eyes twinkled. 'I'm your man. Good day to you both.' He bowed and as the radio played a samba, he danced away down the hill.

They laughed lightly at his exit. 'What a funny little man,' said Jo. 'Funny, but nice with it. And he has a lovely head of curls. Quite unusual.'

They had one last look at the sea. The boat was now out of sight, so they turned and followed Mr Septimus Sparrow at a distance. They arrived at the water tap, which was almost opposite their caravan, and found the Major filling his container again.

He stood erect and clicked his heels, and seemed about to salute but changed his mind. 'Ah, Merryweather again. Major Merryweather. Late…'

'Royal Infantry,' supplied Dick.

The Major stopped the running tap. 'Waste not want not. Can I guess: the professor has been entertaining you!'

'The Professor?'

The Major nodded.

'Oh! The little man with the lovely curls!' replied Jo. She laughed. 'Yes, we enjoyed a little dance.'

'Is that what you call him then: the Professor?' Dick added.

'We do. If it's not music, it's physical culture, or butterflies, or creative writing. Brainy, but barmy, that's the Prof. He changes like a chameleon. Completely harmless, mind you.'

'Well, at least he's interesting,' Jo said. Then she pointed behind them. 'Look, in the distance, over the tops of those trees.'

Well inland from the coast, just beyond the caravan site, stood a narrow forest of trees – beech, birch and oak – defining the perimeter of a field.

High above the trees, hundreds of starlings flew in acrobatic curves, murmuration, producing patterns of black waves in the sky.

'That's how they protect themselves from birds of prey,' explained the Major. 'You have to show the enemy he is outnumbered.'

'While you two are chatting I'll go and put the kettle on. Give me the key, love.' She went up the steps into the caravan.

The Major's eyes widened as he took in her shapely figure.

'Dear boy, your wife is a devilish good looker, what!' The Major took a step nearer and spoke in a confidential manner. 'Is she ever left on her own?'

Dick became slightly alarmed. 'Pardon?'

'Is she ever left on her own?' The Major looked smartly about him, in case an enemy agent lurked close by.

'Well, we haven't been married long, so I don't leave her alone, since…'

'No, no. Not that. Alone. Isolated.'

'Ah! On her tod! Well, sometimes. I do need to go out!' Dick couldn't see where this line of questioning was getting him.

'At night?' persisted the Major mysteriously.

'Well, it depends. I mean… I don't make a habit of, er…'

'Don't hedge, man.' The Major was now back in his regiment addressing a private. 'Tell me. Is she or isn't she?'

'Left alone at night? Well, not all night.'

The conversation took on a conspiracy, at least a whispering campaign. The Major breathed out his whisky fumes; Dick breathed them in, then retreated a step.

'Part of the night is enough. Ten minutes is long enough. I'll fix her up.'

'You what?'

'I'll fix her up.' A gleam invaded the Major's left eye. His right eye twitched. 'With your permission, of course.'

'Oh! That's kind.' Dick wondered if he could recall his unarmed combat tactics.

'Don't worry. Leave her to me. I've fixed up all the ladies who live alone, and those whose menfolk work at night.'

'Have you, indeed!'

The Major seemed to swell. A middle-aged toothy resident walked by, towards the sea. 'Good evening, Major.' She strolled on. He saluted her with his cane.

'That's one of mine,' he muttered. He spoke quieter. 'She still owes me.'

'They pay you?'

'Well, they should do. I've only got my army pension. You see… there's a snooper on the site.'

'A snooper?'

The fumes came again, like a breeze wafting through a brewery.

'A snooper,' asserted the Major. 'A peeping Tom. A flasher. Call him what you will. And I'm out to get the bounder. And when I do, I'll cut his ears off. I'm rigging up an alarm system. Top secret.'

'Of course. Hush-hush, eh!' The man obviously needed pacifying.

'And I'll fix your wife up, too. Permission granted? Good man. Leave it to me.'

Dick relaxed. 'Ah. I see.'

Jo reappeared, but instead of tea she offered a tray of drinks. 'A drink, Major? Only cooking sherry, I'm afraid.'

'Delighted, my dear. Thank you.'

With some relief in his voice, Dick said, 'Who was the woman who passed?'

'Miss Primm. Rather haughty.'

'And you've fixed her up?' Dick said, and watched Jo's face.

'Well, I shall finish her off tonight, I expect.'

'I hope you enjoy it,' Dick said, and, grinning, glanced at Jo's expression, a mixture of horror and intrigue.

'I shall. One has to. Otherwise the job isn't done properly. But she had a nasty shock the other night.'

'I'll bet she did,' said Jo, quietly.

Then, providing the denouement, the Major exclaimed, 'The snooper burst in on her.'

Dick, imagining Miss Primm in her nightgown, with her horsey teeth protruding said, 'I bet he had a bit of a shock too.'

The Major nodded sagely. 'So I'll fix her up good and proper, tonight.'

'Good,' said Dick. 'The best of luck.'

'So...' The Major knocked back his sherry. 'Next time he's on the prowl...'

'Listen for the howl,' said Jo.

'Very apt, my dear… er, Mrs…'

'Coningsby. My Sunday name is Josephine Coningsby. And apart from your military connection, you are…?'

He seemed to wriggle, as though embarrassed. 'Well, I was baptised Algernon Pier, because I, er, was, er…'

'Fertilised under the pier,' she said, with relish.

'Blackpool or Brighton?' Dick enquired.

The Major took it in good spirit and walked away, laughing.

'What was the lewd talk while I was in the van?' she asked.

'He just wants to fix you up like he fixes up all the ladies.'

'I'm flattered, I'm sure. Would that be in lieu of rent?'

Dick laughed. 'That could be arranged, I suppose. No, he wants to fix you up with an alarm system. There's a snooper at large and the Major, even without a platoon, wants to nab him. He asked if you were left alone at night.'

'And you said…?'

'I told him you keep crying out, "Leave me alone, leave me alone".'

She clipped his ear. 'Listen, you get down to that shop we saw in the village. We need bacon, eggs and bread. Meanwhile, I'll tidy up here.'

Dick moved off towards his white van. 'OK,' he called. 'Keep your eyes peeled for the snooper.'

Jo went back into the caravan where she set the table for an early supper. Then from an old-fashioned wattle box she took out a frying pan. Tonight would mark its initial use. She looked at the shiny pan and her reflection looked back at her. It was almost a pity to spoil the newness of the pan. Now she placed cups *and* saucers on the table – which was like a trestle hinged to the wall of the van. *It'll be a nice change from always drinking from mugs,* Jo decided. When she believed all was organised she sat and waited for Richard, as she often referred to him, and leafed through a fashion magazine. Ten minutes later he came in, laden with produce.

'So, the Co-op *was* open, then?' she confirmed.

'Yes. I got everything. It's a clean shop.' He placed a full hessian carrier bag on one of the high stools, then unpacked the contents and placed them on the table. 'That's the lot. Do you think you're going to enjoy it here?'

'I enjoy it anywhere, dear.' She winked. 'Did you notice many people on the site?'

'Not many. It's quiet on the whole. In that nice shop, I spoke to a bloke from this site who told me there's a swimming pool here. That's marvellous, isn't it?'

Jo lit the electric stove and placed the new frying pan on it, then slipped in a smidgen of butter. She placed in the smoked bacon, allowing it to sizzle. 'A swimming pool, eh!'

'Yes. Early morning dips. Think of it.'

'Yes. I'm thinking. If I recall you're terrified of water.'

He bridled. 'Don't be ridiculous.'

'Last year, at Eastbourne, you never went in once.'

As he made a pot of tea and allowed it to brew, he justified himself. 'I paddled.'

'True. In your wellingtons.' She turned the bacon in the pan.

A sulky look caused his face to droop. 'That's due to my feet. I can't walk on pebbles.'

Jo placed the bacon on a warm plate and covered it with another. 'Piffle. You wouldn't even venture out in the speedboat.'

'And why was that? I say, why?'

'Because… you're terrified of water.' She was enjoying this spat. She cracked two eggs into the pan and at once they sizzled. 'Why was it then?'

'Alright, if you really want to know: I had a boil.'

Now she fried two large tomatoes. 'The fresh air would have done it good.'

Dick poured two cups of tea then added milk. 'Fresh air couldn't get to it. Sitting down was quite painful.'

Jo divided eggs, bacon and tomatoes equally on two hot dinner plates. 'Huh, you spent the whole day sitting in a deck chair.'

He sat on a tall stool, folded his arms and tried to look assertive. 'That was different.'

'Richard, don't shout.'

'Sitting down in salt water inflamed it. That is why I decided not to go swimming.'

Jo placed the two plates of egg, bacon and tomatoes on the table. 'You never told me about this boil.'

'Well, we weren't married then.' He cut his bread into squares. 'I mean, one doesn't wear one's heart on...'

'One's bum?' She sipped some tea, daintily.

'It was red and angry. It might have put you off. So, I just bore it...'

'Stoically.' She chuckled, before forking bacon between her lips.

His voice became a grunt. 'It wasn't funny. You don't seem to believe me.'

'I believe every excuse you make, love.' She covered his hand with hers.

He spoke through a mouthful of food. 'I can show you the scar.'

'Now that we're married.' Her eyes showed mischief.

'I can't understand why you've never noticed it.'

'Darling, I've been too modest to look.'

With slight indignation, he said, 'Are you pulling my leg?'

She crept up his arm with her fingers. 'Show me tonight, love.' And whispered, 'A special treat, eh!'

After they had eaten, Dick stifled an artificial yawn. 'I've suddenly come over rather tired. A good meal does that to you sometimes. I think I'll have a little kip.' He rose from the little table and went into the bedroom and sat on the bed. He bounced gently up and down. 'It's lovely and springy in here,' he called.

'Do you need a little company, on your bouncy bed?'

'Oh, rather. Leave the washing up till later.'

Jo went into the bedroom and kicked off her slippers. 'Budge up then.'

❦

Mrs Marks looked about her unkempt shop, when the door opened and Markie, her husband, appeared. He carried a plastic bag from which emanated a savoury tang. He held the bag aloft. 'Chips and fish. All we need is a nice mug o' tea.'

'Thank God for a bit o' common sense. I thought I was going to have to rob the shelves again.'

She brewed some tea and they each sat in an easy chair in the back room. The shop area was actually a lean-to section, added on the caravan, and where they trod from one section to another was in a slight dip because the ground underneath had sunk somewhat. Mrs Marks produced two pint mugs of tea and placed each one on the worn, upholstered arms of the large chairs. For about six minutes silence reigned as husband and wife chomped their way through the fish and chips and slurped tea like wavelets lapping the shore. Then Markie belched.

'That was fantastic – and filling. Nothing makes you feel more comfortable than fish and chips.' He screwed his paper up and threw it in the hearth, or what would have been the hearth in a traditional cottage; instead the area sported a large, gaudy electric fire with a mantle surround behind it.

'We might as well have the beer,' she said. 'Chips make you thirsty.'

Markie hunted for the bottle opener and opened both bottles.

'Hang on a minute,' she said. 'We'll do this proper,' and she produced two glasses, which she dusted with a tea towel, then poured out the beer.

'It tastes just as good from the bottle,' Markie declared.

'We have glasses, we might as well use 'em.' She took a long pull at hers. 'So, fish, chips and beer. Does that mean you're skint now?'

'No, not skint.'

'Well, I am. So p'raps you'd let me have a bit o' folding stuff.' He pulled a face. 'Come on, Markie. Just a tenner. I know you can afford it.'

He handed a note over. 'That means I can't have a flutter tomorrow. What's up, is this shop doing nothing?'

'Not much. We'll have to do summat to get some dosh.'

'Can you not put on a séance like you used to?'

She yawned and farted briefly. 'I suppose I could give it a go. It used to go down well, before we came here.'

☘

Jo was the first to stir. She stretched, touched Dick's arm, then poked him.

'Are you awake?'

'I am now,' he grunted. 'What time is it?'

'You can flash the torch on, can't you?'

He rummaged in the bedside cabinet, found the bike lamp and switched it on.

'Strewth. Half past eleven – at night! Suddenly I feel like a hot chocolate.'

'You feel like a cuddly hubby to me. You don't actually look like a hot chocolate.'

'Stop tickling, Jo. You'll wake me up proper.'

'Well, pass me the lamp, I need the loo. This is the part I don't like. While I'm gone you can make us both some hot chocolate.'

She swung from the bed, slid into her slippers and left the caravan, and Dick prepared the beverage. As he stirred the ingredients with cold milk, he hummed contentedly. Then he heated milk in the pan and poured it out as Jo returned.

'We're going to love it here, you know. It's heaven after that terraced place and your mother's couch. Five folk sharing one lavatory. I hated that – never being able to spend enough time in the loo. Always full.' He put biscuits on a plate.

She washed her hands, picked up her beverage and flopped onto the bed. 'Ours is full, too.'

Dick's chin actually dropped in surprise. 'But I thought it was our own privy.'

'It is.' She took a long drink then sighed. 'Those louts who lived here before.'

'Good God. They're not *in there,* are they?'

'No!' she laughed. 'Nobody's *in* there.'

Dick perched on a high stool. 'But you said it was full.'

'The bucket, I mean. The previous tenants haven't emptied it.'

'Oh no. You mean there's no…' He mimed pulling a chain.

'No. There isn't one. It's an Elsan closet,' she said. 'It has to be emptied.'

'Well go and see Mrs Marks.'

'She won't empty it. You have to do it.'

He took her empty mug, along with his own, and washed them in the sink. 'Dreadful.'

'I'm sorry, darling, but every tenant is responsible for emptying his own.'

'Other folks's as well, according to form. How dare they bog off and leave us with their shi…'

'Effluence, love. That's the technical term.'

He pushed away the plate of biscuits. 'I can't finish that now.'

'Oh, darling, don't be silly. Go on, eat them.'

'I'm not hungry.' Though his stomach rumbled briefly.

'You said you were famished.'

'Not now.' He pulled a face and sighed. 'So, I've got to empty it? I suppose I'll have to get used to it.' He brightened slightly. 'I did fatigues once, in the army, cleaning out the latrines.'

'Oh, that was brave, love.' She smiled, but fondly, not maliciously.

'Well, I reckon I should have got a medal. I was off my grub for a fortnight.' He opened the door a little wider and stared out into the night as if recalling his past. 'Right, where do I empty it then?'

She rummaged in a narrow drawer. 'I've got it written down. The signs are being repainted, y' see. Here we are.' She raised the scrap of paper up to the dim light in the van. 'Turn right outside here. Walk up to the crossroads. Turn right then left at the phone box. Twenty yards ahead is a concrete building. That's it. You can't miss it. Just follow your nose.'

'I can't carry that heavy bucket all that way!'

'You'll have to have spells, love. Little rests all the way.' She mimed sitting.

'I don't mean that,' he grumbled. 'I mean I can't carry it for miles with everybody staring at me.'

'Dickie, dear, everybody does it.' She appealed to him like a beggar asking for alms.

'Well, perhaps they're not as sensitive as me.'

'Conceal it some way.'

'How can one conceal sensitivity?' He sounded conveniently fragile.

'No! Conceal the flippin' bin! Look, there's a sort of Co-op truck under Mrs Marks' shop front. People use it for trundling gas canisters. Secure the Elsan on the truck. In the loo is a plastic sheet. Use that. Tie that sheet around it and nobody will know what you've got.'

'Won't they?' He gawped at her like a halfwit.

'Oh, you do make a fuss. Alright, leave it. I'll empty it. I can manage it, if you'll help me to fix it on the trolley.'

'Don't be silly,' he bridled. 'As if I'd let you do it. It's a man's job.' He seemed to stretch himself as he said this. Then he drooped as quickly. 'If only we had a man about the house. I'll wheel it there in the dead of night, when everybody is watching the telly.'

'Good old Dick. Everybody's hero... Another cup of tea?'

'No. I'll have one when it's over with. Surely some caravan sites are on main drainage.'

'Yes. Most of them are.'

'Then why the hell did we choose this one?'

'We didn't choose it. We were propelled towards it because of this strange job you were offered. They go together. Furthermore, this is not a caravan site. It's a higgledy-piggledy village. And it's been convenient for us.'

'Yeah! The only convenient place without conveniences!'

They stepped outside and walked towards the village shop where, indeed, Mrs Marks did have a truck protruding from under the shop front. As Dick pulled it silently from its den, they heard Mrs Marks warbling a tuneless song. The trolley protested with little squeaks as they wheeled it back to their loo. Dick laid the trolley flat then after a brief wrestling match with the Elsan succeeded in fastening it onto the trolley then covered it with the plastic sheet.

'Well done,' said Jo. 'Do you want me to come with you?'

'No need,' he said. But before he set off he tied a muffler around his face and clipped a clothes peg onto his nose. Then he lifted the handles and pushed the trolley before him.

'Good luck,' she called quietly, and waved him off as he advanced into no man's land.

He jogged along slowly and the trolley bumped over little stones strewn about the narrow, poorly constructed pathway. Because of the darkness he veered from side to side as the Co-op-style truck swerved erratically like its cousin, the supermarket trolley.

Arriving at the phone box, he rested, laying the handles along the ground, like mute wooden snakes. He looked around in the pitch-black night.

'Is it right or left from here?' he asked himself, but his doppelgänger gave no answer.

The only light came from a dim glow inching out from a caravan window. Dick decided to ask the way. He stepped up to the door and knocked. The top half of the door opened slowly, like the entrance to a shippen. Then above the bottom half appeared a grey, bearded face.

Seeing a face covered by a muffler with a peg on its nose, the eyes above the beard became terrified.

'I'm a poor man,' he blurted. 'I have nothing, no money, no jewels. Only a collection of gramophone records. You wouldn't take those from an old man, would you?'

'It's not a hold-up,' said Dick. 'I'm lost.' He removed the disguise from his face. 'I'm sorry, I didn't realise this was your van. This scarf was to, er, keep the night air off my chest.' He forced a brief cough. 'It's my chest. I have to be careful.'

'Ah, now I know you. But how you startled me.

We're plagued by a snooper, you see. Come in, come in. You need a pick-me-up.' He actually pulled Dick inside his van, but not before glancing into the darkness. 'What have you got there?'

'Er… shopping.'

'Well, bring it in. There are light fingers round here, you know.'

'Thanks. Rather not. I don't think pilferers would want my cargo. Still, I'll have that snifter you mentioned.'

They entered the inner sanctum. When Dick looked about him he realised that the Prof's abode was a new caravan, untidy but nice. It was quite warm inside. A log of some six feet long lay stretched between an armchair and the burning fire.

The Prof produced a bottle of whisky, a decanter of water and two tumblers. He poured generous amounts into each glass and pushed one across to Dick, who had sat on a dining chair opposite the armchair with a table between.

'Top up with water, if you wish,' said the Prof. 'But you're not obliged to dilute.' As he sat sipping, he nudged along the log with his foot, and the opposite end crept into the fireplace a few inches. 'Saves all that sawing and chopping,' he explained.

'Good idea.' Dick looked about the room and noticed bundles of newspaper tied up and dumped – in a tidy manner – about the room, so walking about meant squeezing between them. He wondered why they were so dumped, like a paper scrapyard.

As if reading his mind, the Prof said, 'Chap calls for them now and then. Pays me for 'em.'

And Dick had to be satisfied with that explanation.

Dick finished his whisky and felt the warmth surge through his body.

'Thanks a lot,' he said, as he rose to go.

'No, no. Don't go just yet. The night is young.'

'Thank you, but I only called to enquire the way.'

'Do you sing?'

'Not really. Only in the shower.'

'But you appreciate music? Surely!'

'Well, yes. Particularly marching music.'

'Then listen to this.' And the Prof rose from his armchair and turned up the volume of the gramophone, which until then had been humming softly.

The tune surged about the room and Dick thought it might be Wagner.

The Professor handed him a triangle. 'Join me.' He now held a pair of cymbals which he suddenly crashed together. 'Your turn in a second.' The music became gradually quieter – a diminuendo. The Prof held high a baton, turned to Dick and brought the baton down neatly. 'Oh, you missed it. Second chance coming up.' He raised the baton again; as it came down, Dick, feeling rather foolish, struck his triangle. 'Well done, sir.' The Prof nodded appreciatively.

Dick realised the Prof was revved up for the night, so he stood. 'I only came to ask the way…' But his sentence tailed off as Professor Sparrow became carried away, conducting the music and reading the score. He turned to Dick again and brought down his baton.

'You missed the beat again.'

'Sorry. Look, can you direct me to…'

'I am directing you, but you must concentrate also.' He waved his arms vigorously like a living scarecrow frightening the birds.

Dick ducked. 'No, I mean direct me…' The music became suddenly quieter, so the inept triangle player could speak *sotto voce*. 'I need to know the way to the disposal unit.' He moved towards the door.

The Prof turned down his gramophone, and sighed. 'Oh, very well. You're far too agitated to perform. Some other time, perhaps when you're more relaxed.' Even then he couldn't resist grabbing the cymbals and producing one more crash.

'Which way then?' Dick's head began to throb.

'Straight on. One hundred yards. Turn left at the crossroads. Watch out for the snooper.'

Before Wagner could leap from his box once more, Dick picked up the handles and all but staggered along the track. Five minutes later he encountered a concrete building and across its door was painted: 'Disposal Unit'. Underneath was chalked: 'Rose Cottage'. Dick fumbled for his torch and flashed it onto the door. Then he began to untie the plastic sheet.

At that point he heard singing. Strong singing, but wobbly. Drunken in fact. The voice was issuing forth the tune 'Cwm Rhondda':

'Bread from Evans's – cheese from Thomas's,
Be-er from the Royal Oak.'

The singer appeared carrying two buckets and continued to sing.

Dick, who had been a choirboy, joined in the reprise:

'Be-er from the Royal Oak.'

'Well sung, boyo. You're not a fugitive from Cymru too, are you?'

'No, I'm as English as Yorkshire pudding.' Grateful for the rest, Dick took out a cigarette and lit it.

'Don't smoke in there. It'll blow Upsy-Daisy to down under. Methane, you see. I'm Taffy, by the way. Here, hold this door while I empty mine.'

Dick advanced to the door, holding it with the cigarette in his hand. As Taffy entered, he swiped Dick's cig, took two quick puffs then slid it back between Dick's fingers. Taffy took in one bucket at a time, then escaped, gasping. He picked up his second bucket. As he passed Dick to enter, he said, 'God, I need another drag.'

Dick placed the cig between Taffy's lips. The Welshman took two drags, then entered and hurled the contents of his bucket into the interior. He stumbled out again, grabbed the cigarette and took several puffs.

'God, I thought I was going to die. I needed that. The muck needs emptying. The farmer does that, now and seldom.' He took several breaths of fresh air. 'You're new here, aren't you?'

'Yes, how did you know?'

'Oh, it's obvious. Show me your soles.'

'What?'

'The soles of your shoes.'

Dick lifted one foot while holding onto the trolley.

'Oh dear. Oh deary me. That's fatal. Leather you see – smooth too.'

'What do you mean?' asked Dick, putting his foot down.

'It's like an ice rink in there, boyo. You'll fall on your English arse. I'm warning you, no light. Some bugger's nicked the bulb.'

'Does that happen often?' Dick sniffed the air, then stepped back as the aroma from the interior infiltrated the outdoors.

'Too bloody often. But not to worry, I'll tell you what to do, it's as simple as Welsh rarebit. Listen. I'll hold the door. You enter with your load. Take six paces forward. Stop. Throw. Got it?'

'Er, six paces forward…'

'That's right. Here, try it with me, here… without your bucket. Right?'

'Right!'

'We push open the door,' Taffy grunted. 'Forwards: one, two, three, four, five, six. Stop. Throw.' They threw imaginary contents. 'That's far enough. Now, try it on your own.'

Dick lifted the Elsan from the trolley. 'Hellfire, it's heavy.' He staggered forward.

'Door open,' called Taffy. 'Enter.'

Dick staggered through.

'Go. One, two, three…'

'I'm slipping,' Dick cried.

'Four, five…'

The Elsan clattered to the floor and Dick went down on his backside. The contents splattered all over the place and Dick dragged the Elsan outside and stood, drooping.

'Lucky you didn't fall in. You need a shower.'

'What's going on here?' came a strident voice.

'Ah, Major Merryweather.'

'Oh, it's you. Leave him alone, you great Welsh bully.' The Major raised his stick threateningly.

'I was helping him,' Taffy said, taking a step back, 'and he slipped.'

'Who is it?' asked the Major, and flashed a torchlight into Dick's face. 'Oh, it's you, young fella.'

'Yes. It's me. Richard Coningsby. I slipped. It's my soles. Taffy was helping. Take six paces and throw, he said, but…'

'Six?' queried the Major. 'Did he say six paces?'

'Six, yes.'

'You only take four,' the Major balled. He faced Taffy, pointed his stick and thrust it forward like a rapier. Taffy stepped back. 'Four is the maximum. Otherwise you're in it.'

'You can say that again,' said Dick, spreading wide his arms and displaying his damp clothes.

'Four normal paces!' emphasised the Major, glaring at Taffy.

'Normal! Yes, normal,' said Taffy. 'I grant you. But his aren't. He takes little paces, like this.' And Taffy demonstrated six effeminate steps.

'Oh no I don't!' Dick now sounded quite distressed. 'I don't, do I, Major?'

'I jolly well hope not. Can't say I noticed you did.'

'You do,' stressed Taffy. 'When I saw you walking along, pushing your trolley…'

'Ah! The trolley,' said Dick. 'That's it. You can't walk otherwise with a trolley, else you'd bump your shins. Look!' And Dick went quickly to the trolley and pushed it a few yards, taking small steps. 'You see.' He left the trolley and walked back to the others, exaggerating his steps. 'That explains it, surely.'

'Of course it does. Sorry, boyo. Sorry for that grave mistake.'

'He'll have to explain his grimy condition to his lovely wife,' the Major pointed out.

'Ah! Lovely wife,' echoed Taffy.

'So you'd better make amends. Your premises are just there,' the Major said, pointing to a ramshackle wooden erection. 'So, supply our friend with soap and towel. Guide him to that apology for a shower and I'll bring a pair of army breeches.'

The Major marched away to fulfil his promise.

'The shower is just round the corner,' explained Taffy. 'I'll bring soap and towel. Off you go. You need a good soaking. I've not finished painting the doors yet, so the paint might not be dry.'

Inside Miss Primm's caravan, her dog started yapping and pulling at the bed sheets covering her.

'Be quiet, Candy! What a time of night to wake me up. You need a wee, do you? Well, if you must you must. No, I'm not going to scold. Come along then.'

She picked up her pet and opened the door. 'When nature calls, we must obey.' She placed the little dog on the grass and it ran under the caravan and she went round the side of the van to supervise it. 'Good little dog.'

Dick hurried towards the showers that were in a poor condition. He paused between two swing doors; one had been newly painted and displayed the word 'Men', but the letters indicated only half of the word, the other half had not yet been painted. Dick, desperate for a wash, breezed through the swing doors.

Immediately facing him were two occupied cubicles, each with cowboy-style saloon-type doors. Both showers were full on, and steam was issuing forth, shrouding the occupants. He pulled open one of the doors and tapped the occupant on the shoulder.

'How long are you going to be, mate? I'm filthy.'

The occupant turned, covering her bosoms and screeched, 'You certainly are. Get out of here.'

The woman in the next shower screamed, 'The snooper. He's here.'

Both women began screaming, 'Help, help!'

Dick quickly made for the exit. He rushed outside and ran a few yards, expecting a posse to follow him. He saw a caravan lit up and made for the steps, and sat, panting, on a chair.

Miss Primm re-entered her van with the little dog brushing past her.

'You really did want to go. What a good little chap you are.'

She closed her door then turned round to face her unexpected visitor.

'I can explain,' said Dick. 'Don't scream, please. I can't stand it.'

Miss Primm seemed to swell. A look of satisfaction invaded her face. She raised her arms and stepped towards him.

'Ah! Our handsome young newcomer. I've been dying to meet you again.'

Then she stopped in mid-stride, her nostrils dilated and she sniffed. 'What a dreadful smell.' Her features took on the look of someone about to receive an injection.

'It's me,' he whimpered. 'I slipped into the cesspit. I need to get cleaned up.'

Relieved at what he believed to be a narrow escape, Dick stood erect and went towards the door. Miss Primm, hand over her mouth, stepped back and the unhappy muck spreader left the caravan, retrieved his trolley and shuffled off homewards.

'What a start to a new home,' Dick muttered to himself. 'I wonder what else this place has in store for us.'

THREE

Upsy-Daisy had been a railway terminus since 1925. It was a hamlet built on a promontory in East Anglia. Because its access to the coast was its attraction, big business had tried to develop it into a seaside resort and built a few guest houses in the nearby village of Down Daisy.

Previously, Upsy-Daisy had been a salt-mining area, and a railway junction had evolved about 300 yards from the headland. In 1940 the railway lines were removed to become scrap metal for the war effort. Indeed, the iron railings round the guest houses in neighbouring villages had also been cut down to provide crude steel for counteroffensive measures. The only relic remaining to testify to Upsy-Daisy's railway history was a dilapidated railway carriage, circa 1920, which was now used by vagrants and drunks. Even these did not escape Mrs Marks' sales ability if she thought dropouts were lurking inside. Her approach was simple: 'Buy or bugger off.'

She had just investigated these insalubrious premises and was walking down the slope towards the centre of the site where a resident was hosing down his caravan as Mrs Marks sauntered by.

'Morning, Wally.'

'It's going to be lovely day.'

With fag dangling she shuffled towards the new van occupied by Professor Sparrow for whom she cleaned once each week. She earned a tax-free income cleaning for various caravan dwellers. She knocked at the door and entered.

'Morning, Professor. It's Tuesday again.'

'Yes, I know. It's Tuesday all day.'

'Well, I do for you on a Tuesday, don't I? And you're supposed to leave your bed down.'

She struggled with the bunk bed, lowering it down from the wall. The Professor sat at his table finishing his breakfast.

'I don't suppose there's any tea left in that pot, is there?'

He raised the lid, and, with a mouthful of breakfast, nodded. She helped herself.

'And don't forget to pay me this week. Being absent-minded must be very handy at times.'

She began to clear up the breakfast things then paused to peer inside the Professor's teacup.

'I say, look here. It's very vivid inside your teacup this morning. Would you like a reading?'

'Is there a fee?'

She raised the cup as he peered myopically into it. 'Well, I'm not a charitable concern y' know. Tell yer what, I'll help meself to a slice o' bread and marmalade and we'll call it square all round.'

Without receiving consent, she swiped a square from the wrapped sliced loaf and buttered it then spread it with preserve.

'Square all round!' echoed the Prof. 'That's an interesting shape.'

He went into a daydream conducting a square with his right hand and describing a circle with his left. He found it difficult and shook his head.

'Hm… Interesting but nigh impossible. It would need plenty of practice.'

Mrs Marks raised his empty cup and scrutinised the messy interior.

'Here, you're going to 'ave a very unusual day. Now what is that shape? Looks like a number fifty. The figure fifty,' she declared dramatically, 'is going to loom large in today's activities.'

'The figure fifty?' he queried. 'Naturally it will. It's the number of my caravan. But I cannot remain here discoursing upon my horoscope, whatever may be in store for me. I must away to see my dainty darlings.'

She looked askance at him and shrugged. At that moment, the postman pushed a letter through the letter flap. The Professor picked it up.

'Oh dear, dear. How irritating.'

'What's up, Prof? Not bad news, I 'ope? Not a bill?' She almost cringed as she said the dreaded word.

'Both,' he said, sounding deflated. Then he paced his reply. 'At… one… fell… swoop.' He palmed his forehead like an overplaying actor. 'It means I shall have to remain here today. And I did so want to see some tits.'

She placed the teacup back on the table and gripped both sides of her ample waist like a strapping toby jug. She glared and challenged him.

'I beg your pardon. There is a lady present.'

But Professor Sparrow did not seem to see one. In fact, he seemed about to cry.

'I wanted to look at some tits today.'

'Disgusting,' she retorted. 'I will not stay here a minute longer.' She donned her voluminous coat. 'I thought you were respectable, and all the time this caravan is a den of iniquity.'

Her heroics seemed to bring him back to earth – or rather the interior of the van.

'My dear woman…' He placed a fatherly hand on her chubby arm. 'I assure you…'

'Don't you touch me.' She shied away from this electric shock. 'I may be ancient, but I am pure,' which was the first of her Tuesday red herrings.

Professor Sparrow was utterly bewildered; he understood women not at all.

'What on earth is the matter with you, Mrs M? I merely mentioned that I would not now be able to visit my birds.' He waved aloft the letter in his hand.

Still standing like a toby jug, with her chin thrust out resolutely, she quivered, as best her size would allow her, and actually looked down on the Prof.

'I know full well what you mentioned. Indeed,' she said, a word which she seldom uttered, 'I am surprised at you. Hin the presence of a lady too!'

'Mrs Marks. Please.' He advanced kindly towards her.

'Keep away, else I'll scream. And I thought you were a gentleman. I won't stay here a minute longer.' Like a corpulent Queen of Sheba, and probably imagining she was, Mrs Marks swept from the Prof's tiny dwelling... Within ten seconds she had returned. 'One pound. If you please. And don't come too close.'

'But you haven't done for me!'

'Done for you! Done for you!' She took a deep breath, deeper than she had taken for many a day. 'Let me tell you, Professor Sparrow, if you don't change your habits, I've done *with* you.'

He reluctantly handed over the money, she marched out, and he glared at his letter and shook his fist at it.

Mrs Marks continued to amble along the narrow paths of the site until she arrived at Taffy's caravan, which was in a drab condition. She knocked then entered.

'Morning, Taffy. It's me.'

Taffy, sprawled across his tiny table, was reading the racing column of the local newspaper.

'Morning, Mrs M. I rather fancy a flutter this morning. But I'm not sure about these nags.'

She snatched the newspaper from him and spread it out, bringing it back and forth before her eyes.

'Quick, I've got one of me feelings coming on.

Now what's this horse called, third line down? I ain't got me specs on.'

He snatched the newspaper back and ran his eyes up and down the column.

'Here, let's take a gander. I Ain't Got Specs On? There's no horse called that.'

'Don't scoff at the disabled, 'specially them wot has feelings coming on.'

Taffy lowered the newspaper to look down at his visitor.

'Oh, ah, Blodwin. I see what you mean now. Third horse down: Home On Wheels! Well, I'll run to Betws-y-Coed! That is appropriate.' He tapped the paper excitedly. 'This is our horse.'

'Told you so,' she smirked.

He sank back into his plastic chair; his disenchanted face virtually dropped to his knees.

'There's only one snag.'

'What's that?'

'I'm skint.'

'Well, don't look at me. You already owe me a fiver.'

Taffy looked at his watch. Then folded the newspaper and placed it on the table.

'Yeah, well, Blodwin…'

'Don't keep swearing like that.'

'See you. I've got to go to work, otherwise I'll be late.'

He set off to earn a crust and she put her feet up and began to squint at the paper. Prior to mounting his cycle, Taffy began to wheel it, when he noticed the Prof coming towards him, holding something aloft and waving to him. As they met, Taffy saw that it was a letter the old guy was waving, rather agitatedly.

'Oh, Taffy, say that you'll do it for me,' he panted. 'There's a good chap.'

'Aye, aye, I've heard about your sort,' Taffy said with a grin. 'First thing of a morning too.'

The elderly gent hardly heard him and placed a hand on the handlebars. He looked up, almost pleading, into the Welsh dragon's grinning features.

'You see, I must go and see those birds today.'

'Blimey, you are in earnest, you frisky old devil. Any chance of their phone number?'

'Oh dear, this really is a nuisance. Confound this letter.'

Taffy stood his cycle stationary with the stirrup, but held it in case his acquaintance leant on it.

'Hold it, Professor. The more you say, the less you tell me. Now, take a deep breath and start at the beginning.'

'Well, I had arranged an ornithological expedition today. And now...'

'Orny what?'

'Birdwatching. A birdwatching session. You know, our feathered friends. But I'm obliged to take this account,' he glanced at the letter, 'to Grabbing and Gloat, the brokers in the High Street in Down Daisy. If I go, it will take me all day, and I shall be obliged to postpone my studies. I was there the other day,' his face became suddenly elated, 'and I saw a beautiful pair of tits.'

Now it was Taffy's turn to look elated.

'Oh, I do so want to see those tits again.'

'I'll bet you do,' said the Welshman.

'Don't you think blue tits are wonderful?'

'Blue? Naw. They might be suitable at the North Pole. Mind you, I don't object to a nice pair o' chocolate brown, boyo, but not blue. Blimey, that's getting far too kinky. Anyway, I'll have to be off to work.' He mounted his cycle again. 'I'll take your letter for you. I'll make a slight diversion and go down High Street.'

The Professor thrust the overdue account at him and almost danced on the spot.

'I say, would you?'

'I've just said so, haven't I?'

'There's one other thing,' said the Prof.

'Oh gawd. You don't want me to go to the Co-op as well.'

'The Co-op? Oh no. Some other time.' The Professor took out a ridiculously large purse and extracted £50.

'Hey, there's no need to give me a tip… well, not this time. What's it for?'

'I owe it to them.'

'What fifty smackers?'

'Yes. That's my final instalment.'

'OK then. So I give 'em the account and hand 'em fifty quid?'

Taffy brusquely grabbed the money, stuffed it in his windcheater pocket, put the account in his bike bag and pedalled away.

Professor Sparrow returned to his caravan, humming happily now. He entered the van and placed the letter on the table. Then he changed himself into clothes suitable for birdwatching and vacated the van again, hiding his key under the mat. As he began to walk away, he heard a loud gunshot. He had arrived at the Major's caravan so he cowered behind it, peeping for the sharp shooter. Then he heard the angry voice of Major Merryweather.

'You damn varmints. I'll get you yet.'

The Major pointed a blunderbuss skywards and blasted off another volley. The pigeons he had missed wheeled away towards the sea.

'Blast the blighters,' said the Major. 'I've missed 'em again. I'll have to invest in a new rifle.'

He turned abruptly and made for his caravan, holding the gun pointing forward. In that moment the Professor, investigating this disturbance, peeped round the corner of the van, only to come up against the Major's gun.

'Oh, don't shoot, don't shoot. I'm innocent.'

This encounter shook up the Major somewhat.

'Good God, man, you gave me a turn. You mustn't go lurking about the place like a fugitive, like a convict on the run. That's the way to get ammo up your arse. When I was in India, I've blasted intruders for less.'

During this monologue the Professor had been shaking considerably.

'Is the snooper on the loose again?'

The Major patted his weapon affectionately and laughed.

'Oh no,' he said, 'it's those damn pigeons. They're spotting the caravans. The roofs will cave in one of these days. Lime is very corrosive, you know.'

'Surely you are not shooting them with a gun?'

'Well, I'll never get 'em with a blasted bread knife, will I?'

The Professor held his head theatrically and swayed from side to side.

'Oh, my poor feathered friends,' he gestured skywards, waving with both hands, 'fly high in your azure world, away from murderous mortals.'

The Major felt suddenly uncomfortable. He shuffled and fingered his collar in embarrassment.

'I say, Professor, steady on. We have a right to protect our domain, you know. It is our duty to keep our homesteads clean.'

The Professor earnestly felt he was entitled to offer counselling.

'You need not use a gun. Use a hosepipe.' He pointed to several caravans along where Wally, sometime handyman, was hosing his van.

'Oh, come, come,' said the Major. 'You would never reach them with a hosepipe.'

'You misunderstand. Use a hosepipe to wash away the droppings from the caravans.'

'Ah, but of course. And preserve our wildlife.'

The Professor's whiskery features broke into a smile and he nodded animatedly.

'I suppose you are right,' the Major said. 'They say the golden eagle is almost extinct. And I admit, I wouldn't relish being responsible for exterminating the wood pigeon. Oh yes, we must preserve them: the robin, chaffinch, wheatear...'

'Kittywake, blackbird, white arse puffin...'

'Steady on. That's a bit coarse. There may be ladies within earshot.' He peered about him then grinned slyly. 'Did you say Kitty Wake has a white arse? Does she live on the site?'

The Professor became slightly flustered.

'No, no. I merely stated that the kittywake must also be preserved. Then you mentioned wheatear. So I was illustrating that white arse is the real name for the wheatear, a bird the Scots refer to as whey terse,' and he said this in broad Scots. 'And wheatear is a corruption of this.'

'The Scots. Huh, damn foreigners. Their pronunciation is thicker than their porridge. Anyway, getting back to the point, I'll arrange for the caravan roofs to be swilled down with a hosepipe. I don't know why I didn't think of it earlier.' He walked towards the handyman. 'I say, Wally, do you think I could borrow the hosepipe sometime today?'

As the Major approached Wally, the Professor walked to the edge of the site and went through a side gate into the woods. Feeling at one with the birds he so loved, he began to sing, 'The cuckoo is a pretty bird'.

The postman arrived at Dick's van and pushed letters through the door flap. Inside the van Dick heard the flap drop and dragged himself out of bed and picked up the letters.

'What have you got?' asked Jo.

'You remember when I spoke to old Simpson about me collecting insurance premiums, and credit drapery payments on this site? Well, he said he'd transfer some of his customers to me.'

'Oh, good. We'll need all the money we can get to buy that swanky new caravan.'

Dick was busy examining the details of each customer. He groaned.

'Well, old Simpson is not as daft as he looks. There are a hell of a lot of arrears on this site.'

'But I'm sure you'll persuade them to pay up, my love. And Mr Simpson is an elderly chap. Perhaps it got a bit of a drag for him to collect up here. It doesn't actually cost you money, does it?'

'No, not really. And my motto is: Pay on the dot, else that's your lot.'

Jo got out of bed and plugged the kettle in.

'And that's a very good motto. You'll cope.'

'I'll have to,' he replied, pulling a face. 'Anyway, make me a good breakfast. As the Major tells us: an army marches on its stomach.'

Taffy had by now arrived in High Street in Down Daisy. He dismounted from his cycle to enter the brokers, when he quickly realised the betting shop was next door. He stood back and looked at both shops. He took a coin from his pocket, tossed it in the air, caught it and examined the result.

'Ah well. It could have been heads.'

From his inside pocket he took the £50 the Professor had given him, shrugged and entered the bookies. He checked the clock on the wall. 9am. He approached the counter.

'Fifty quid on Home On Wheels.'

❦

Mrs Marks was as busy as she personally could be, sweeping the inside of her shop, when the phone rang. The phone was more agreeable than a broom, so she propped the latter against the counter, picked up the grimy instrument and articulated in her posh voice, reserved for unknown callers, 'Hellew. Upsy-Daisy Emporium. The manageress speaking.' She wrinkled her brow. 'Yer want me to get who?' she replied, lapsing into the vernacular. 'The site manager? You want me to go and get 'im? Will you pay my fare? Why? 'Cos he's in Majorca. Go and get who? Get Professor Sparrow instead? Well, he ain't in either. He's gorn off for the day. You're a-doing what? Repossession! Oh my gawd.'

She slammed down the phone and made for the door. Then she stopped. A feeling of effrontery came over her and she scuttled back to the phone, picked it up, and without even dialling she articulated in her posh accent, 'By the way, we are not, repeat not, message minders.' Then she dashed from the shop.

Mrs Marks hared past several caravans until she came to Major Merryweather's residence.

The Major was standing on top of his van hosing bird droppings off the roof. 'That's it. Clean at last.' Fatal last words, for a particularly large dollop splashed down on his van. 'Damn you.' He looked up and shook a fist at the seagull. 'Thank God cows can't fly,' he muttered.

Below him, Mrs Marks looked up, seeming most agitated.

'Major, what shall we do? What on earth shall we do?'

'Do? Shoot 'em. My good woman! What the deuce is the matter? Standing there, wringing your hands as though you've lost hope.'

'The Professor's lost hope. The bailiffs are coming to tow his van away.'

The Major threw his hosepipe down to squirt all and sundry.

'Turn that damn tap off, Mrs Marks, will you? Hang on while I disembark.' He clambered from the roof to stand beside her. 'Now what's this you say?'

'The bailiffs are coming to tow the Prof's van away. Repossession. They say the stupid man owes them money. They've just telephoned. He's ignored their letters. He received one this morning which seemed to upset him.'

The Major tightened the water tap firmly. 'Did it, by Jove?'

'But only for a minute,' she explained.

'Naturally. I had better investigate this. Come with me, Mrs Marks.'

They walked a few paces to the Professor's van and peered in through the window.

'Well, well,' declared the Major, 'there *is* a letter on his table.' He tried the door but found it locked. 'I'm surprised he even bothered to take trouble to lock up.'

'Oh, he does. He's very careful.' She stooped, lifted the door mat and produced a key.

'So I notice,' said the Major.

They both entered the van where the Major at once read aloud the demand notice.

'Dear Sir, You have chosen to ignore every notification we have dispatched. Unless the final instalment of £50 is to hand by 4pm on Tuesday of this week, we shall have no alternative than to repossess your caravan. Yours faithfully, Grabbing and Gloat, financial advisers.'

The Major replaced the letter and looked round the new but cluttered caravan.

'Good God! Did he buy the blessed thing on hire purchase?'

'Don't we all?'

'Certainly not, madam. However, never let it be said that I failed to rally to a cause.' He now stood to attention just as he had as a young professional soldier, years earlier. He stood so, because he was about to give an order. 'Now, Mrs M, could you undertake a quick recruiting campaign? Gather together as many people as are available on the site. Tell them to bring their weapons.'

Mrs Marks had in fact been on her mark, ready to dash out through the door, but hearing the word 'weapons' she halted mid-stride.

'Weapons, Major? We ain't got no weapons!'

'We have! Rolling pins, garden equipment, clothes props. A sickle can be very useful, efficiently handled, of course.'

'Here, there ain't going to be no violence, is there?'

He ignored her complaint and ushered her out of the van.

'I hope so,' he muttered. 'Just like old times.'

He spotted a file, a wire threaded with bills and letters. He lifted the file from its hook and examined it.

'I'd better check if there are more documents of war,' he told himself. '"Dear Sir,"' he read. '"Thank you for your donation of £5…" Mm, I see. Dr Barnardo's.' He unthreaded another 'document'.

'"We gratefully acknowledge your cheque for £6… The RSPCA." Good grief, no wonder the blasted bailiffs are after him. The clown is giving all his money away.' The Major halted his tirade, shook his head and sighed. 'He's actually not a bad old stick,' he told himself. 'Let's see, my monthly annuity is due tomorrow. Now, if we can hold those blighters off for twenty-four hours, I'll be able to loan him the money myself.' He replaced the file, chuckled, took out his pocket watch.

'Twelve noon precisely. Zero hour is 16.00 hours. That gives us four hours to plan tactics. By Jove, it's just like old times.'

🌳

After Taffy had collected his winnings from the betting shop, he went straight into the Diving Duck pub and ordered two pints of best bitter, a pork pie and a Scotch egg. By the time he came out, he'd forgotten what had happened that day. All he knew was, he felt happy, and that was all that mattered.

Now, rather sloshed, he cycled his wobbly way through the caravan site, and as he cycled he sang, 'Dear old pals, jolly old pals.'

On arriving at his own caravan, he dismounted by cocking off and in the process almost fell off the machine. He retrieved his door key, which hung on a string inside the letterbox. No sooner was he inside than he fell on his bunk and began to snore the sleep of the dead.

❦

The shop bell tinkled and Dick entered. Mrs Marks was busy leaning on the counter.

'Afternoon, Mrs Marks. You'll be interested to learn that all the credit subscriptions and insurance premiums on this site will now be collected by me and not Mr Simpson. All in the cause of economy.'

'Good. Well, you'll be interested to learn that I'm economising too. So you'll have to miss me this week.'

'I see,' he said, with a sigh. 'By the way, what's all the commotion at the far end of the site?'

She exhaled cigarette smoke, dropped her fag end on the floor and trod on it.

'The Major is organising a revolution. He wants you to enlist as soon as you can. You have a gun, have you?'

'A gun? Afraid not.'

'Well, take a carpet beater, you can use that.'

'I see. It sounds a rum do. Anyway, I'll see you in the trenches.'

He left the shop wondering what the fuss was all about and made his way to Taffy's caravan where he banged on the door several times.

'Come on, Taffy. I know you're in.' He noticed the cycle discarded dangerously. He banged the door again then went inside.

Taffy was lying on his bunk, snoring his head off. The place stank of alcohol. Dick prodded him with a firm middle finger. Taffy grunted and turned over. Dick prodded again and Taffy grunted.

'Holy Holywell. It's not morning already, is it? What day is it?'

'It's pay day. You pay me. Come on, cough up. You're in arrears.'

'Call again.'

'When?'

'Next year.'

'Not good enough, Taffy.'

Taffy thrust his hand in a pocket and pulled out a bundle of notes.

'Here. Take what you want and leave some change.'

Dick was surprised but did as requested, recorded the amount in his book then left the caravan. He went to his next customer. A note was stuck to the door with chewing gum:

'Credit collector. Call again next week. Am a bit stuck.'

Dick continued and achieved some success then went home.

'Ah, a cup of tea. And I'm ready for it.' He sat down at the table.

'Had a bad day, love?'

'Mixed,' he said. 'But it's "Call back next week. Me old man's been off work." I bet old Simpson is laughing his head off, exchanging my clients for his duds.'

'Be fair, Dick,' said Jo. 'You can't honestly say that all your other customers were good payers. It is possible that the caravaners have had a difficult week.'

'Old Taffy surprised me. He forked out a fortune. If that money represented his wages, he's on a good screw.'

'There you are then. You'll just have to be more firm with your difficult clients.'

He pushed his empty tea mug away and rose from the table.

'Well, I'll try again,' he said, 'and go and see what the Major wants at the same time.'

He left their van and went towards the sound of the crowd. Several neighbours had thronged round Major Merryweather who was giving them a pep talk. They were gathered about the Professor's van, armed with rakes, pitch forks and cricket bats. The stentorian voice of the Major rose above the rabble.

'Don't forget, if we allow these bully boys to get the better of us,' he waved the Prof's letter above his head, 'many of you can expect to be harassed in future.' He noticed Dick had joined them. 'Ah, Richard, my boy. You have been briefed?'

'Yes, Major. Mrs Marks said something about

these tactics of yours. But should we be taking the law into our own hands?'

'We have to do something! We either hold them off until Professor Sparrow returns, or until my monthly annuity arrives.'

Dick could feel the agitation of the site members around him. They seemed impatient for action.

'When is that?'

'Tomorrow,' replied the retired army major. 'I think. You're not afraid, are you?'

Someone in the crowd called, 'Not him. He's an ex-soldier. Served in Afghanistan.'

'Hear, hear,' some shouted. Two or three clapped. Dick was elevated to hero on the spot.

'Well, no,' replied Dick. 'I'm not afraid. Not really, but...'

'Good man,' called the Major. 'Here, take this whistle. Stand a couple of vans away and when you spot the enemy, blow it.'

The Major then shouted up to Wally, the handyman, who still stood on top of the Prof's van holding the hosepipe.

'Don't forget, Wally, you are our rear guard. You command a forceful weapon. Use it... Any questions, old chap?'

Wally looked critically at the hosepipe and opened his mouth to speak, but a great 'Hurrah!' from the group drowned what he might have said.

'Good,' said the Major. 'That's settled then.' He checked his pocket watch. 'Huh, it's four o'clock already. The devils are yellow.'

Again, there came an appreciative roar from the growing crowd.

Taffy was about a hundred yards away from the Major's mob, and, recovered from his earlier boozing, was strolling towards the commotion when a jeep pulled up beside him. Inside were the broker and the driver.

'Excuse me,' said the bailiff, 'can you direct me to the caravan occupied by someone called Sparrow?'

He wore a stiff flat cap and had a dark whiskery smudge about his top lip. To Taffy, he had a Hitler look about him. Taffy disliked him on sight.

'I'm going in that direction myself,' said the Welsh elbow-bender, 'I'll direct you there.'

He stood on the step of the jeep, which began to bear down on the Major and his mob. The shrill sound of a whistle stirred the crowd into action. The Major, seeing Taffy hanging onto the jeep, sprang to the wrong conclusion.

'Quisling,' he shouted. 'Traitor. Coward. Let 'em have it, Wally.'

The handyman, standing proud on the Prof's caravan, obeyed the order and squirted forth a strong surge from his hosepipe. Unfortunately, it was badly aimed, or not aimed at all, and Taffy became the surprised and drenched recipient.

The bailiff, who had encountered various resistance techniques during his career, shouted to his driver, 'We'll have to take the initiative with these loonies.'

The clamour increased. People waved their weapons like savages.

The jeep backed up to the caravan and the bailiff jumped from the vehicle and started to tie a towing rope to the front of the van. His bravery had to be admired. The other end of the rope had long been tied to the front of the jeep. The bailiff climbed back into the vehicle, which began to pull slowly away. Mrs Marks, who had been standing to one side, waiting for an opportunity, stepped forward, and almost casually snipped the towing rope with her garden shears. The jeep shot away for a few yards, then stopped; the bailiff jumped down again. He pointed a slightly trembling arm at the opposition.

'Right, Sparrow,' he shouted. 'You fancy yourself as a game bird, so I'll bring the police. They'll pluck your feathers for you.'

'*I* am not Sparrow,' returned the Major. 'Yet at this moment I am a bird of prey, ready to swoop to the assistance of a comrade.'

Taffy, now off the jeep's fender and standing damp on terra firma, yelled, 'Can somebody tell me what's going on here?'

'We have simply come to repossess this caravan,' said the bailiff. 'The owner owes a final instalment of £50, yet still sees fit to withhold it, in spite of several warning letters from us.'

A slow, cold dawn was beginning to materialise in Taffy's cranium; recent past events were starting to surface, swimming through his bitter beer and whisky chaser.

'Who? Do you mean old Sparrow?'

'Yes. Exactly that man.' The bailiff turned side on to Taffy and faced the crowd. 'If you are all so concerned about his welfare,' he continued, facing the crowd, 'why don't you club together and lend it to him?'

'That would have been the sensible thing, Major,' said Dick. 'Much simpler.'

Major Merryweather huffed and grunted and examined the ground in embarrassment.

The bailiff stretched to his full height with righteousness – and arrogance.

'Where is this Sparrow anyway?'

'He, er, flew off earlier this morning, and… er… you've not called for that fifty quid, have you?' said Taffy.

He recalled the broker's premises were next to the betting shop. The phrase 'Home On Wheels' percolated slowly into his fuddled mind. This was nudged aside by another phrase that registered: 'Fifty quid at ten to one.'

'Of course they have, man,' barked the Major, still smarting under the bailiff's suggestion and Dick's concurrence. 'What the devil do you think all this fuss is about?'

'Well,' drawled Taffy, 'why didn't you say so?'

And from his pocket he revealed a bundle of notes and peeled off fifty smackers.

The crowd, of course, assumed he was using his own money.

'Good old Taffy. Well done the Welshman.'

'Is it a loan or a gift?' Dick asked him.

Taffy wasn't sure, but he passed the money over to the agent who shook his head, bewildered, but was lucid so far as money was concerned and gave Taffy a receipt. Without more ado, he climbed back into the jeep, which moved quickly away, followed by a final squirt from Wally's hosepipe.

'Well done, Taffy. I must say, perhaps I've misjudged you at times.' He slapped Taffy on the back. 'Very generous. I never thought you had it in you.'

'He hasn't,' said Mrs Marks. 'He has it on him. The money, I mean.' She stood glowering, swinging the garden shears casually back and forth. 'Now, crafty Taffy, where did you get all that dosh from?' She shot menacing glances at him.

'It's mine.' He didn't fancy being clipped by the shears like a docile sheep, so he tried to brazen his way out. 'I won it on that nag you mentioned, Home On Wheels.'

'Really? That was ten to one. You didn't by any chance win £500, did you?'

She turned and appealed to the others with a gesture; many of them were aficionados of the turf, gamblers to a man. They caught on quickly and eyed Taffy with suspicious orbs. Only Dick and the Major seemed puzzled.

She chanced a guess. 'And where did you get your fifty quid from?'

'I... er... I...'

'You borrowed it from the Professor, didn't you.' It was a strategy she would use herself... on the quiet, of course. 'It was to pay off his caravan, wasn't it?'

'Well, yes, but I didn't think...'

'You never do, Taffy. That nag could have lost.' She turned to Wally, still standing on top of the Professor's van holding the hosepipe. 'Rear guard: fire.'

Wally aimed the nozzle at Taffy; the jet of water caught him full on the chest and he was knocked onto his rear end that was already damp from the previous soaking. As he fell, he opened his fists and the money fluttered all over the caravan site. The caravanning combatants broke ranks and gleefully gathered it up.

Mrs Marks snatched a few notes for herself, only to be approached by Dick.

'I suppose it'll be convenient to collect the fire insurance, Mrs Marks?'

Reluctantly she handed over two £10 notes. And as the others scooped up what they could, Dick extracted money from his bad payers.

Taffy sat dejectedly on the step of the Professor's van; he looked as though he was about to cry.

At home, Jo said, 'And so everybody got what was due to them?' She laughed. 'Well done.'

Dick placed his money on their small table.

'Yes, in more ways than one.' He sniffed exaggeratedly. 'By Jove, there's a nice smell in this little van of ours.'

'Yes? Well, while you've been gathering your dough, I've been baking mine. So give me a tick while I bring in some smalls off the line, then we'll have an early supper.'

As she was removing the washing, she saw a figure walk dejectedly by.

'Hi! Is that you, Professor?'

He stopped and looked across at her, absently, like someone meeting a stranger.

'Ah, dear lady. Good evening, if indeed it can so be termed. It has been a boring day, nothing has happened.'

'Many people would disagree with you, Professor. You do look fed up.'

He sighed, raised his arms then they flopped down again.

'I would hardly use that phrase. I'm too hungry even to feel fed up. I haven't eaten all day. However, I did feed the beautiful birds… Gorgeous creatures.'

His complaint was reiterated by a distant grumbling overhead. Jo looked up at the frowning sky.

'What's that? Distant thunder I would say.'

'It could have been my stomach, craving attention.'

'Then come and be our guest. We are about to have supper.' He didn't need asking twice and followed Jo into her caravan. As they entered she said, 'I've brought a friend of yours. He's hungry.'

'That makes two of us,' said Dick. 'Sit down, Professor, here, at the table.'

As the elderly sage sat with them he beamed at the neatness.

'How beautifully tidy everything is. My residence is a tip in comparison.'

'Well, a woman's work is never done,' said Jo, lost for a suitable reply.

'To break bread with friends is indeed charitable.'

'Well, supper first, Professor,' said Dick, 'save the communion service till after.'

Jo placed a plate of hot pie in front of their guest.

'I thought I heard shooting earlier on,' the Professor said.

'Yes. It was the Major firing his gun, willy-nilly,' explained Dick.

Professor Sparrow sat, his left arm poised, holding a forkful of pie before his open lips.

'That's why we're able to offer you *pigeon* pie,' emphasised Jo.

The Prof's wrinkled face became even more crumpled. He groaned in protest, dropped the fork and clutched his throat with his other hand.

FOUR

Major Merryweather strode out briskly, enjoying his morning walk. On his right-hand side the ground sloped upwards, causing him to sway slightly. Nevertheless, with his stick over his shoulder, rifle style, he sang as he strode out.

'In a cavern by a canyon, excavating for a mine; Lived a miner forty-niner... or thereabouts,' he added, relapsing into speech.

Suddenly he stopped in his tracks at the sight of Professor Sparrow tunnelling into the sloping hillside. The Prof had in fact dug a small cave and was on his knees shovelling away, making the hole deeper. On his head he wore a miner's helmet.

'Morning, Sparrow. How are you?'

The Professor ignored him and was in fact now digging fervently.

'Eureka! Eureka!'

The Major stepped up to him and sniffed.

'You don't smell too fresh yourself, old chap. You're not starting another Channel Tunnel, surely!'

The Professor looked up; his face was streaked with sweat and he panted repeatedly.

'This, my dear fellow, represents weeks of patient research. I have of late been studying an old geological map of this area. On it, potholes were indicated. But, though caverns were shown, the entrance to the cave itself wasn't indicated. It's an ancient salt mine.'

'Ah! In the days before refrigeration, eh?'

'Precisely.'

'And that which was holed up is now uncovered!'

'Exactly.'

The Major stepped nearer and stooped to examine the hole markedly.

'By Jove. That's jolly interesting.'

'Come inside,' the Professor invited. 'Come inside and examine the strata.'

The Major retreated quickly as though avoiding a smack across the head.

'Ah! Fascinated though I am by your diligent labour, I must decline a conducted tour.'

'But it is quite safe.'

The Major stepped forward again and prodded the top of the hole with his stick and a lump of clay fell off. He wagged an admonishing finger at the digger.

'Oh, merely subsoil,' explained the Professor. 'I guarantee it's as safe as, er, a caravan.'

'Without wheels, fastened to a trailer, driven by a maniac. No thanks.'

Professor Sparrow shrugged then with difficulty; like an escapee crawling up the muddy bank of a brook, he climbed from the hole.

'Well, the ground where the caravans and shacks are situated is quite safe. And this cave, when I actually locate it, leads to the site.'

'Good grief,' the Major exclaimed, 'y' mean we're living on a pothole?'

The Professor became ecstatic and all but trembled.

'Not one pothole, several. The site is honeycombed, I should think, according to this old map.' From his back pocket he produced a tattered, ancient map.

'Good God! After what you've said, tonight I shall feel vulnerable. Instead of cocoa and sleepy-time, I'll imagine I'm camping on a beach, waiting for the tide to come in.'

But the Professor wasn't listening; he ignored second opinions.

'I shall call it Sparrow's Hole, because I found it.'

'You're welcome to it, old bean. If you're so concerned about it, take it indoors before some blighter runs off with it.'

The Major laughed at his own whimsy and made as if to move on.

'Don't go,' pleaded the Prof. 'Stay. I shall need assistance in my survey. Surely you'll join me?'

'If I join you, Sparrow, I might get separated from everyone else. However, should you start selling coal, I'll give you my custom.'

Now the Major did move off, shaking his head at the Professor's stupidity, and yet admiring his courage.

'What a man. Potholes! Whatever next?' he muttered to himself, a person he enjoyed talking to. 'However, it's logical. If a nun inhabits a nunnery and a parson a parsonage, I suppose – as old Sparrow's potty – he *should* live in a pothole.'

He walked back between the huts and caravans and came across Mrs Marks who was examining the wheels of her caravan, which had sunk below the ground. As she bent over, she revealed her large posterior, which, bedecked in bright blue, attracted the Major's attention.

'Oh dear! I spy a stern expression. Are you having trouble, Mrs Marks?'

Now he also bent to examine the wheels.

'Do you think I'll have to put a dick under it, Major?'

He jerked back up in surprise, like a parson finding a sticky bun on a pew.

'I beg your pardon?'

'Does it need a thingy under it?' she said. 'Y' know, a whatsit? A Dick, a Joe, a…'

'A jack! You mean a jack. Yes, you'll have to get it jacked up. Your wheels have sunk.'

'That's all? Thank gawd for that.'

'And your bottom's touching the ground.'

Mrs Marks at once clutched her backside, squeezing hard with both hands.

'Major!' she scolded. 'That's not very nice, is it? I can't help having…'

'The bottom of your *van*. The floor – inside. It'll collect damp. Once that sets in, it could cost you a pretty penny. It might mean a new van.' He leaned closer, spoke quietly. 'It could mean…'

'Yes?'

'Mr Marks working overtime.'

Leaning on the van, she pushed herself up, shook her head, smiled sardonically. 'Overtime!' she echoed. 'It will mean Mr Marks getting a job first.'

At that point their regular postman arrived.

'Ah, good day to you, Fred,' the Major greeted. 'Right on time again, I see. I'll take my mail if you like.'

'Oh, ta,' said Fred. 'And here's one for old Sparrowlegs too. What's he up to these days?' he asked, handing over the letters.

'He's not up to anything,' the Major replied. 'He's underneath it.'

'Underneath what?'

'About fifteen ton of rock, I should imagine. I'll explain it all another time. Must go. Need the whatsit and to listen to the radio.' He started to walk away, then turned his head and called, 'Don't forget, Mrs Marks, get your underneath parts painted with creosote, otherwise you'll cave in.'

The Major strode away, whistling the march, 'Blaze Away'.

The postman looked Mrs Marks up and then down, and took a step back, like a quantity surveyor assessing an old rustic cottage – or perhaps a stockman appraising a poorly Aberdeen Angus.

'Not been having one of your turns again, have you, missus?'

'Me? No. But somink will have to be done abaht this bleedin' box I'm living in. You coming in for your cuppa, Fred?'

'I'll just finish delivering this lot. Then I'll nip back to wet me whistle.'

'But I've just brewed it.' (Ten minutes ago.) 'Come and drink it while it's fresh.'

'OK then. Just to please you, mind.'

The postman followed Mrs Marks into her caravan. As he crossed the living room area, his foot went through the floorboards.

'Oh, me ankle.' He stumbled and gripped his lower leg. 'I've sprained me flippin' ankle.'

Mrs Marks replaced the teapot back on the table and rushed to his aid.

'Oh dear, I am sorry, Fred. Could you crawl to the couch? Sit down and I'll bring a bowl of cold water before I hand you your tea.'

'Blimey, I'm not all that thirsty!'

'For your foot, I mean.'

Tetchy, grumbling, Fred reached the couch, crab-like, flopped onto it and removed his shoes and socks. Then he gingerly placed his sore foot into the cold water and snatched a quick breath as though it were hot.

'This will put paid to my delivering,' he moaned.

She reheated the tea and treated him to a tea tray piled with teatime sustenance.

'I do feel terrible about that, Fred.'

'Huh! I don't feel delighted meself.'

'No, seriously, I'm sorry about it. Major Merryweather had just been advising me about having the van hijacked.'

'When? On the way to the scrapyard?'

He removed his foot from the bowl and gingerly stood erect to test his ankle.

'I'll just about be able to hobble back to me post office van, but I'll never get round with the rest of these flippin' letters.'

'Have you a lot left?'

'Only about half a dozen.'

'I'll deliver them, if you like.'

'Oh, I dunno. The post office is touchy about that. All these are private, you know.'

She cocked her ears at this and a slight twitch played about her lips.

'It's Her Majesty's mail, y' see. She's touchy about that.'

'Oh, Fred! Do you think you could get me her autograph?'

He had a slurp of his tea then dunked a shortbread biscuit.

'I don't mean it that way,' he remonstrated peevishly. 'I mean, us postmen are sort of, well, top dogs, so far as letter delivering is concerned.'

Her eyes narrowed as she cogitated – craftily.

'After all, Fred, I caused you to fall. So I don't mind delivering 'em, even though my back is playing up again.' She arched her back and scratched what waist she had and grunted. 'Just look at this floor. I shall have to get Wally to attend to it until I can afford to get it mended properly.'

'Hey, that's not saying much for... 'Ere, I didn't know your old man was called Wally.'

She picked up the tray's contents he'd finished with and plodded into the kitchen with them.

'He ain't,' she said. 'I'm talking about Wally the handyman.'

The postman put his socks and shoes back on.

'Is your husband not a handyman?'

'Not him. He's more of a randy man. No, I shall have to get some dosh from somewhere. I'm as skint as a dressed rabbit at present.'

Fred liked that and showed appreciation with deep chuckling. He stood up from the couch.

'You'll have to tell a few fortunes like you did in the old days.'

Her eyes lit up like a child's at Christmas. She rocked back and forth, smiling.

'Cor, that was a lark. I used to sit in me little tent with the billboards on the outside.' The memory of it deepened her recollection. She gestured towards an imaginary cameo. 'Mrs Marks of Margate. Clairvoyant and Palmist...' She turned to the postman. 'Yes, I think I will, Fred. I'll organise a séance this very night. It should bring in a few quid. I won't have to let Markie get his hands on it, though.'

'I must admit, Mrs Marks, you do have a gipsy look about you. Have you lived in a caravan all your life?'

She winked at him, and would have twitched her ears if she could.

'Oh no, Fred. Well… not yet.'

'Any road up,' said Fred, 'if you do deliver these letters, do you swear you'll carry out the job to the best of your ability?'

Mrs Marks raised her right hand; the gesture seemed to come easily to her.

'I swear to tell…' She stopped suddenly, remembering where she was.

'You don't swear to tell anything. You just deliver these letters. Now, I'd best be getting back to me van. Me foot seems to have swollen. Hey, I might get a few days off! Still, I don't think head office will sue you, Mrs M… Cheers.'

And Fred limped outside, hoping he'd qualify for a few days' respite.

Mrs Marks, taking pique, mimicked him, nasally: 'I don't think head office will sue.' She addressed her remarks to the closing door. 'They can please their bloody self.' She leant on the counter and lit a fag. 'If they come to me for money, I'll help the buggers to look for it. Huh, I've a good mind not to deliver his flamin' letter… Hang about!' The crafty notion persisted.

Letters. Information!

She picked up the batch due for delivery.

'Let's see, there's one for Wally. Blimey, I didn't think he could read! One for Taffy… all the way from Wales. Now who could be writing to him?'

She weighed the letters in her hand.

'Now, if I knew what's inside, I could forecast brilliant horoscopes.' She held each letter up to the light. 'I wonder if there's a penalty for peeping? Fifty hours' community work, perhaps. There are four for young Dick. They'll be about his agency collecting, I expect. And a letter for Jo. Hello, hello, hello. As the copper said to the triplets, this letter's open. It weren't properly licked. They must ha' run short o' spit. I wonder what it says?'

She gingerly shook the letter from its envelope. Then she opened a drawer and pulled out a pair of rubber gloves and unfolded the letter.

'No, I better not. It might be private. Then again, it might be urgent. In which case it should be delivered straight away. But how do you tell if a letter is urgent, wivaht reading it?'

She locked the front door of her caravan, then spread the letter on the counter, read it and began to chuckle. 'Well, well. Lucky little cow.'

❧

Dick and Jo were enjoying morning coffee when they heard letters drop through the letterbox. Dick gathered them together and opened his own.

'Anything exciting today, love?'

'Huh, pep talks by post! What next? "To all agents: Concentrate on fire and burglary insurance this week, we are well below target," blah blah blah. It's called general branch.'

'But you do concentrate on fire insurance,' she said, 'especially when I feel like a night out.'

'True. The commission's very handy. Hello, here's one for you.' He tossed the letter across to her.

'They certainly didn't intend anyone but me reading it. It's sealed with Sellotape.'

She read the letter while Dick put the kettle on for dishwashing.

'Hey, listen to this,' she said. 'It's from Auntie Alice. "… Also you will be delighted to know that Grandpa left £6,000 to be divided between his four grandchildren. This means you will receive £1,500."'

'But that's wonderful.' Dick poured hot water into a large bowl. 'Now, if only the rest of our relatives could behave in such a sensible way, I wouldn't need to flog any more dodgy items.'

He finished wiping the pots, put them away then slipped on his outdoor coat.

'What, and have you grow fat on inherited money? Now nibble your toast and get your skates on.'

'I never realised you loved and respected me so much.' He held up a slice of burnt toast.

'How much?' she asked.

'Enough to give me a burnt offering every morning.'

She pushed his briefcase under his arm and chivvied him from the caravan.

'Oh, get off with you. Go and sell yourself.'

'Don't you think it would be more profitable to raffle me off?' he called over his shoulder.

Dick walked a few yards then called on his first prospect. The resident knew him and listened to what he had to say.

'So if you have a burglary, the company will meet your claim.'

'No, thank you, dearie,' she replied. 'If a burglar breaks in here, I'll go halves with anything valuable he finds.'

'And you can pay your premiums monthly, at no extra cost.'

'Call when my husband is home,' she suggested, and gently but firmly closed the door on him.

Dick walked away, already feeling disheartened. He became almost angry and kicked at a stone. The projectile bounced towards a stroller approaching him.

'Good morning, Richard. I say, you are looking decidedly despondent.'

'Oh, good morning, Major.' He held up some leaflets. 'I'm having some trouble with general branch.'

'General Branch? Never met him. I knew a Brigadier Twigg. Could it be the same family tree?'

'No,' said Dick slowly, wearily. He offered a leaflet. 'Not General Branch,' he replied, in *largo tempo*. He took a deep breath and at presto snapped, 'General branch. Insurance, fire, burglary – as opposed to life assurance.' He stopped for a breath.

The Major was taken aback at Dick's quick-fire delivery. He feigned a little sidestep.

'Oh, you bamboozle me. Anyway, I'll be quite well off when I've snuffed it.' As usual he tittered at his clever wit and swaggered away, swinging his stick.

'Well off when he's snuffed it!' Dick muttered. 'What the hell is he on about?'

He walked on, shaking his head. He approached another caravan and knocked at the door. A woman answered, holding two empty milk bottles. Dick gave her his broadest smile and said, 'I've called...' She shoved the bottles into his hands, went back inside and shut the door. Sighing, Dick withdrew and dropped the bottles in the waste bin. He trudged a little further and arrived outside the Prof's caravan. He knocked.

The Professor opened the door and bobbed his head round, wearing a miner's helmet, complete with a lamp.

'Ah, Richard, dear boy! You are just the person I wish to see.'

Dick stepped inside, believing his luck might have changed.

'Oh, good. Now what was it, fire, burglary, motor?'

'Potholing,' replied the Professor, beaming.

Dick opened his briefcase and rummaged among his leaflets.

'Good, good. I'll just see if... pot what?'

'Holing,' and the Prof sat down and removed his helmet.

'I suppose we must cater for that,' Dick muttered, continuing to rummage. 'Perhaps there's a leaflet for unspecified items.' To himself he muttered, 'I've just got to break me duck.' He looked up. 'I think perhaps I'll have to get in touch with the inspector who deals with...'

'Potholing.'

'Quite. Accidents?' suggested Dick.

'Yes. Now you mention it, an accident could occur.' The Prof's eyes lit up. 'But then, that's all part of the excitement, isn't it? But you will help?'

'Of course. If I can. It might be expensive.'

'Expensive?' The Prof's happy face seemed to fade to be replaced by a worried frown, a bit like a torch going suddenly dim. 'But I don't understand.'

'Expensive,' Dick pronounced clearly. 'Costly. Dear.'

'Ah, dear. Yes. You obviously understand. It *is* very dear to me.'

Now Dick's face changed, from pleasure to puzzlement, just as it did at school at the start of a maths lesson.

'Of course. Expensive, but valuable.'

'Absolutely.'

'So, how far are you prepared to go?'

'As far as possible,' said the Prof, dreamily. 'It will be marvellous.'

'You'll fork out then?' Dick asked, hopefully.

'Definitely. Forking out and shovelling. And you also will need adequate cover.'

'Eh! No,' said Dick. 'You'll need the cover.' He waited, poised with notebook and pen and put misunderstandings down to the client's age. 'Now what do you actually need?'

'I definitely recommend some form of protection.'

'We've established that,' said Dick, recalling that his wife had said her granddad went very queer before he popped off. 'Look, for example, do you need third party?'

'Oh no. Just you and me.'

Dick actually shouted, from frustration, 'You agree you need protection! I agree you need protection. Now, what sort of protection?'

Professor Sparrow picked up the compressed plastic hat and cap lamp.

'A helmet!' Dick dropped his pen and book on the table and threw up his hands in despair. 'Professor Sparrow. You are puzzling me. Perplexing me. Blinding me with…'

'Oh, sorry. I didn't realise it was switched on.'

'It isn't,' Dick shouted.

'Then I do not comprehend the…'

'Neither do I,' Dick yelled. 'Listen, our lines are crossed. Let us start at the beginning… Now, I am trying to sell you an insurance policy.' He spoke with exaggerated embouchure. 'And – you – are trying – to…'

'Get you underground.'

'Pardon?'

Now the Professor spoke with exaggerated embouchure.

'Potholing. Underground. In caves. Our own personal grotto.'

Dick raised his eyebrows in surprise and pointed to the floor. The Professor nodded his head delightedly but Dick shook his slowly.

'No fear. I once lived in a flat and got locked in the cellar for two hours. Never again.'

'Pity,' said the Prof sadly.

'Ask Taffy. He used to be a pit prop in the Rhondda Valley.'

Dick zipped up his briefcase and made as if to move off.

'I don't suppose you deal in motor insurance?' asked the Prof.

Dick wheeled round quickly, thinking, *Is this it?*

'We certainly do, and at very competitive rates. And I collect your premium monthly. No need to pay it all at one go.'

'Then we'll strike a bargain,' said the Prof. 'Your commission for my commission?'

Dick gave a sickly smile, yet he needed the custom. So they shook hands.

'Is it dark?'

'Only when the lamps go out.'

'But I've no helmet,' Dick protested. Although he towered over the old guy, he gesticulated meekly. 'So you see I couldn't possibly...'

'Problem solved,' said the Prof. He placed the miner's helmet on Dick's head. 'You will be adequately protected in that. I will search for something else.'

He rummaged under the bunk bed, which was down, and brought out a chamber pot. He raised it as if to try it on, then shook his head.

'No use. I take a six and seven eighths... Ah!' He looked up at a row of pegs holding all manner of hats. On the last peg hung a horned Nordic helmet. 'The very thing. I bought it at a car boot sale.' He popped it on his head. 'I had forgotten about this.' He turned to Dick and smiled, like a juvenile at a party.

'We don't have to cross a three-acre meadow to get to this pothole, do we?' Dick asked.

'No. Why?'

'If the bull's grazing, and sees you, it might start getting pally.'

Mrs Marks was stacking a shelf behind the counter; a fag drooped from her dry lips. She removed the half-finished fag, trod it into the floorboards and warbled a song:

'I could have danced all night, I could have danced...' A spate of coughing halted her rendition. 'Bloody fags! What do they put in 'em these days?' She lit up another.

The door creaked open and a traveller entered. 'Morning, madam. I'm Rigby. Coughing better, I see... I'm the public health inspector.'

Mrs Marks became flustered, snatched the cigarette from her mouth and tried to conceal it. In her panic she backed away onto the bacon slicer. She rebounded sharply, clutching her backside. 'Oh heck,' she muttered, and as she did so cigarette smoke spiralled from her open mouth in a surprised curl.

'Do be careful, madam, or else your customers will get a little behind with their orders.' He laughed over-loudly at his flippancy. 'Sorry for the ancient chestnut.'

'You startled me,' she said, feeling quite cross.

'Relax, love. Don't snap your garters. I'm not an official, and it's a good job I'm not, the way you're standing there chuffing like an oily exhaust.'

He approached the counter in a swaggering manner.

'I think you had better state your business before

I lose me temper,' she said, recovering and beginning to bristle like an irate rhino.

'Can I speak to the manager?'

'I'm acting for him.' She swelled her generous bust.

'Acting! Look, darling, I've not come to hold auditions. I need the owner. I only deal with people at the top.'

She now felt quite hurt. 'At the top of what, a ladder?' She scrambled onto the counter and thrust a broom at him, like Boadicea. 'The top! Am I high enough for you now? You cheeky sod.'

He backed away sharpish. 'Nothing personal, ducks. Only it's a matter of business.'

She lowered herself onto terra firma. 'Anyway, he ain't here. He's on holiday.'

'Abroad?'

'He might be. He's visiting foreign parts.'

Rigby thought impudence was clever. 'Foreign parts or foreign tarts?'

'Careful… there's a lady present.'

Rigby took a risk and looked about the shop, searching for camouflaged crumpet.

'Really! Anyway, to business. A new van will be sited here next week,' he said confidently. 'And I've called to discuss the part exchange with the buyers. Name of Coningsby.'

'Oh yes. That's Richard and Josephine, a young couple. Having a new van, are they? Huh, lucky for some.'

'That's the way it goes, love. Some of us were made for success. I've put a few vans on here over the years.'

'I thought I'd seen you before.'

Rigby made a mock bow. 'My face is familiar, is it?'

'Yes, and from what I've heard, so are your hands.'

'Well, well. Envy, eh? Such a remark is praise in disguise. Anyway, I expect, like me, you're on commission, so I'll give you some business before I hop it. A packet of twenty, please.' He placed a £20 note on the counter. 'Sorry, love. I've no less than that.'

She picked it up. Held it up to the light. 'Well, I can't change that.'

'Oh! I'll have 'em on tick then.'

Mrs Marks pointed to a large card behind the counter on which was printed: 'NO TICK THE CLOCK HAS STOPPED'.

Rigby shrugged, picked up his £20 note and made as if to leave the shop.

'Hang about a minute,' she said. 'Just before you bugger off, come and look at this.' She led him into the living quarters and showed him the weakness in the floorboards. 'What can you recommend for this?'

Rigby stooped and examined the rot.

Anticipating a sale, he waxed lyrical, 'I recommend a new caravan, dear lady.'

'Aye, and dear is the key word. I can't afford it.'

He looked about the tatty premises. 'Yes. I believe you, missus. Hire a carpenter as soon as possible.'

With that, he doffed his hat, walked out, sought the Coningsbys, who were not at home. 'I'll call again,' he grumbled.

Dick and Professor Sparrow were standing outside the hole the Prof had dug earlier. Dick was wearing the coal miner's hard hat and his learned companion sported a Nordic horned helmet.

'Now there is nothing to be afraid of,' the Prof assured him.

'If I had any horse sense, I wouldn't be here.'

'Horse sense! Nonsense, my boy. After all, horse sense is merely stable thinking. And you and I are not cattle. We dwell in caravans. Modern gypsies. I would not have troubled you except that there is a ledge and, if I am to investigate properly, I shall need your assistance. Indeed, you are privileged. I would not have asked anyone else. Now let us enter. Be not faint of heart.'

'Oh, I'm willing to go into the cave. It's me legs that are the cowards. Cripes, I could murder a double brandy.'

The Professor rummaged in his haversack. 'Then quell your violence on this.' He passed a brandy flask to Dick, who took a thirsty guzzle.

The Prof crawled into the cave, turned as best he could and beckoned Dick to follow. They crawled a few yards in.

'Imagine you are a Colditz hero.'

'Aye, but they were crawling out. Ye gods, it's as black as night. Everything is closing in on me. I feel I'm dying.'

'Well, I'm trying to help you… Here have another drink.'

Once again he passed the flask to Dick, who took a further satisfying gulp.

'You will never regret this, dear boy. You will behold many of Nature's wonders. Look at those, stalagmites and stalactites.' The Prof turned his cap lamp on them. 'I don't suppose you have seen such beauties before?'

'Oh, I have. *And* I know the difference. Mites go up.' He gesticulated insects with his fingers. 'And tights come down.' He mimed a woman removing her knickers.

🌳

Mrs Marks arranged a row of chairs in her living room and stepped back to appraise them. Markie, her husband, was walking about in his underpants.

'Where've you put 'em? Where's me bleedin' kecks?'

He shuffled around, huffing and puffing, looking behind cushions, under chairs and in cupboards.

'They're where you'll never find 'em. They're not in our van. You are not traipsing off to some boozy do tonight. You've got to help me with this séance.'

He flopped into a chair just in his shirt tails, and, pretending he was modest, held a cushion over his manly parts.

'Huh, it's a bloody liberty.'

'Now quit squawking and come over here.'

Mrs Marks had earlier erected a curtain, behind which stood a chair. She paddled a hand, ushering him along as though he was a child. Then she pointed to the seat and obediently he sat.

'And don't forget, no funny tricks this time, otherwise you don't get paid. When I call, "Is there someone here?"' – declared in a wavering voice – 'you do *not* reply, "Aye, but only for the beer."' She reminded him of this by flicking his head with a hard, cruel finger. Then she returned to her place.

He stuck his head round the curtain.

'It was only a bit of fun, liven things up a bit.'

'This is not fun, it's business. We are skint. We need the van repairing. Wally now works for the council. And you're too idle to get one of your mates to come and look.' She thrust sheets of paper at him. 'Now, here are some notes I've prepared for you. Here is a torch what you must cover with a hanky… if you have one. You've done this before. You know what to expect.'

'Expect! Expect! *I* didn't expect you to confiscate me breeches, but you have done.'

She grabbed a thick book off the shelf and threw it at him.

'We need the brass, Markie. It's for your benefit as well as mine. Now for once, try to be a normal husband and co-operate.'

'What's it worth if I do?'

'It's worth a thick ear if you don't.'

❦

Squashed together with Richard inside the pothole, Professor Sparrow indicated a small hole with the light from his torch. The hole, however, could only be reached by climbing onto a ledge.

'There you are, Richard. That is the inner cave I was telling you about.'

Dick, having drunk all the brandy, waved the empty flask about as he spoke.

'Alright, cock, you having found your hole, now...'

'Sparrow, if you please.'

'Alright, cock sparrow, you've found your hole. Now, letsh go home.' He placed his wrist watch in the beam from the torch. 'Itsh past midnight.'

'No it isn't,' the Prof corrected. 'Whether or not you promised your wife you would be home by midnight.'

'Thatsh true. So it can't be midnight, 'cos I'm not home yet.' With his right hand he felt his left arm. 'I'm still here.' He shook his head and puzzled wrinkles furrowed his brow.

'Now, I am unable to enter this cave unaided, Richard. So be a good chap and support me.'

Dick took another hopeful swig at the brandy flask, but finding it empty he flung it at his feet.

'Support you? You support your bloody self. It takes me all my time to support my wife.'

'Just crouch here for a moment.' The Professor gently pushed Dick down on all fours against the wall of their tunnel, then clambered onto his back. 'Nearly there.' He stretched up unsteadily.

'What's the use of him bringing an empty brandy flask?' muttered Richard, quite maudlin.

Inside Mrs Marks' caravan, her séance customers sat in a tight semi-circle round a small table. Jo sat in the centre of the semi-circle, with Major Merryweather on her right and Taffy on her left. Next to the Welshman sat Wally the handyman and then Miss Primm, who did not manage to escape as the proprietor bolted her shop door. Markie sat in an easy chair a few feet away.

'And you really have contacted people from the other side?' Josephine asked.

'Course I have, dearie. Reglar as clockwork.'

The Major snorted. 'Rubbish!'

'I tell you I have.'

'I heard it said she has,' asserted Wally, scraping dirt from under his fingernails with a pocket knife.

Jo watched him and squirmed.

'Who, then, have you contacted?' Major Merryweather's voice was loaded with contempt, like a child who doesn't believe in Father Christmas.

'Well, my first husband, as a matter of fact. When *he* was alive I had to be a magician as well as a fortune teller.'

This sounded more veracious to the Major. 'You mean you performed tricks?'

'Yes. Every Friday I had to trick him into parting with his wages.'

Taffy and the handyman and Miss Primm tittered at this.

'But you always led me to believe your first husband was a military man,' pursued the Major. 'I imagined him to be upright and smart in his bearing. You know, something like…'

'Something like yourself, Major,' said Taffy, whose face remained deadpan, but whose eyes betrayed mischief.

'Absolutely.' The Major sat suddenly upright in his hardback chair.

'Smart? Smart?' echoed Mrs Marks, who now did speak more honourably than usual. 'He was the scruffiest chap you ever clapped eyes on.'

'I heard,' put in Wally, 'that the nearest he ever got to being tidy, was when he drank his whisky neat!'

Jo burst out laughing. 'Oh, you're exaggerating, surely?'

'You told me he was a musician,' Taffy said, sounding piqued at some past deception.

'What I said was, at night he'd go out as fit as a fiddle and return as tight as a drum! Anyway,' said Mrs Marks, 'if we keep discussing him, he'll spoil it all by appearing and he'll borrow a fiver off somebody. So let's get down to business… erm… research. Now, don't forget, your fingertips must touch each other's so that the spiritual current can be circulated.'

'Aren't you going to go into a trance then?' Jo asked.

Taffy nudged her and indicated Wally, who was enjoying a quiet doze.

'Some folk are in that state permanently, aren't they,' he said softly.

Mrs Marks was now rocking slightly in her chair and beginning to groan.

Jo turned slightly towards Taffy and placed fingers on her lips.

'Sh. I think she's going. We'll have to stay quiet.'

In a voice like a husky contralto, Mrs Marks began to perform. 'All is dark. Dark. Is anyone there?'

Markie was sitting behind the curtain with a script in his hand and holding a shaded torch. He too produced an unfamiliar voice, yet it was still oiled and greased by alcohol and roughened by nicotine.

'Hello, Josephine. This is your grandpa here.'

'Oh! Oh, heavens.' She clutched at Taffy's arm, thus breaking the spirit circle.

'Oh, this is so sudden, my dear,' Taffy responded, stroking her hand.

'Sh, be serious,' the Major reprimanded, 'give the thing a trial.'

In a wavering voice Mrs Marks moaned, 'The circuit is breaking.' Now her voice died away, 'Breaking... is breaking.'

Jo whispered to Taffy, 'Oh, sorry.' She pulled herself away from him. 'We've got to touch hands.'

Taffy chuckled sensually, his imagination running away with him. 'This is the best part of it.'

Mrs Marks came through again, as though her voice was kept in a drawer. 'That is much better.' She swelled on the syllables. 'Much – better – now.'

When Markie spoke, Mrs Marks mimed him. 'Are you there, Josephine?' he asked. Hidden behind his curtain, Markie was swigging a bottle of beer between his lines. 'I would like to speak to you...' He took a quick swig. '... Josephine.'

'But this is incredible,' Jo gasped. 'It sounds just like him.'

'I hope, dear Grandchild, you were pleased with the little windfall I left you in my will?' Granddad's question was followed by a hefty belch from Markie.

Taffy, man of the world, sceptical about everything, muttered, 'Windfall is the right word.'

Jo gasped. Her hand flew to her throat. 'It is him. Nobody else could possibly have known. It is him.' She clapped her hands like a child receiving a wanted gift. 'Oh yes, Grandpa. I was pleased when I was included in your will. Oh, I was.'

Taffy's eyebrows shot to his hairline. He leaned away slightly from Jo and looked cautiously at her. Then he glanced towards the curtain and his bushy brows dropped again as he frowned.

A slight cough preceded Grandpa's next comment: 'It will help you get what you want.' Markie inserted an unscripted line. 'Don't forget your friends…' The voice boomed again. 'Do I read your mind correctly when I say that you are going to have a new home?'

Jo all but fainted. 'Yes. Yes, you do.' She ratified her feelings to her neighbours with a gesture. 'But this is fantastic.'

The Major leaned over to Jo. 'Surely you are not leaving us?' he whispered.

'No,' she murmured, 'we're getting a new caravan.'

'Sh. Quiet,' Taffy muttered. He was now unsure of himself, hesitant about the reality.

'Well, I'd best be going now, Josephine,' Granddad told her. 'There's a queue up here waiting to speak to their friends down there.'

'Oh, couldn't you stay a little longer, Grandpa?'

'No. Not tonight, Josephine.'

There was a rustling around Mrs Marks as she fumed at Markie's flippancy.

'There is something decidedly odd about all this,' asserted the Major.

Fearing the Major's suspicion, Mrs Marks went into moaning mode again.

'Oh, oh… Another voice is coming through. It's struggling to get through.'

Markie picked up his cue promptly. 'Hello there, is that you, Llewellyn bach?'

'Huh, they must be on the wrong wavelength. There's no one here of that name.'

'There is, you know,' said Taffy, with a spurt of excitement. 'It's me.'

'You!'

'Yes, Major. It's my middle name. I don't use it much.'

Major Merryweather burst out laughing. 'I should think you don't. Llewellyn. Oh dear.'

'And what might your bloody middle name be?'

'Enoch.'

Markie, Taffy and Wally laughed their heads off, the tittering coming from all directions, causing the Major to look about him suspiciously.

The veteran shook his head. 'I don't like it at all. I don't like it.'

'Then why don't you change it?' Taffy sniggered vigorously.

'Quiet!' Jo commanded. 'Control yourselves. Grown men, quarrelling over names. You'll frighten the spirits away.'

Taffy (and Enoch) muttered apologies, and actually hung their heads.

'Is that you, Llewellyn?' came a voice, sounding suspiciously like Grandpa.

'Oh, get on with it.' The Major was now irritable.

'This is your uncle speaking.'

'Which one?' Taffy asked. He wagged his head at the others. 'I have so many, you know.'

'Huh, Celts,' muttered the Major. 'They breed like Welsh rarebits.'

'I'm your Uncle Morgan Davies,' moaned Markie, carefully.

'Good God,' exclaimed Taffy, 'only last week the folks back in Pontypridd placed a stone on his grave.'

'But they were too late,' said the Major with a smirk. 'It seems he got out.'

'I thought I'd let you know I'm doing alright up here. Decent beer,' Markie added, sliding from the script.

'Good digs have you got, Uncle?'

'Good digs!' the Major remonstrated. 'Really!'

'Or whatever they call it… up there,' said Taffy, sheepishly.

'Yes, thank you, boyo. Not like Wales, mark you. But it's a heavenly little place. Reminds me of Prestatyn.' This also was unscripted.

Mrs Marks exhaled a deep sigh of resignation.

'Listen, Llewellyn, you'll be having a visitor next week,' Markie went on.

'Oh, who will that be then?'

'It'll be your finance... er, fiancée, Blodwin.'

'Stone the crows, so I will. It's a fact,' he explained to the others. 'I got a letter about it only this morning.'

The Major's jaw dropped. He nodded towards Mrs Marks. 'Then she is genuine?'

'Of course she is,' asserted Taffy. 'Every damn word.'

Ensconced in the dimness of the caravan, Mrs Marks smirked, enjoying the performance.

The Major crossed himself quickly. 'Then I take back all I've said.'

'Oh, it's too late now, boyo,' Taffy insinuated.

'Watch her, Llewellyn,' the voice cautioned. 'Watch that fiancée of yours. She's out to stir up trouble.'

'What sort of trouble, Uncle?'

'Can't say.' The voice became fainter. 'Must go.' He began to sing quietly. 'We'll keep a welcome in the hillside...'

Mrs Marks rose from her chair. 'There seems to be another message for someone.' She walked towards the curtain as though in a trance, and under cover of the gloom she thrust her hand through the curtain and slapped Markie across the head. 'The message is for Major Merryweather. It says: "Do not scorn the unknown. Mock not that about which you are ignorant."'

Outside, the rain beat heavier on the caravan. There was a sudden flash of lightning, then a roll of thunder.

Mrs Marks continued her moral tale with ghoulish cadences. 'As well as those above who try to help us, there are those below who would tempt us.'

The séance assembly then heard rumbling and scraping under the floorboards.

'And it sounds as though they intend to join us,' Jo observed.

Another flash of lightning blazed by the window, reminiscent of the Blitz, and the table began to wobble.

'It could be worse,' the Major said. 'We could have drummed up Old Nick on the Ouija board.'

Jo clutched his arm. 'I think we have.'

The wobbling table now fell over and a splintering of timber was heard below where the table had been. Suddenly the Professor's head popped through the hole, complete with horned helmet, closely followed by Dick wearing a miner's helmet. Jo screamed and sprang up, staggered forward and clutched at the curtain, which fell, wrapping itself around her. Markie's face was petrified. Miss Primm, sitting on the end, woke up. 'Oh! Have I missed something?'

FIVE

Rigby strolled casually among the caravans and shacks of Upsy-Daisy. He shook his head in disgust, and a sense of revulsion raised the left corner of his top lip, revealing a small tunnel of distaste.

'What a dump. Still, their money is as good as anybody else's.'

He saw the caravan he was looking for, a tiny tourer, not even fit for a mucky weekend, in his aloof opinion. He walked round the side and then the back, noting the blemishes. Then he stepped onto the iron grid and knocked. The door opened.

'Oh, hello,' Richard said. 'You must be Mr Rigby? We got a letter from your firm saying you'd call on us.'

'Well, it's not my firm… not yet.'

The mindless boast went unnoticed by Richard. 'Come in, come in.'

Rigby entered the van. 'Very small, isn't it?'

He didn't wipe his feet and Josephine noticed. She also spotted his fancy shoes, which only an egotistical holidaymaker would wear, in her opinion.

'It is small,' she said. 'But we've grown to like it.'

Rigby looked at the young woman and was halted in his tracks, for he was blown away by her beauty, and for a few seconds stood gaping.

'Well,' he said, recovering, 'if you've grown to like this, you'll flourish in one of ours.' He sniggered at his own wisecrack. 'I believe you have visited our display area?'

'Oh yes,' Dick said, 'and very nice your vans are.'

Jo had decided she didn't like him on sight; nevertheless she invited him to accept a mug of 'Tea of coffee, Mr... er?'

'Lionel,' he announced, 'sometimes Leo. Named after the mountain lion.'

He looked about him for an ovation, but Jo saw only a peacock. 'Well?' she asserted.

'Ah yes. Coffee, please.'

'Have a seat, Leo...' Dick glanced at Jo who glared. 'Mr Rigby,' he corrected himself.

Rigby settled at the tiny table and once more savoured Josephine's appearance.

'What we need to know is how much can you offer in part exchange?' Richard said.

Jo placed a swiftly concocted mug of coffee before him and the salesman took a quick gulp at it. 'Biscuit.' It sounded more like an order than an invitation.

'Why not,' the lionheart responded. And he reached for a coconut crumble and dunked it into his beverage.

This made Jo shudder so much she had to turn her back on him.

He masticated the biscuit and talked at the same time. Watching him, Dick was reminded of a concrete mixer as Rigby, quite unaware, sprayed damp crumbs across the table.

'I checked your van over before I came in,' Rigby said. 'It needs a lot of attention… You bought it from Vic Venables, didn't you?'

Richard nodded.

Josephine enlarged. 'There's not much point in doing anything if one intends to buy a new one, is there?'

Rigby was obliged to hum and haw at this. Then he committed a mortal sin. He took out a packet of cigarettes, offered them; the offer was declined, so he lit up, quickly, like a well-practised conjurer.

'This is a no-smoking establishment,' Jo almost bellowed.

The lion quickly became a rabbit, and Rigby deftly pocketed his addiction.

Richard was anxious to learn the details of a financial transaction. 'So what can you offer?'

'A hundred,' Rigby said. 'It needs a lot of work.'

'A hundred!' Jo echoed. Now she liked the bloke even less.

'Well, I'm governed by the firm I work for.'

'And we are governed by what we can afford,'

Richard said. 'So, how much is a new caravan likely to cost? Your lot were very cagey when we called. Mrs Marks said you would be.'

'Well, prices vary.'

'And part exchanges don't, I suppose.' She looked at the table top, then grabbed a dish cloth, snatched the empty coffee cup and wiped his crumbs off the table.

'Well, there's the cost of towing it away,' he began, 'then repairing and respraying. Then there's…'

'But a hundred quid is your limit, is it?' Richard asked.

'OK, I'll go up to £120.' Rigby shrugged his shoulders to display his co-operation and generosity.

Jo was by now quite irritated by his attitude. 'We're not prepared to settle for that either.' She demonstrated her anger by snatching his now empty mug from the table and banged it down on the draining board.

'Well, my offer is the best you've had today,' he said conceitedly.

'Wrong, Mr Rigby,' Jo replied. 'Your offer is the worst we've had today. Thank you and close the door on your way out.' She turned her back and began to wash the crockery.

Rigby, used to winning sales and therefore surprised at his defeat, rose from his seat and retreated from the caravan.

'I thought you were a bit rough and ready with him, love,' Richard said.

'I was certainly ready for him. I'm just about weary with con men.'

'Well, you're right about that,' he said. 'Fancy shoes and flashy ties.'

'And he had dandruff on his collar.'

❀

Everyone admired Taffy's caravan; some residents admired what he had but they didn't know the truth. So it had to be whispered: 'It is not Taffy's caravan.'

'Are you sure?'

'Positive. The mobile home he swanks about in fact belongs to Blodwin, his girlfriend.'

❀

Taffy looked through the caravan window and saw Rigby walking by looking quite despondent, resentful even.

'He's a sulky-looking bugger, and no mistake,' Taffy mumbled.

From the table he picked up the letter which had just been delivered, sniffed it, as a bloodhound would, and said (as a bloodhound wouldn't), 'It's from her! It's from Blodwin.'

He sank the mug of tea he'd just brewed then slumped into the armchair and opened the letter.

It contained a lot of yakety-yak, plenty of tittle-tattle, some scandal then the main event:

'So I'll arrive late Tuesday afternoon. No need to meet me. I'll hire a taxi from the station. All my love, Blodwin.'

A look of alarm swept across Taffy's tanned face and the tip of his ruddy nose like a draught wafting over a cherry cake.

'Good God. That's today. I'd best tidy up a bit,' he muttered. 'She doesn't like her van being mucked up.'

He set to with a disgruntled effort. Blodwin, whom he often referred to as his fiancée, was a very tidy person and quite fussy about the condition of her caravan.

This irked him like a tiny pebble in his shoe. In earlier days Blodwin won a considerable amount on the lottery; it wasn't enough to buy a small house but sufficient to purchase a large caravan. Furthermore, she nursed a desire to leave Wales and live within commuting distance of the bright lights, posh pubs and swanky shops of London. And via a caravan magazine she had located Upsy-Daisy, which was situated about eighty miles from the capital, certainly nearer than Aberystwyth where she lived at present.

When his back started to ache through pushing the Hoover and he'd swilled – rather than washed – the pots in the sink and flicked cobwebs from the window panes, Taffy paused for a breather, made a cup of tea and a slice of toast, and sat down to watch the news on the telly… his telly, he thought, smugly.

'A convict has escaped from Berwyn, Wrexham,' the announcer said. 'He is not considered to be violent, but anyone who sees him should contact the police.'

A mugshot of the escapee was shown… and Taffy gasped. 'Good God. It's Bryn Jenkins,' he told himself. 'I knew he was doing time.'

Taffy, however, was only half pleased at Bryn's escape, because in earlier days the convict had been over-friendly with Blodwin; and it was only through Bryn's incarceration that Taffy had been able to muscle in on the Welsh wench and take the felon's place, just like a latecomer to the theatre bagging the sole seat on the front row.

It was shortly after becoming affectionate with this attractive Welsh cleaning woman that Taffy learned she had won the lottery; and before long – encouraging her to shell out on some accommodation – he had a permanent roof over his head.

After a few weeks of an unauthorised honeymoon, Blodwin presented her news about relocating. 'Wales is boring,' she maintained. Initially Taffy was surprised she wanted to live further afield, and a teeny bit vexed if the truth were known. But since he enjoyed free lodgings and regular rumpy-pumpy, he had to agree to her terms. He also believed Blodwin still had some lottery money left over.

'If you settle in the van, it'll give you time to find a job. There are lots of roads in England so there'll be vacancies for roadmenders.'

And that was that.

What she omitted to communicate in her letter, which Taffy read twice, was that she had spent a few days in hospital recovering from spots. The medical term being Rocky Mountain Spotted Fever. It was quite infectious and recognised by red spots invading the patient.

Taffy now switched off the telly, made some sandwiches and scribbled a note, which he propped up against a book strewn casually on the table:

'Dear Blodwin, Thank you for your letter. I'm afraid the firm I work for are completing a stretch of road on the A11. We have to live near to the job until it is finished. Wot will be a while yet. Make yourself known to the folks in Upsy-Daisy. They are a nice bunch. See you wen I get back. All Yours, Taffy.'

He packed his lunch and some clean clothes for the pub after work. Then he scribbled another note, which he fastened to the knocker outside the door. He slammed the door shut and walked up to Dick and Jo's small caravan. He knocked.

'Sorry to trouble you, love, but will you hand this key to my, er, fiancée when she calls later today?'

'Oh, righty-ho, Taffy,' Josephine said. 'Going off, are you?'

'Yes. We have to finish a stretch of road. And if I don't turn up, I'll get sacked. Thanks a lot.' And off he trudged towards Daisy Hill village where the lorry would pick him up and transport him to the site.

About the same time that Taffy was climbing aboard the transport lorry, Blodwin was just a few miles away, hailing a taxi. 'Do you know a place called Upsy-Daisy?'

'I certainly do, ma'am. Jump in and I'll have you there in half an hour. I'll put your cases in the boot.'

Blodwin settled herself in the back passenger seat and they were off. The taxi driver knew a few shortcuts and he transported his passenger there in record time. At the entrance to the higgledy-piggledy village, the driver went slowly so that Blodwin could identify the address of each caravan. Then she began to scratch herself.

'Oh no. Not again!' She scratched some more and sighed.

They drove up the slope between the vans.

'This is the one. Thank you very much.' In appreciation for the safety and speed of the journey she gave him a tip, and he heaved her luggage beside the steps then drove off with alacrity.

The first thing she noticed was the note fastened round the door handle:

'Dear Blodwin, Sorry, but I had to dash off to work. I'll be gone about three days. The key is being held by Dick and Josie, on the opposite side, further along. It's the small caravan. Love, Taffy.'

Leaving the luggage on the steps she trudged up to the small caravan and knocked. The door was answered by an attractive young woman.

'Sorry to trouble you, dear.' She scratched her itchy arm. 'Are you Josie?'

The woman anticipated her. 'Have you come for Taffy's key?'

'Yes, please. Although it's my key, not Taffy's.'

Josie ducked back in then bobbed out again, handed the key over then noticed the woman was scratching. 'Are you alright? Would you like to come in?'

'No thanks.' Tears welled up in Blodwin's eyes. 'It's the spots. They've come back again. I'd best be off.'

As she moved away, Jo pushed the door to and peered through the gap.

'That woman seems to have a flea, or something,' she said to Richard, then closed the door again and shuddered.

Blodwin unlocked her door, humped the cases inside, kicked the door shut then flopped onto the bed and wept. 'Oh God. Not another dose? They said I was cured.'

Although Josephine – in the odd manner that some women assess their own sex – decided that Taffy's fiancée was a tart, she nevertheless felt sorry for her, and wondered how the Welshman's moll would cope for food and perhaps minor medication. So an hour after the woman had called, Jo decided to investigate. She strolled down to the flashy caravan and peered through the windows, shading her eyes with a cupped hand. The woman was prostrate on the bed and the shaking of her body suggested she was sobbing. Jo tapped on the window. After a repetition the woman turned, then came to the large and filthy glass pane. Her face was covered in spots.

'Are you alright?' Jo asked, knowing she wasn't.

The woman shook her head and pointed to her spots. 'I've been in hospital with Rocky Mountain Spotted Fever. I thought they'd cured it. But it's come back. I can't open the door because it's contagious.'

Hearing this shouted through the glass, Jo actually stepped back with a slight gasp. She thought, *She looks dreadful.* Then went up to the window again and mouthed, 'Do you need anything?'

'I've no food. No bread or milk. I also need a doctor.'

Jo pondered this. Provisions she could acquire. Medical aid was more difficult. 'What's your name?' she asked, as well as miming.

'Blodwin… What's yours?' The spots did a little dance on her top lip.

'Jo. Short for Josephine. I'll see what I can do.' She offered a weak smile then walked away, back to her own caravan. Seated inside, she explained the problem to Richard.

'Spots, eh!' he echoed. 'Why did she come here then?'

'She thought the hospital had cured her. Honest, she has a face like a Christmas pudding. But instead of raisins she's got these spots. They're dreadful – and catching. But we can't let the poor woman starve.'

'Right. Well, we'll feed her then send for an ambulance.'

They ambled over to Mrs Marks' tatty shop and explained the situation. The cautious retailer at once turned to her notice hanging behind and above the counter. It proclaimed: 'NO TICK THE CLOCK HAS STOPPED'.

'I've been conned before,' she said. 'I don't wish to seem unkind, but I'm not giving credit to somebody I've never even seen.'

'But it's Taffy's girlfriend,' Dick explained.

'Precisely. Therefore, no tick.'

'OK. I'll pay.' He took out his wallet, and turned to Jo. 'What do you suggest we get her?'

'Bread, milk, a pot of jam. Tea, coffee, packet of butter.'

'Boiled ham, a nice slice of cheese, chocolate to perk her up,' added Mrs Marks, sensing a killing.

'Hang on. I'm paying for this,' Dick emphasised.

Eventually they settled on half a dozen items and Dick settled the bill. The groceries were secured in a plastic bag with a handle, which Mrs Marks had secreted from the Co-op. The squiggly handle was tied into a knot.

They were about to leave the shop when Jo suddenly said, 'We can't ask her to open the door, her spots might…'

'Fly out and contaminate us,' Dick said, exasperated.

'Well, I'm not doing it,' she maintained.

'Look, we'll place the parcel on the step, walk away, and she can open the door.'

'Oh! Of course. Why didn't I think of that?'

He turned to Mrs Marks. 'Do you sell ointment for a mental blockage?'

After some mild thumping and squabbling they left the shop, followed by the nosey Mrs Marks. They arrived at what was earlier known as 'Taffy's van'. They saw Blodwin through the large window and at once noticed her spots, like dots on a Dalmation. Jo held up the carrier bag for the dejected patient to observe.

'I'm going to place it on the doorstep,' she mouthed. 'Then you open the door when we have moved away.' All this was spoken with embellished enunciation, as though talking to a deaf person who might also be a bit thick. And Jo pointed to the bag she held and the location of the doorstep.

Blodwin understood at once. After all, as a youngster she passed for the grammar school. She held up two thumbs, signalling her understanding.

Josephine placed the bag in front of the door with the care of a footballer taking a penalty. She stepped back, looked at it, then the heroic trio moved on a few paces, stopped, turned to glance at the door. But it didn't open. They looked at each other's blank faces.

'I'll go back and see what's up,' Jo declared.

'Take care,' Richard observed, as though to a bomb disposal expert.

'Avoid the spots,' said Mrs Marks, thinking the pustules might spit at her.

Jo actually crept up to the window, pointed to the door, then became a mime artist and acted out a dumb show about unlocking the door.

Blodwin motioned desperation with a begging gesture. 'I've lost the key,' she wailed.

The rear guard advanced. 'What's up?' Dick demanded.

'She's mislaid the key,' Jo explained.

The three of them gawped through the window like rubbernecks at the zoo. Their inquisitive crouch was joined by curious neighbours.

'Something amiss?' asked Major Merryweather.

'What's up?' said Wally the handyman.

'She lost her key,' Mrs Marks explained.

Professor Sparrow tut-tutted and added, 'Dear me. How awful.'

'Some people are so careless,' pronounced Miss Primm.

'Trouble is, she's not well,' Dick told them.

At that, everyone stepped forward to glance at the sufferer – then stepped back smartly when they saw her spots.

'Blimey, she's in a mess,' said Wally. 'Looks like a tattoo gone wrong.'

'And we've got to get this food to her,' Jo explained, holding up the plastic bag.

'Ask her to open a window,' the Major said.

They did – too many of them, all standing in front of the main window, signalling, shouting, miming, like a company of clowns on speed.

Inside the van, Blodwin returned their gestures with her own signals.

'I can't understand what she's getting at,' Wally complained, 'waving and pointing like that.'

'That's because she's Welsh,' Mrs Marks said.

Richard shook his head with exasperation. 'Look, we're getting nowhere. It needs only one of us to explain what we mean.'

'Good man,' the Major agreed. 'I suggest you take control, Richard.'

'Hear, hear,' the Professor added.

For a few seconds everything went quiet, then Dick went nearer to the window. As if giving him encouragement, Blodwin thrust her spotted visage close to the glass.

'Open one of your windows,' he said simply.

'I can't,' she replied. 'They are all locked, too.'

'Stupid cow,' grumbled Wally.

'Well, she's Welsh,' asserted Mrs Marks.

Richard stepped back among his neighbours and looked up at the caravan.

'There's a fanlight on the roof,' he said. 'If she can open that we could lower the plastic bag inside.'

'Good man,' the Major repeated.

'We don't call them fanlights,' said Mrs Marks.

'They're known as fannys,' Wally explained, with a grin. Whereupon he went up to the window and pointed upwards. 'Open your fanny,' he shouted.

Inside the van Blodwin bridled visibly.

'Uncouth lout,' the Major snorted.

'She should be so lucky,' Miss Primm sighed.

Jo went closer to the window. First she waved, then smiled. Now she pointed upwards to the van's ceiling. 'Can you open that little window at the top?' She stated her enquiry slowly and with clarity.

Inside her mobile home, Blodwin searched for, and found, a broom. She held it by the head and poked the wooden handle upwards, and located the hatch. She pushed gently and the little window opened slightly wider.

Outside everyone cheered.

'Fannies have to be loose,' Wally said, 'to let fresh air in and foul air out.'

'Absolutely,' the Major agreed, and slapped the handyman on the back.

'The next problem is to get this parcel through that opening,' Jo said, holding up the plastic carrier bag.

'Climb on the roof,' the Professor suggested.

'Too bloody steep,' said Wally.

'Huh! So much for fancy caravans,' Mrs Marks declared.

'We must lower it through the hole,' Richard announced slowly.

'That will be difficult,' Miss Primm responded.

'Easier said than done,' Jo added.

'A fishing rod will do it,' Professor Sparrow suggested.

'Well spoken, that man,' the Major commended.

'Wally's the fisherman,' Mrs Marks informed them.

So the handyman went to collect his rod and line, and the others pondered and rebuked the new neighbour in their midst, who was causing them so much aggravation; the new neighbour, of course, couldn't hear them. The angler returned with his tackle.

'Give it here,' he commanded, like a conjurer about to present his best trick. He hooked the handle of the plastic bag onto the end of his line and swung it up and over the caravan; then lowered it steadily over the hatch. But it refused to enter the hole.

'It's too big!' the Prof sang out, to be augmented by a cry of dismay from everyone. 'Bring it back.'

'Bloody bag. This one, I mean. Not her indoors.' And Wally swung his line away and reeled in the bag like a disappointed angler who's hooked flotsam instead of fish. 'I'll have to send 'em up one at a time.' He unhooked the bag.

'Try the loaf,' Richard suggested.

Which he did. The bread was two small bun-loaves, unwrapped. Nevertheless, Wally hooked one on and swung it high in the air, enjoying the familiar feel of the rod; he was a master of the sport.

Blodwin was not the only one wanting bread. Hungry, circling above them, pigeons and seagulls invited themselves to the party. Just as Wally had steadied his delivery over the hatch, and was lowering it to enter the hole, a ravenous gull darted in and pecked at the bun, which swung off course.

'Gerroff,' Wally ordered, and snatched the rod to one side. The fishing line, with the bread on the end, now swung like a pendulum over the hatch.

More birds joined the function, enlivening it by challenging each other. Then, as birds do, they began bombing those below. One white, well-aimed bomb caught the Major on the forehead and slithered down his nose.

'Whatever it is these vermin consume, certainly keeps them regular,' he said, wiping his hooter.

'They're not vermin, Major,' the Professor complained, 'they're just birds.'

'They are vermin and I am angry.' And the Major began scrabbling up the gravel from the path and throwing it at the enemy, which squawked, dodging the stones. 'Come on,' he commanded, 'we can beat them.' By now other residents had been bombed, and saw no other way of retaliation; so they formed a platoon, and with handfuls of gravel, gave as good as they got. Within a short while, the terror from the sky got the message and flew out of range.

'Well done, everyone. They know we mean business,' said Major Merryweather gleefully.

Meanwhile, throughout this bombardment and counterattack, Wally, because of his expertise, had managed to lower the groceries down the hatch; and inside the van, the grateful Blodwin stretched up and reached each parcel as it was delivered. When it was all over she came to the window and blew kisses from her hands. Wally noticed the length of her fingernails.

'My God, look at them red nails. How the hell does she manage to wipe her arse?'

Having completed the job of food delivery to their satisfaction, the residents moved off to attend to their own business, all except Josephine; she was quite concerned about the Welsh woman's welfare. She approached the window again and tapped on it. Blodwin stared out at her, looking like an exotic fish ensconced in a large glass tank.

'Have you still not found your keys?' Jo mouthed.

Blodwin shook her head then shouted through the glass. 'No. I've looked everywhere.'

Jo stepped away from the window and suddenly a thought crossed her mind. She recollected what she did when she used her own loo – the shed. So she went into Blodwin's privy; and there, as she guessed, was a large purse, very like her own. Inside the purse were various toiletries a finicky woman could not manage without; and among the contents were the keys. She returned to the caravan and unlocked the door from the outside then dropped the purse on the mat, stepping back sharply in case Blodwin appeared, preceded by her spots. As she walked away, the Welsh visitor – or probably new tenant – appeared behind the window holding the keys gratefully and waving thanks with the other hand.

Feeling sorry for the woman, Jo knew what she had to do. She picked up her mobile and dialled. The clinic responded at once.

'Hello. I'm speaking from Upsy-Daisy village. We have a lady here covered in spots. Could you kindly send a doctor or an ambulance or something. Sorry, I've no idea what it is. Later today? Oh, thanks.'

Two hours later, a physician did appear: Dr Patrick Mackistry, better known as Dr Paddy MacWhiskey because of his acquaintance with the hard stuff. He wore a well-worn brown suit with a check waistcoat, the squares incorporating brown, blue and red. Its usefulness was more important than its appearance, for the capacious pockets were filled with loose tablets. If he was uncertain about a diagnosis – and he often was – he'd advise the patient to rest, drink plenty of water and 'take two of these for three days'. And impersonating an expert magician he conjured six untethered tablets from his waistcoat pocket. These pills were, of course, placebos.

In every job, trade or profession some candidates slip through their final assessment, and MacWhiskey was no exception. He'd joined the Royal Navy and in 1960, at the age of thirty, he managed to scrape through his medical examination and was awarded an MD. He then obtained a position as a ship's doctor in the Merchant Navy. Because it was a small crew, and little medical work was involved, he was expected to muck in with the sailors. After he had seen quite a bit of the world, and been paid for it, he applied for a hospital post on terra firma.

The years rolled by and eventually, because of a shortage of doctors, he was accepted into a clinic in East Anglia, even though he was well over retirement age. And serious cases he passed on to a more experienced practitioner.

His weakness for 'the bottle' was acquired during his leisure time in the Merchant Navy. Because of his taste for the hard stuff, and the soft as well, his nom de plume, Dr Paddy MacWhiskey, was made welcome in Conservative, Liberal and Socialist clubs, where complimentary drinks awaited him.

He arrived at Upsy-Daisy in his Morris Shooting Brake, the exhaust belching fumes like an indisposed elephant. His appearance caused residents who knew him and his jalopy to stand at their doors, for he was always welcome; so they approached to snoop who his patient might be.

When it was realised he was visiting Taffy's spotty diva they sidled up to her caravan. Josephine was already waiting.

'I'm the person who telephoned,' she said.

'Ah yes. Thanks,' he said, unsure if he could cope. He approached the caravan cautiously, exactly as one would approach the plague. He went up to the window. 'Show me your arm,' he mouthed. Blodwin smiled and stretched out both arms. 'Oh Jaysus. You'd best come to the door, but I won't come in.' He turned to Josephine. 'No one from the site has been in, have they?'

'No. We've kept well away.'

Blodwin opened the door and the Doctor stepped well back.

'Have you received any treatment?'

'Yes. I was kept in hospital in Wales.' She recited the address. 'They said it was Rocky Mountain Spotted Fever.'

'Ah yes,' he said, quickly writing down the illness and the name of the medical centre Blodwin had quoted, and thinking, *I'll phone them tomorrow.* 'Did you receive an injection from them?'

'Oh yes. Twice. In my bottom.'

By now several residents, many who knew Dr MacWhiskey as a drinking crony, had gathered inquisitively about Blodwin's caravan.

'In which case I will continue their treatment.' He bent down and took a syringe from his old-fashioned doctor's bag, which he sometimes used to carry his bowls, as Paddy loved the ancient game, particularly the drinks that followed. 'Turn your back to me and bend over.' He donned a pair of transparent plastic gloves. As he pulled them on he said to the crowd, 'Do you mind, this is private.' So, taking the hint, they averted their gaze by swivelling round. But as soon as he began the injection, they swivelled back.

Blodwin had obediently turned her back with her face towards the interior; and the door being ajar, she was unaware of the spectators. She now dropped her kecks.

Wally whistled softly and muttered, 'What a nice round arse.'

The Doctor executed a skilful injection, having practised on sailors' bums for years to rid them of a social disease caught while off duty. Immediately following this minor surgery, a cheer went up. The Doctor assumed it was for his painless dexterity; but it was really for the once-in-a-lifetime's sight of Blodwin's spotty posterior. He then removed his gloves and chucked them in the nearest bin. The relieved resident closed her door – and that was that; but not before Wally had called, 'See you in the club later, Paddy.'

And satisfied with what they'd seen, the residents shuffled away, thinking, *Well, that's that...*

But it wasn't.

❋

Bryn Jenkins experienced porridge for a minor offence. The judge, however, seemed understanding, for he said, 'I am recommending that you be placed in custody for a brief period so that you may ruminate on your foolishness, and never again commit a similar offence.'

But the custard Bryn thought he was to be placed in never materialised; still, the brief period suggested was briefer than expected – because on a charitable half day out, for personal shopping, Bryn extended his absence... in a word, he scarpered.

He sneaked briefly into his village where he learned that his poppet – the one who'd won the lolly – had also decamped. But a day later he acquired her new address from an avaricious cousin who was vexed on receiving nix from Blodwin's winnings. This time, instead of an afternoon initiative, Bryn did a moonlight flit.

After changing trains, riding on a bus and cadging a lift, Bryn found himself trudging up the same slope traversed by Dr Paddy MacWhiskey a week earlier to jab Blodwin's now smooth, chubby cheeks.

'I visited the nick,' she told Bryn, 'but they said you'd done a bunk.'

'Too claustro-whatsit,' he explained eruditely. 'And it was a nice day, so I thought I'd visit you. Seen Taffy lately?' he asked, changing the subject suddenly.

'No,' she said, 'lately' implying the last ten minutes. 'But,' she countered, 'I don't want you ushering the woodentops in my direction, Bryn. You can stay one night, then you bugger off.'

'Don't say that, Blod. I've been looking forward to this.'

'Anyway, I'm leaving tomorrow. Urgent business.'

'Where?'

'Miles away. Starting afresh.'

'Oh no, Blod.'

'Oh yes, Bryn.'

He pleaded with her but she was adamant and wouldn't divulge where she was going. So, he made the best of it, as he usually did. They spent a pleasant evening together, after which Bryn was pleasantly spent. He slept soundly and when he awoke… she'd gone.

For a whole day he did what he did best – nothing. Then in the early evening, as he was chomping a slice of toast, he saw a police car sidle slowly by. His pulse quickened and fear gripped him almost as firm as Blodwin had gripped him the previous night. He quickly packed his duffel bag and made a swift exit.

By now it was dusk and televisions were being switched on. At the far end of the site, car headlights pierced the gloaming. The door of a caravan opened and a woman stood on her caravan steps. She noticed a figure loitering and addressed him.

'Excuse me, but do you know anything about televisions? Mine is on the blink.'

Bryn looked into the distance; the lights of a car were approaching slowly.

'I'll have a look at it,' he said. 'But I can't promise anything.' He moved quickly and went into her caravan.

'There it is, in the corner,' Miss Primm directed. 'While you're busy I'll make us a cup of tea.'

Bryn approached the set, holding the remote control, pressed a few buttons, then realised the TV wasn't plugged in. Without a word, surreptitiously, he rectified it, and when she returned with the tea, the picture was bright and inviting.

A car with lights full on drove slowly past.

'Oh, *Coronation Street*. My favourite programme.'

'Mine too,' he lied.

'Really? Well, you must stay and watch.'

When they had seen the programme, Bryn glanced round the van.

'I see you have a shower. That's unusual in a caravan.'

'That's why I bought this particular model. Would you like a shower?'

'Oh, yes please. That's very kind.'

'Well, one good turn deserves another,' Miss Primm assured him.

After the shower she noticed how crinkly his hair was and complimented him on his lilting voice. 'Are you Welsh?'

'Originally,' he affirmed, 'but these days I'm freelance.'

'Well, feel free here,' she exclaimed then clapped a hand to her mouth. 'Oh, I'm sorry, that sounds very forward.'

'I'm in no hurry,' he assured her.

In fact he spent an unexpectedly comfortable night. His Welsh cronies would have called it a one-night stand, except they were lying down. In the morning, after a substantial breakfast, they noticed a low loader trundle past, and before long Blodwin's caravan was secured on the long skeleton of the loader then carted away. Bryn didn't go outside to enquire about its destination in case the Old Bill returned; he had no immediate desire to return to the jug; life had to be lived outside.

So he bid a fond farewell to his unexpected paramour and promised to visit again, 'When business brings me to these parts.' He'd had a good time and wasn't called Jammy Jenkins for nothing.

It was some three hours later, when standing before a large mirror in the station waiting room, he noticed spots had appeared on his face.

*

Richard was busy collecting caravan insurance from his customers, paid – extortionately – on a monthly basis. He knocked on Miss Primm's door. When she answered, he croaked, 'Oh my God.' And fled. He stumbled into their small caravan, breathing heavily, and flopped heavily onto a chair.

'Have you seen a ghost?' Josephine asked, her eyes wide open with anxiety.

'No, but I have seen a woman with spots!'

'Not Blodwin again?'

'No, she's vanished, along with her caravan. The person I saw was Miss Primm and she doesn't seem to realise she's infected. And talking of caravans we can't site our new one until we've got rid of this tiny hovel.'

'It's not a hovel, a kennel perhaps.' She laughed lightly. 'But we have been comfortable here.'

'True. But your granddad's money came at just the right time. Then we'll be more comfortable still. We've got to dispose of this first.'

'I still don't understand why the firm won't take ours in part exchange.'

'They did explain. They sell new vans as cheaply as possible, which means there's no cash margin for a part exchange.'

As the Coningsbys were discussing their problems, Taffy had his own to contend with – but he didn't know it yet. He had actually completed his work schedule the previous evening and clocked off. He slept reasonably well, in the roadmender's cabin, then after a massive roadmender's fry-up, he climbed aboard a juddering lorry and along with his workmates was transported home, until the following week when his work schedule would start again. To save time and money, the lorry dropped them off close to their homes.

'Whatchu getting up to during your break, Ernie?'

'I'm off to Newmarket tomorrow, Taffy. There's a promising nag running in the two thirty. Have you anything planned?'

'I'm hoping to enjoy meself too, boyo. My girlfriend has come over from Wales.'

'That's the spirit, Taffy. After a week at home you'll probably be too tired to return to roadmending.' They both had a good laugh. At that point the lorry pulled up and Taffy said, 'This is where I get off.'

'Strewth. What a godforsaken place,' Ernie said. 'Still, everybody has to live somewhere.'

Taffy climbed out, the truck pulled away and Taffy made for the Diving Duck, where he wet his whistle, bought the landlord a drink, then with compelling steps made his way to Upsy-Daisy. As he stepped out he thought about Blodwin, and felt sure she would feel pleased at his return. He felt like a sailor home on leave, and this thought led to him feeling frisky. As he passed the toilets and showers he popped in to check out their condition.

'Wally seems to have cleaned up lately,' he told himself. 'I'll look forward to a shower after.'

After what? he ruminated, and grinned to himself. He turned a corner into his site.

'What the hell!' The caravan had gone and standing sitting squat on the concrete raft was his television. 'She's gone.' He felt like a tired boxer in the tenth round when an opponent lands a final, brutal jab in the solar plexus. 'The bitch.' He sat down on the concrete and tears welled up and smarted his eyes.

'What do I do now?' He looked up and along the dirt road. Someone was emptying rubbish in their bin. It was young Josephine. 'She might know something.'

Muttering unkind thoughts about Welsh women in general, he clambered to his feet and shuffled towards the Coningsbys' tiny caravan. He stepped up to their door and knocked. Richard answered.

'Oh, hello, Taffy. Can I help you?'

'My caravan has gone – well, her van, actually. Any idea what's happened?'

'Jo, will you come out here a minute? Taffy has a problem.'

Josephine appeared and explained about the low loader arriving and taking the van away.

'I mean, it was none of my business, so I kept away.'

'I've nowhere to kip down now,' Taffy moaned. 'What am I supposed to do?'

The Coningsbys looked at each other and shrugged. 'Well, er, buy another?' Dick suggested, lamely.

'I can't. I'm skint.'

'Can you afford to pay rent?' asked Josie.

Dick looked aghast at her, thinking she was about to invite him to stay with them.

'We hardly have room for ourselves,' he said, admonishing lightly.

'Come in, Taffy. You're obviously upset. We'll all have a cup of tea.'

Dick thought, *Dear God, she gets these ideas about good deeds in her head and there's no holding her back.*

Taffy sat at the small table and Dick sat opposite him. Jo brewed three mugs of strong tea and placed them on the table, along with a packet of chocolate biscuits, then she sat next to her husband.

'The thing is, we're collecting our new van this afternoon.' Dick looked up to interrupt but she kicked him under the table. 'Instead of doing a part exchange with them, we could rent out this van to you. It's ideal for a single person. We could have this moved to your site and our new van can be placed here. We'll work out a reasonable rent.'

A smile settled on Taffy's Welsh features, like the morning's rays settle on a sunflower, and nettles too, of course. 'Oh, you are so kind.'

'Well, it's a business arrangement really,' Dick said, wishing to be involved.

Josephine looked straight into Taffy's eyes. 'But any missing rent and you're out.'

SIX

'And the young couple are having their baby christened,' Josephine said.

'Great. That's nice,' Richard replied. 'Which church are they going to?'

'Well, they're Church of England, but the parish church is being repaired inside because of storm damage, so the little one is being baptised here, on the site.'

'Good grief! Let's hope they have a nice day for it then.'

The couple in question were the 'D's': David and Doreen Dewhurst. They were both twenty-four and had come to live in Upsy-Daisy because they couldn't afford to buy a house and didn't have the wherewithal to rent traditional accommodation.

Several members of the higgledy-piggledy village had helped them to site their van, especially Wally, who was experienced in caravanalia. The couple were so delighted with the reception and help they received that they had asked Wally to be godfather, particularly as their family lived miles away.

'Wally, a godfather!' the Major scorned. 'Surely they could have asked someone with a little more decorum. Someone with higher standards.'

'How high do y' want 'em?' Markie asked as he placed the Major's groceries on the counter.

The Major, detecting flippancy, growled, 'It is not the height, it's the depth that matters.' He struck the area of his heart, slightly above his prominent belly, with a clenched fist. 'The depth of feeling.'

'Make your mind up, Major. Is it height or depth you're after?' Markie, a fag dangling from his lips, twitched them as he calculated his customer's order. '£25 exactly, sir.' He emphasised the formal address with a touch of sarcasm, but Major Merryweather didn't notice.

In fact, the Major conjured up his calculator and itemised each purchase.

Now it was Markie who felt affronted. 'I'll bring the missus in to double check, if you like.'

'No thank you. This appliance is more reliable than a human calculator.'

'Is that so? Can it assess how many beers I've had on a Saturday evening? 'Cos my missus can.'

The Major ignored him and continued his inventory. Satisfied he hadn't been diddled he packed his purchases in his worn rucksack and marched from the shop. 'Good day to you.'

Markie muttered a mouthful, which the Archbishop of Canterbury would have censored.

Rucksack over shoulder, the Major strode smartly along the narrow walkway between the caravans. As he walked, he ruminated – but could not have explained why – about Wally and thought, *A mere handyman becoming a godfather. Whatever are things coming to?* Then, as though this thought conjured up the image, he almost bumped into the factotum.

'Morning, Major. Nice day.'

'What, oh, er, yes. Ah! Wally.' The handyman was almost past him when the Major added, 'I, er, I hear you are, er, acting as godfather on Sunday.'

Wally stopped, retreated a pace, looked down in a friendly manner on his neighbour and replied, 'Yes, that's correct, Major. But I'm not really *acting* as godfather, I'm actually fulfilling that important role.'

'Do you know these new people?'

'Well, I do now. They were strangers when they arrived and they obviously needed assistance. So I helped them settle down, and that's how I got to know them. They're young folk. Nice people.'

A little hesitantly, the Major enquired, 'Have they no relatives they could ask?'

Wally appeared to bristle slightly. The Major seemed to shrink. They resembled a St Bernard towering over a Pekingese.

'Their families live too far away. I suppose that's why they asked me. Any road up, I'm already a godfather to my sister's kid.'

'You are?' The Major sounded incredulous, as if Wally had climbed Everest.

'Well, it's no big deal. But it is nice to be able to offer advice to the youngsters as well as slipping them a few bob now and then. You've been asked yourself then?'

'Well, army life abroad, y' know. It makes such activities impossible. I was a *professional* soldier, you see.'

'So was I, Major. My coconut shy was the Falkland Islands.'

'You actually fought in the Falklands?'

'I certainly did. In fact, I was one of the few Redcaps there.'

This info threw the Major somewhat. He'd assumed he was the only veteran in the area. He reasserted himself. *But Wally! Military police!*

'Ah, well, I had the weight of the regiment on my shoulders.'

'The regiment! Make that a platoon and I'll believe you.' Wally saw his neighbour was about to swell and splutter, so he added, 'Will you be attending the christening on Sunday? It's here on the site, you know, not in church. Give the little bug… beggar a good send off, eh? It costs nothing, p'raps a collection. Nice drinkies after.'

Wally could not have mentioned a better invitation.

The Major should really have said, 'Now you're talking.' Instead he postured. 'Quite. Well, I'll get my business wrapped up early. Then I'll tootle along.'

'Well done, General. Oh, and don't forget your gift.' This last remark sent the Major rigid. 'We all know you're noted for your generosity,' added Wally slyly. Then he moved on.

Major Merryweather, feeling pigmy-like, watched Wally stride on, and noted his retreating shoulders were broader than Yorkshire. The Major felt he'd been caught out, caught for a duck. He snorted and walked towards his caravan, vexed, muttering, 'Xto#^kI/!'

Meanwhile Wally called in on the young couple to whose child he was going to be godfather: David and Doreen Dewhurst, or Dave and Dreen as Wally called them. He knocked.

'Come in,' called a female voice.

Wally entered and ducked, as he did by habit.

''Lo, Dreen. How's the little 'un?'

She placed a finger to her lips and whispered, 'He's sleeping, thank goodness.' She pointed to a tall stool on which Wally parked his ample bottom.

'Where's the other little fellow?' he asked softly.

'David's gone to collect him from school. They should be back any time.'

'Can I peep at my protégé?' he asked, smiling in anticipation.

She pointed towards the far end of the caravan where a cot was hunkered down between a table and a bunk. Wally stood and the van seemed to rock with his bulk. He crept surprisingly daintily for a big 'un, and peered into the cot at the pink, sleeping cherub. He turned to her. 'Can I touch him?' he murmured. She smiled and nodded. Wally held his muscular arm over the sleeping infant then with a middle digit as thick but as light as a chocolate finger, he touched the baby's brow. 'My little friend,' he whispered.

At that point the van door flew open and in bustled Benjamin, but on seeing Wally he stopped abruptly. 'That's my brother,' Benjy said, with forewarning colouring his six-year-old voice.

'I promise I won't hurt him,' Wally said.

The child's father entered. 'Oh, hullo, Wally. Come to visit us?'

'No fear. I've come to visit this little chap.' They laughed at this.

'I bumped into the vicar at the school,' Dave said. 'While we were chewing the fat she mentioned she would like a little chat with you. Apparently she'd been telling the kids a story.'

'Oh, the vicar is a she... is she?'

'Yes,' Doreen said. 'She's nice, you'll like her.'

'Oh, I like all the lassies,' Wally replied with a grin.

'She's a brilliant musician too,' put in David. 'Last time I went to talk to her she was playing the church organ. I assumed at first it was the regular church organist until she stopped playing and came down the steps to meet me.'

Wally stooped to talk to Benjamin. 'And what sort of a day have you had, Benjamin?' The little fellow became suddenly shy and walked to the safety of his mother.

'Benjy, tell Wally what you did at school today.'

'I sat at my desk.'

'Who do you sit next to, Benjy?' Wally asked, trying to be friendly towards the child.

'Stephen.'

'What's his second name?' his mother asked, wanting her child to communicate.

'It's just Stephen.'

'Oh, right,' Wally contributed. 'Is he nice?'

'Sometimes.'

The adults looked at each other and shrugged. This was going to be hard work.

'Was Stephen nice today?' his father asked.

'No.'

'Why not?' asked his mother, with just the slightest sign of anxiety.

The child looked up at them and casually said, 'Because he farted.'

And in spite of themselves, they were reduced to laughter.

🌳

Wally left the Dewhursts' caravan, still laughing. 'Kids!' he grinned. The young vicar was expecting him, so he decided to shoot off straight away. He changed into a tidier pair of trousers, a clean shirt, rescued his bike from the chaos of his shed and pedalled away.

The Anglican church of St Aidan was situated in the next village of Down Daisy, which lay in a lower land mass than Upsy-Daisy. The river Babbler twisted its way through, making it popular for picnics.

Wally saw the church spire and headed for it, although he was familiar with the area. He dismounted his bike and secured it to wrought-iron railings inside the church grounds. Even from outside he heard the organ being played, and it sounded as though it was being well played. He went inside and wiped his feet on a large doormat. He noticed at once that the church interior was being renovated.

The Vicar spotted Wally as soon as he entered and stopped playing. She switched off the sound, and the organ lights, and came down the steps to greet him, shaking his hand warmly.

'Hello, Vicar. Oh, the lady with the slack bike chain. Well, well. Pleased to meet you again.' Wally admired her at once. She was quite tall, wore her auburn hair short, and her pleasant features broke into a smile that was as white as her clerical collar.

'Call me Miriam. And you're Wally. I've heard a lot about you.'

'Don't believe most of it,' he joked.

'It's all good, I promise you. Let's sit here, shall we?' She walked towards the altar and sat on the front row.

Wally thought, *Blimey, we're going to pray*, but they didn't.

'Now, you're going to be the child's godfather, I believe, Wally?'

He smiled and nodded. Was she going to explain how to guide youngsters in this wicked world? Was she going to tell him what the church expected of him? He suddenly went slightly hot then cold. Would she suggest he started attending church? But she didn't. Miriam, priest of Down Daisy and surrounding areas, said, 'Forgive me asking this, but do you know what the child's name will be?'

He looked up, surprised. 'Course I know. Andrew James. Well, Andrew James Dewhurst.' His reply was accompanied by two semi-circular eyebrows over each eye – two thick, sandy arches, almost like horizontal question marks.

'I ask that,' she said, 'because so many godparents don't know, or at best, momentarily forget.'

'Blimey, I would never have thought it.'

'What did you work at, Wally, before you became handyman on the caravan site?'

'As well as being handyman on the caravan site, I also work for the council. Before that, I was a regular soldier.'

'Good grief.' She sat up and looked at him with new interest. 'So was I!'

His face widened with genuine surprise. 'A padre?' he asked.

'No fear! A proper soldier. A lorry driver.'

Wally became close to Christianity as he almost sang, 'Well, I'm blessed.'

'You are, Wally. You certainly are. I don't need to advise *you* on counselling children.' She stood up suddenly. 'Come on, let's go for a drink. The Diving Duck is just round the corner.' And without more ado, she led Wally down the aisle, through the church door, round the corner and into the pub.

'Hello, Miriam,' the landlord said. 'The usual?'

'Yes please, Toby.' She turned to her new-found companion. 'What's your poison, Wally?'

'A pint o' bitter, please. Oh, and a bag of cheese and onion crisps.'

The Vicar introduced Wally to Toby, the landlord, and priest and protector found themselves a seat in a corner of the recreation room, with its snooker tables and dartboard. Each one eagerly clutched their tankard when the drinks arrived and took a gulp.

'Down the hatch, Wally. I got a taste for this when I was billeted in Caterham, Surrey.'

They sank their first drinks; Wally ordered seconds and they discussed their experiences in the armed forces. Soon, however, their exchanges became difficult to follow, as a brass band commenced rehearsals in a room over their heads.

'This band practises here once each week,' she said.

Wally, who was not unmusical, listened like someone acquainted with the sound of brass. 'That's "Blaze Away". But there's too much of the umpah – although the principal cornet's good.'

'You sound as though you know something about brass playing. Were you in a military band?'

'No, I was in the Redcaps.'

'Ah, the military police,' she said. 'I didn't realise that lot were in the Falklands conflict.'

'Well, wherever there are military you have to have a means of controlling the hooligans. There is a Royal Falkland Islands Police force, of course, and I was in a platoon that was despatched to augment them.' He fell silent for a while, apparently listening to the band rehearsing above them.

Miriam, the Vicar, said, 'Right… But what's that got to do with brass bands?'

'Well, when the band rehearsed I went with a mate of mine, who was in the band, and I became their librarian – you know, putting music stands out, handing out and collecting the music. And I used to listen to what their conductor said.'

'So a bit of knowledge rubbed off onto you?'

'Yeah, you could say that.' He took another gulp of his beer. 'But this lot!' He pointed to the ceiling and shook his head.

'So what's your reaction when I tell you they are playing hymns and that for the Dewhurst baptism?'

'Bloody hell! Oh, sorry.'

'You're right, Wally. It is bloody hell. But David Dewhurst works with the lead cornet, who offered to bring a sextet, not all the band, thank goodness. You see, the lead cornet is new to the band and didn't know the other players.'

'Otherwise he wouldn't have offered their services.'

'Got it. The problem, as no doubt you will have gathered, is the bass trombone. He seems to think he's a soloist.'

'Right. Did you know the bass trombone is the second least important member of a brass band? A player they could manage without.'

'Really? Which instrument is the least important then?'

'The third tenor horn.'

'And this fellow,' she pointed towards the ceiling, 'is a bit of a boozer, to boot.'

'Is he now. So he'll come in here after their rehearsal?'

'Nothing is more definite. Anyhow, I'm afraid I can't linger,' she said. 'I have one or two parishioners to visit. So do feel free to visit me again. Alternatively, I'll see you on the day.' And she rose, patted him affectionately on the shoulder and left the pub.

To pass the time, Wally walked over to the dartboard, took the arrows from the little wall cupboard and practised his dart playing, a game he indulged in regularly in the army. On one throw Wally scored a bull's eye and he was so pleased with himself – but regretted no one was there to notice it – he awarded himself another pint.

'Another bitter, Toby.' He put the money on the counter. 'It's a good games room you've got there.'

'Enjoy it while you can. The band'll be invading shortly.'

'They sound as if they have a good principal cornet.'

'So they say. A new bloke, apparently.' He sniggered. 'They might improve a bit now.'

Wally returned to the games room and threw a few more darts. Then the band arrived, almost one at a time. They all held a full glass and placed their instrument cases around the wall. With a sixth sense Wally noticed the bass trombone player at once; he held a pint glass of beer in either hand. The next thing the ex-Redcap noticed was that the bloke had a lot to say for himself.

'Nobody playing snooker then?' he said loudly.

'Not tonight, Bob. I've got to get home and take the dog out.'

'How about you, Brendan? Fancy a game?'

'No thanks, Bob. My little girl is not well. That's why I was late arriving tonight.'

Wally walked round the snooker table. 'Hiya. You're Bob. Bass trombone, I reckon. I'll give you a game… Wally.' He held out a hand; Bob shook it.

'Oh, right. New round here, are you?'

'Not exactly,' Wally said. 'I'm from Upsy-Daisy.'

'Ah, on the site. We're playing there, apparently, a week on Sunday. At a christening, would you believe. Anyway, the loser gets the drinks. Get your money ready.'

Wally produced a coin and they tossed for first turn. Bob called heads and won. As he leant over the table, his backside reminded Wally of a baby hippo. Bob sawed his cue back and forth then struck. On his first and only strike he struck too hard and the cue ball, after bouncing from the cushion, rolled into a pocket.

'Hard lines,' Wally said, and thought, *He bangs at it. He's too rough. He's as coarse playing snooker as he is playing trombone.* Meanwhile he rubbed chalk on his cue.

'These bloody cues are not straight,' Bob grumbled. 'They need replacing.'

Wally eyed along the cue, as if lining up a rifle. 'They seem straight enough to me, Bob.' He retrieved the white ball, planted it on the baize again, cued up and struck the white, dead centre. The white sped along the green baize and smacked into the batch at the end, scattering several balls and propelling one into a pocket. What followed was the result of hours of practice in a large shed in Stanley, the principal town on East Falkland.

Within minutes Wally cleared the table. 'Mine's a whisky,' he said.

'I thought you were on shandy,' Bob said, his face drooping like a spaniel.

'Beer when I'm practising, but whisky when I've won.'

'I reckon you're a pro.'

'No, I'm not,' Wally assured him. 'But it's like playing a musical instrument: the more you practise the better you become.' He nodded towards Bob's trombone, standing against the wall, waiting to go home. 'How often do you practise that?'

'I've been playing for fifty years, Wally. I don't need to practise.'

Wally looked at him and thought, *Least said, soonest mended.*

'Well, if you don't mind I'll have me whisky, then I'll set off. I have to pedal up a hill.'

Muttering and grousing to himself, Bob went to the bar to pay for his forfeit. And a young man approached Wally.

'Did I hear you say you were from Upsy-Daisy?'

'You did, indeed. I live in a house on wheels.'

'So does a mate of mine: Dave Dewhurst. In fact, a few of us are coming to your place to play for Dave's child's christening.'

'So I believe. What's your instrument?'

'I'm principal cornet. I've only recently joined this lot.'

'Right. I heard you all playing, earlier on.'

'I'm Malcolm.' He looked round to see if the other players could hear; but many of the band had gone. They shook hands. 'What did you reckon about the playing?' he almost whispered.

Wally kept his voice low. 'Bloody awful. Well, you were alright. But the bass trombone spoils it.'

'I know. I didn't realise he was so bad. Had I known how they sounded, I wouldn't have joined. But, I must admit, I wanted to be a principal.'

'Can't you get rid of him?' Wally asked.

Malcolm shrugged. 'Dunno. I'm still new. I don't know the setup.'

At that point, the maestro himself appeared, carrying two drinks, so the conversation was altered.

'So, you've met Malcolm then?' Bob said.

'Yes. And I heard him play, earlier on.'

Bob patted the young man's shoulder. 'Yes, he's good. Well, a bit more experience, and he will be.'

Wally felt he couldn't stand any more. He knocked back his whisky. 'Well, I'll see you two gentlemen in Upsy-Daisy, in a few days. Cheerio.' He retrieved his cycle and pedalled off home.

The following day, at breakfast, David Dewhurst said, 'I hope a few folk from Upsy-Daisy come to our little one's christening, if only for the sake of the Vicar.'

'Yes, she's been so considerate about it,' Doreen added. 'Perhaps we should make some sort of effort to persuade them.'

Both of them stared into space; in reality they looked at the morning light as it beamed through the small transparent hatch in the ceiling of the caravan. The ray of brightness obviously inspired Doreen for she suddenly exploded with an idea.

'Let's invite them. We could wheel our little one round the site in his pram, encourage the neighbours to look at him and invite them.'

'Good idea. But we won't just ask them, we'll deliver an invitation. I'll type out invitations on the laptop then print them out on thin card. I've got some cream-coloured card I used for those Christmas cards last year. Then we'll cut them out.'

'In the shape of a cradle,' she added. 'Hey, that's great.'

Dave went to work at once. His simple invitation read:

'You're invited to witness Andrew James

Touched with water, and receive his names.'

When the cards were completed, and while young Benjamin was at school, they wrapped their newly born into a shawl, placed him into his pram and set off round the site.

'We could just pop these invitations through the letterbox,' Doreen said.

'What, after all the trouble I've taken to make them? No fear! If we want a good turnout, we deliver them personally – unless they are not at home.'

The first prospective guest they called on was Major Merryweather. He opened the door and smiled warmly, then twirled his moustache.

'Good morning, Major,' Doreen said. 'You're looking quite perky this lovely morning.'

The Major thrived on flattery.

'My daily military regime keeps me in the pink, you know.' And without more ado he began running on the spot on his doormat. Then to display his flexibility he stooped to touch his toes, then yelped. 'Strewth, I've put a sprain in me back.'

The visitors were desperate to titter. Instead Dave said, 'Better sit down for a minute, Major.' And he slid a chair under the veteran's hindquarters.

'Get me a glass of water, please,' announced the old soldier. Doreen quickly did as she was bid and handed it to him.

'I expect you experienced much worse in the old days,' David suggested, which was fatal, for the Major, after gulping down the water, began a running commentary on his exploits of yore. The visitors hadn't the nerve to leave him to his bluster, so they drew up chairs and were obliged to listen until a sudden whiff suggested to Doreen that the real celebrity needed changing.

'We'll take him home again,' she said. 'He needs changing.' And off she went.

David lingered awhile, and when the Major paused for another gulp of water he thrust out the card. 'We thought you might be interested in this little get-together, Major.'

Major Merryweather scrutinised the invitation. 'Ah yes. I heard about this. Yes, I'd be delighted to attend, dear boy. I'll wear my medals, that should bring the children along.'

And before the old soldier could trot out more of his exploits, Dave slid from the caravan, back to the safety of his own hearth… in reality the stove.

Doors and windows were flung open, then the youngster was changed and the miniature compost heap wrapped and thrown into the black bin. Then, after tea and toast, the young couple tumbled outside with their precious stink bomb and continued their patrol, handing out invitations. Their child was going to have the best christening ever.

SEVEN

Sunday arrived and Wally played chess with the borrowed chairs until the arrangement suited his purpose. Then he manoeuvred the font – in reality a clean bird bath – until, to his soldier's practised eye, it was winsome. This marshalling was carried out while the residents slept.

The wretchedness of the brass band's playing still irked him, and he rightly believed it would spoil the day and blight the ceremony. So he walked round the site, up one path and down another, like a man in a maze, contemplating the problem. Gradually a plan formed, which would need an accomplice… Who?

'Markie is the man,' Wally told himself. 'He'll commit perjury for a drink.' He laughed. 'Huh, he'll carry out an assault for two.'

But first he had to set in motion his plan.

As a Redcap, Wally had tolerated many a dust-up with his detainees. So to avoid regular dust-ups, he and his captors had invited their captives to an unexpected drink. But these tasty tipples had been previously laced with diazepam, a drug that encouraged sleep – a better remedy than handcuffs. So Wally returned to his van, rummaged under the sink and found the green beer bottle he had used so often. He then went to the site shop to outline his plan. Markie knew everybody who frequented the Diving Duck.

'Oh, I know *that* Bob. He plays yon big trombone. He's a bloke to be avoided.'

'Avoided! In what way?'

'He drives the band's bus. He's to be avoided,' he echoed himself.

'What, when he's driving the bus?'

'No. In the Diving Duck. He orders a round, goes for a pee, comes back then makes out you ordered. Then he will order. Then it's your turn again. He's to be avoided. It's his bus y' know. He drives roadmenders to their work and home again. And when the band go on gigs he drives. He only charges petrol. He's cheap, like. So the band…'

'Have to tolerate him. Aye, I get the picture,' Wally said. He bought some bread and a tin of beans. 'What's his poison?'

'Y' what?'

'His drink. What does he sink best?'

'Oh! Owt. Anything, if it's free. I should say best bitter.'

'Right then. So I'll take one bottle of best bitter and three bottles of, shall we say, light ale. Then a small whisky.'

A broad smile lit up Markie's face like a stripe on a melon. 'Expecting visitors?'

'Yes. And you're the guest of honour.' And without more ado Wally outlined his plan to a chuckling Markie, then returned to his van and sloshed out a few drops of diazepam.

At two o'clock the band's coach arrived, with Bob settled at the wheel. He pulled up near the roofless meeting house and the bandsmen unloaded their instruments. Then Bob drove his vehicle higher up the slope towards the established sand dunes feathered with tall fescue grass.

No sooner had he parked than he had a visitor holding a hand-woven shopping bag. ''Lo, Bob. See you're on time then?'

'Ah, Markie. Yes, we're ready for the off.'

'I usually have a nip this time o' day. Like to join me?' He took Bob's silence as assent and relieved the shopping bag of two tall glasses and a bottle of light ale. Markie glanced at his quarry and noticed the drinker's twitch, a spasm Markie was acquainted with.

Bob had indeed begun to salivate. There was no rule against wetting your whistle before a concert, although it wasn't encouraged. 'Well, I'm not sure if I…'

But it was like dangling a lamb chop in front of a hungry hound. 'OK. But it'll have to be a quick one, the lads are setting out the instruments.'

Markie poured the amber liquid from the bottle into Bob's glass. As he poured he slowly raised the bottle up and down, creating a miniature waterfall; the beer bubbled like a fetching fountain. He dropped the empty bottle into his basket then poured his own from a different bottle first, smacking his lips. By now, Bob was really thirsty. Markie gulped his own beer again. He knew what made a boozer drool. Bob almost grabbed his drink and gulped it down like a parched priest breaking a fast. In fact the beer disappeared quicker than emptying a drain.

'By heck, I didn't realise I was so dry.'

'Wait till you've tippled this down you,' Markie said, and poured Bob a liberal measure into a clean glass from the green bottle. 'By heck, this is good.' He took another pull. 'I'm supposed to be helping set the instruments out.'

Markie had his extra refreshments from the brown bottle. 'Oh, let 'em get on with it. You do a lot for this band.' He then emptied the suspicious contents from the green bottle, Bob's bottle! And the trombonist knocked it back.

Then the sharp taste took control and his head lolled back.

'Just before we shoot off, join me in a tot of Irish,' and Markie conjured a whisky bottle from his basket.

Bob always ended a booze-up with short stuff. It was a habit, and today he didn't break this pattern. He had one mouthful – always a danger – and slid to a recumbent posture on the back seat.

As Markie stepped down from the coach, he heard Bob snore, and knew his job was complete. He walked to the open-air service to hear the Vicar announce, 'We'll now sing the children's hymn "All Things Bright and Beautiful".

The outdoor congregation sang it well, and the band sounded better than they ever did. Markie glanced at Wally, who nodded with satisfaction.

Miriam, the Vicar, gave her short address which was mainly about children, and went on to talk about how they should be guided. 'Not just by parents, but by godparents. When kids go wrong,' she said, 'whatever "wrong" happens to be, it's often because parents, perhaps to avoid arguments with growing youngsters, have allowed their offspring too much time to themselves. Children of all ages need to be included. So, if you want your children to turn out well, spend twice as much time with them and half as much money.'

Mrs Marks, sitting three rows from the front, frowned at this. She wanted the site children to spend as much as possible. Most folk seemed to agree with the Vicar. The ad hoc outdoor service did not follow the normal protocol that occurred in a usual church building. This service was free and easy, as was the music. Several small children were there, sitting cross-legged on the ground. So it was mainly for their benefit that the band struck up, 'The Wheels On The Bus'... When they'd enjoyed this unexpected song, Miriam said, 'I bet they're not singing that in York Minster today.'

She got several laughs for her quirky remarks and knew, Wally realised, how to make ordinary folk feel at home.

She carried on. 'Did you hear about this small child in church for the first time? He was watching the ushers pass round the offering plate. As the ushers approached their pew, the child piped up, in a loud voice, "Don't pay for me, Daddy, 'cos I'm under five."'

Again she received a ripple of laughter from her caravan congregation. Then she added, 'It's now my pleasure to ask the child's godfather to pass on some welcome advice.'

Wally stood and stretched himself to his full height. 'I'm glad I was asked to do this job.' The congregation at the back craned their necks, wondering what words of wisdom the handyman could offer.

'I look at present-day kids and realise things have changed since my day in short pants and red knees. In my younger days, a youngster was a person between a child and an adult. These days a youngster is a creature that stands halfway between an adult and a telly.' This wasn't what the congregation expected, but it was something they appreciated. 'Although I'm a godfather,' Wally continued, 'I don't think I'm competent enough to offer ideal advice – only personal experience. For example, I was always kept short of pocket money. My mother reckoned that the more money I got, the more I wasted.' He looked up and noted several nodding in agreement. 'I was forever skint. But now, when a youngster knows the value of a pound, they often start asking for two. That never happened when I was a kid, because my family were always hard up.

'These days it's not cash that's lacking, it's discipline. But there is one thing in support of unruly kids! It gets their parents home from the pub earlier.

'But I musn't be too dismal. Youngsters do brighten up a home, if it's only by leaving the lights on. We were all young once and had our own personal problems.'

Major Merryweather thought, *What on earth could Wally's problems have been?* To himself, the Major admitted he was enjoying the service.

'Y' see,' explained Wally, 'I was often lonely as a child. So I invented two imaginary friends. Trouble was, they preferred playing with each other.'

This caused a few giggles and even received a brief round of applause. Wally thought he'd said enough. 'Thank you for coming, and God's grace to you all.' He bowed briefly and sat down.

This reverent adieu was gratefully noted by the Reverend Miriam who got briskly to her feet. 'I reckon Wally has missed his vocation,' she said with a charming smile. 'However, we haven't quite finished. I thought I should ask the oldest among us what childhood was like in his days of yore. Please welcome Professor Sparrow. And I've no idea what he's going to say.'

The small, elderly resident got to his feet, seemed to wander towards the centre of the group, and actually leant on the font. A few sighs were heard from those expecting to be bored.

'I don't believe anyone here actually knows my real, baptismal name. So I'll start at the beginning… Before, and even after, I was born, we lived with my grandparents, because we were strapped for cash. Now, my granddad had a dog, a Jack Russell terrier. The old chap used to sit in his rocking chair, nursing his dog, rocking to and fro singing, "Jackie-o, Jackie-o". Then one October the dog died and I was born in November. From force of habit owd Jem rocked me. "Jackie-o... Hey, let's call him Jack." So it was agreed.

'Now, Granddad was a local preacher in the Primitive Methodist Church. And in those days, late 1920s, early 30s, local preachers had free rein, perhaps because they came cheap – no fee. They could baptise, marry, bury the dead, and so on. Owd Jem baptised me "In the name of the Father, and of the Son and of the Jack Russell terrier." And that's how I came to be called Jack.'

The congregation loved it.

EIGHT

'Good morning, everybody.'

'Good morning, Mr Watson.'

'While you were writing up your diaries,' Wally said hesitantly, 'I marked up the register. I know who you all are because of your name tags. So, we'll start the first lesson, shall we?'

'If you say so, sir.'

Wally approached the cheeky chap who'd offered his opinion, and peered at his name tag. *Ah, he's a Charlie.* Wally, the temporary teacher, returned to his hastily assembled desk and stared about the room – the hut they were in. It was quite good for a temporary structure, assembled yesterday by council workmen. It was quite cosy inside – better than its external appearance suggested. Wally glanced at his quickly scribbled notes.

'Right, we'll begin by discussing last week's visit to the farm. Although I wasn't with you, I do happen to know the place. But don't call out. If you have something to say, raise your hand. Now, what did you enjoy best?'

A boy with short, ginger hair raised his hand. Wally took a step forward and peered at his name tag.

'Well, Harry, the way you've been flapping your hand about, you're obviously excited about something. What did you like about the farm trip?'

'I enjoyed me sandwiches, sir.'

Wry surprise visited Wally's face. 'Good grief, lad, surely you have sandwiches every day?'

'I know, sir. But yesterday were me birthday and our Lily put a chocolate bar in me lunch box.'

'Ah! I see. Well, many happy returns, Harry. And how old are you now?' Wally sat back on the Windsor chair the Vicar had provided him with.

'I'm nine now, sir.'

'No, he's not, sir. He's nine and one day old.'

The caravan site's handyman glanced at the cheeky chap again. 'Well done, Charlie, you're quite right.'

'For once.'

'Thank you, Michael,' said the teacher, peering at the boy's name tag. 'But even you are incorrect... Now, class, why are Charlie and Michael wrong? Come on, think about it.'

'Please, sir, because Harry is only nine years old and half a day.'

'Well done, Tracey. Harry is nine years old and half a day, because it is still only the middle of the morning. Now, what else interested you all yesterday? Yes, Sarah?'

'I liked the little yellow chickens best.'

'They're not much cop though, are they?' This was the birthday boy's assertion.

'Why is that, Harry?' Wally relaxed and sipped his water.

'Well, sir, they're nobbut fluff. My dad reckons poultry are only useful when they are laying. You know, sir. Eggs.'

'Well, there is something in what you say. Farming has to be productive.'

🌳

Walter Watson's venture had begun on Friday night when he seated himself at the bar in the Diving Duck. He liked this pub. Unlike other modern beer houses, it still resembled a tavern. The appliances in the bar area were brass and shone with regular buffing. Oak arches supported the ceiling, and faded photographs of the area were displayed about the room.

Wally took another gulp from his glass. 'This is a nice bitter you have here, Toby.'

'Aye. It's become very popular,' the landlord agreed. 'And here's somebody who'll second that.'

Wally swivelled on his tall stool slightly. 'Oh, hello, Vicar. I didn't expect to see you again so soon.'

'Ah, bad habits are hard to conquer. But, please, call me Miriam, so I don't feel I'm on duty.'

Wally smiled and pulled a stool nearer the bar for her. 'Right. Settle yourself here, Miriam. What is it, half a pint or a big boy's glass?'

'Oh, that's kind. I'll try a half of the same bitter you're obviously enjoying.'

'A half pint, Toby, and top up mine.'

The landlord became almost reverent as he placed a clean glass under the tap and unhurriedly pulled down the polished wooden handle. The beer issued a squishy sound as it oozed into the glass – a welcoming sound, promising dewy pleasure. The two customers watched with eager anticipation.

'After a demanding day, that's one of the nicest sounds you can hear,' Miriam asserted.

The landlord placed the full glass before her then topped up Wally's.

'You've had problems then, have you?'

She sipped her beer rather than gulping. 'You can say that again, Wally. I don't just prattle from the pulpit, y' know.' She took another drink, obviously mulling over her problem. 'I'm also a school governor.' She sighed. 'Like the church, the school is being altered, and adapted. And until it's complete we need another classroom.'

'Aye,' said Toby, unable to resist an opinion, 'you have a lot more kids than there used to be.'

'It's not her fault,' snapped Wally, becoming Miriam's defender.

'I know. It's just that they make more noise than they did.'

'The more kids, the more noise,' she said plausibly.

The landlord twirled a little finger in his earhole. 'Yeah, I know. But the language they come out with.'

She gave him an admonishing look, so he meekly muttered, 'Another one – on the house.'

'We'll both have one on the house,' she demanded, and emptied her glass. 'Anyway, to come to the point: we're getting an extra classroom next week, but we need somewhere to put it. The playground's not big enough and it's too near to the road. That's dangerous.'

'Ah!' Wally sighed, from either his free drink or his understanding, 'it's one o' them cabins, is it?'

She dabbed at her mouth with a clerical white handkerchief, wiping away froth, for which many a tippler would have used a sleeve. 'Yes. Cabins are OK as a temporary measure, but unsatisfactory as a permanent fixture.'

'But t' building's not arrived yet, has it?' Toby enquired, his prying disposition getting the better of him.

Wally offered the Vicar some crisps from a newly opened bag. She took just one, gazed at it then munched it in a pensive manner.

'If you're really stuck, we've space on our caravan site.'

She placed her half-empty glass on the counter, and grabbed Wally's arm with an animated gesture. 'Cool, Wally, that would solve the problem. We could transport the kids up there in the school bus.'

'Yeah! It would only take about six minutes.'

'I'll see what I can do,' he offered. 'Would there be a few bob in it for Mrs Marks?'

She chuckled. 'Well, I'll see what *I* can do, too. Oh, and there'll be two powder rooms.'

'Eh?' Wally's eyebrows challenged each other like feuding caterpillars.

The landlord, mopping his counter, leaned in towards Wally and mumbled, 'They'll need a couple o' khazis.'

Over the weekend a three-man firm arrived, and on behalf of the local council erected the wooden buildings: a schoolroom cabin and two toilets. Desks and chairs were also installed.

※

On Monday the Reverend Miriam Peach appeared, but her fruity name wore a sour look.

'Now then,' said Wally, 'you look as though you've lost a tenner and found a fiver. What's up?'

'I thought things were running too smoothly,' she moaned. 'We're two teachers down but I can't provide cover for these kids because I'm committed to officiate at a funeral at half past ten.'

'Oh dear. Have you prayed about it?' he asked cheekily.

'Yes. And him upstairs suggested I came to you.'

Wally actually took a step back in surprise. 'Are you serious?'

'Course I am.' The ex-soldier in her materialised. 'A bloke who buggered up his misspent youth fighting in the Falklands can surely look after thirty kids for an hour.'

He knew then they were buddies. 'Blimey! My flabber has not been gasted like that since I was wrongly placed on jankers. Well, General, what do I do?'

'Just follow the instructions.' She handed him a file. And no sooner had he opened and read some of it, the school bus trundled up the slope to the caravan site.

As the children disembarked, he heard her say, 'Listen, everybody. Your teacher this morning is Mr Watson. So behave yourselves.' And she mounted her bike and road away.

And within minutes, Wally had taken charge. 'So let's keep rigidly to last week's visit to the farm.'

'Please, sir.'

'Yes…' He checked her name. '… Carol?'

'Last week, at the farm, I enjoyed the piano music coming from the farmhouse.'

'Good. Yes, I have heard about it. It seems the farmers, Mr and Mrs Bradshaw, have a talented fourteen-year-old son called Rupert. So, as you were walking past his house last week, you would hear him practising his pieces for his next exam. I'm glad you enjoyed his playing, Carol.'

'He goes to the same music teacher as I do, sir.'

Several young necks turned towards her… towards this cocky little classmate, in some young minds.

'Oh, so you're learning the piano as well, are you, Carol?'

'Yes, sir.' She was an attractive child and wore a white bow in her hair. 'I have been learning nearly a term. But I still hate those sharks in flats.'

'I think you'll find, Carol, that it is sharps and flats. They show you what key you are in.'

'Huh, I think Rupert is a daft name.'

'It's not as daft as yours, Charlie Wrigley. Yours is a funny name.'

'OK, Bernard. That will do.'

'Well, folk sometimes call Charlie, Chucky. Now that is a daft name.'

'Now listen, everybody. No more talk about names. We're supposed to be discussing last week's visit to the farm.'

'Please, sir, I liked them two farm dogs best.'

'Yes, they are excellent dogs, Jonathon. I noticed them when I visited a while ago. Two quite obedient animals.'

'My dad reckons dogs are only useful if they are working dogs.'

'There's something in that, Jonathon. Incidentally, would anyone like to comment on working dogs? Yes, Tracey. Now is your hand up or down?'

'It's on the end of her arm, sir.'

'Huh, you need a different scriptwriter, Clever Clogs.'

'I'm not wearing clogs.'

'Will you boys pack it in? Yes, Tracey!'

'Police dogs are working dogs, sir.'

'Quite true. Police dogs are certainly working dogs.'

'Huh, her's only saying that 'cos her dad is a copper.'

'I'll have you know my father is a police sergeant.'

'He's still a copper.'

'And one of these days he might arrest you, Charlie Chuckle Head.'

This remark caused a deal of tittering.

'Huh. He'll have to catch me first.'

'OK, Charlie, that's quite enough.' Their teacher sighed and slumped in his chair.

'It's not breaktime, is it, sir?'

'Not quite, Bernard.'

'Please, sir, I think a guide dog is a working dog.'

'Well done, Marion.'

'So she should be,' someone muttered.

Wally almost jumped from his chair. 'You, yes, you. You impertinent boy. See me afterwards.' He looked round the class, noticed how some kids were better dressed than others. 'Do you know, the Guide Dogs for the Blind Association train a dog for two years before they match it up with a blind person?'

'Sir, how do you match a dog to a blind person?'

'A good question, Harry. Well, if the blind person is tall, for example, he or she would need a big dog in order to feel the pull from the dog as they walked. So in this manner, the dog is matched to its new and suitable owner.'

'I would only want a big dog.'

'Don't make me laugh, Charlie. You're not tall enough for a big dog.'

'I'm as tall as you, Harry Prescott!'

'No, you're not. Any road, you have to be blind too.'

'I sometimes think he is.'

'What's that supposed to mean, Smithie?'

'It means, Charlie Chuckle Head, that in our last match, wot we should have won, you missed a goal by a mile. You were blind then.'

'I was dazzled by t' sunshine.'

'Sunshine! It were raining, you clown.'

'OK, OK. Let's not argue… What's the matter, Marion? You're pulling an awful face.'

'It's terrible, sir, isn't it, Bernard?'

'I'll say. It's Charlie, sir.'

'What about him?'

'He's farted. He's always farting.'

'Can't you choose a better word, Bernard? Well, Charlie, do you need to leave the room?'

'Not now.'

'He just needs another fart.'

'That will do, Bernard. And stop calling out.' Their teacher stood again. 'Now then… where are you two girls going?'

'We feel sick, 'cos of the stink Charlie has made.'

'Everybody farts.'

'Not like you, Charlie,' continued Bernard, warming to the subject. 'You stink like…'

'A midden,' someone shouted.

'A compost heap,' another kid called.

'Rotten eggs,' suggested a third.

The teacher raised his hands, took a step forward – then he retreated as he had once or twice in the Falklands, when the stink of cordite and scorched earth overwhelmed them. But this disgusting stench, trumped up by this whippersnapper, was more than a veteran soldier could bear. He stepped back.

'Strewth. I think you're right, Tracey. Right, emergency stations, everybody. Marion and Tracey, step outside and leave the door open. Platoon,' he barked, 'dismiss.' And all the kids followed him outside. After he'd inhaled a few fresh breaths he said, 'Dear God, Charlie, what on earth did you have for breakfast?'

'Just a treacle butty.'

'Well, tomorrow, try jam, and make sure it's fresh. Leave that cabin door open,' he called. 'Right, follow me. We'll walk smartly round the caravan site.' He strode on with the kids scuttling beside him.

'Charlie's farted, Charlie stinks.'

'That will do, lads. If we're going to sing, let's choose a proper song. Come on: Onward, Christian soldiers, marching as to war...'

One kid leaned towards his pal's shell-like ear. 'Hey, Harry...'

'What you muttering about?'

'I can't say it out loud, else owd Watson will hear.'

The kids moved in a flock like sheep surging towards new pasture.

'Whassup, Mickey?'

'Start us off wi' a chorus. Mek summat up.'

'OK. But join in... Charlie's farted, what a smell, when he dies he'll go to hell.'

All the lads – except the scoundrel – chanted the impromptu lyric, which became their anthem for weeks to come. They were allowed only three choruses.

'OK. Cut that out, lads. If you must sing, choose something we all know.'

'We all live in a yellow submarine.'

'Well done, girls. Everybody: We all live in a yellow submarine… Left, right, left, right. Come on, step out smartly… A yellow submarine.'

'… Go to hell.'

Tramping round the site had been a mini route march and many of the kids were breathless. But the effect had been to gradually quell their exuberance.

'Right, up the steps and back into the classroom. You can stop singing now. You lads, cut the cackle. Last person in, leave the door open. We'll have a window open too. Sit down, quietly and calmly, please. Now, we'll take a little rest, then carry on where we left off… So, we were discussing your visit to the farm. Any further comments?'

'Please, sir.'

'Yes, Peter! You haven't said anything yet. What did you enjoy last week?'

'I liked that large oak tree. My cousin – who's in the top class at our school – reckons it's 150 years old. I went and stood underneath it.'

'That's how you get all covered in bird muck.'

'Charlie! You and your muck. Shut up. So you stood underneath the tree, Peter?'

'Yes. When you keep still and listen quietly, you can hear the leaves murmuring to each other.'

'Oh, lovely.'

'Yes, Peter is quite poetic, isn't he, Marion? You obviously like trees, Peter.'

'Not all trees. Privet and such are rubbish. But I like the stately oak. They shed hundreds of acorns each year.'

'They're not as good as chestnut trees.'

'And why is that, Charlie?'

'Well, sir, they don't drop conkers, do they? I mean, you can't play conkers with an acorn, can you?'

'Sir, you wouldn't expect an oak tree to shed a conker. That would be a quirk of nature.'

'That's true, Peter. Oak trees have given good service over the years. I'm glad you are fond of trees.'

'Yes, sir. I am. When I'm older I'm going to work for the National Trust in one of their forests.'

'Well done. Now, can anyone tell me anything about last week's farm visit that is as interesting as that?'

'I liked the look of that bull best, sir.'

'Oh, very nice, Bernard. Can you tell us his pedigree?'

'Yes,' came the prompt reply. 'He were a Hereford. He – were – massive. He had a ring through his nose.'

'So does my sister.'

This caused much tittering.

'Thank you, Charlie. The ring through the bull's nose is so that his keeper can control him.'

'Same as me sister. Me mam holds it when her's stupid.'

'Why does that not surprise me! Yes, Tracey. Is your hand raised?'

'Charlie was quite rude yesterday. He kept on about bulls and cows. Coupling, he called it. Then he said people do it.'

'My parents don't,' Marion asserted.

'Huh! You think they don't, Marion. You tell 'em, sir. You're an adult. It's all about nature, innit?'

'Well, now, er, Charlie…' The hooter from the sugar beet factory sounded. 'Ah, breaktime.'

The children sprang to attention. Breaktime meant playtime, and they wanted to roam round the caravan site.

'Leave the classroom quietly, and as quickly as possible. There's a shop here if you want to visit it. Charlie, visit the boy's toilet before you come back in.'

The kids trooped outside, ready to explore.

'Ye gods, that was damn close. Kids! They know more than I do.'

⁂

On her way home, the Reverend Miriam Peach called at the Co-op for bread and fresh fish. In front of her stood an individual loading his shopping bag with candles. As he passed Miriam on his way out, she noticed he had an odd, slightly deformed face, and she silently denounced herself for thinking this.

'Who's that customer, Bob?' she asked the manager.

'His name is Grimshaw, and he works for the council. He's a strange cove,' said Bob. 'Best left alone. He's actually the Pastor at that little church called The Sanctuary.'

She left the shop not realising that Grimshaw would have a disagreeable effect on her life in the near future.

NINE

A friendly rivalry existed between the villages of Upsy-Daisy, Down Daisy and Daisy Hill. Each year a fete was organised and this rivalry reached its highest during the various contests and competitions. These events ranged from cake making to joisting, egg throwing, pillow fighting, flat racing, darts, hoopla, arm wrestling and weight lifting.

Points were awarded for every activity, which was adjudicated by an independent judge. Throughout the afternoon, a radio announcer made corny observations.

A pillow fight sounds like a cosy pastime, something like fighting with balloons on sticks, but at the Daisy Fete it had dangerous connotations. These pillow fights were often as fierce as locked antlers, but not as firm or compact. They were fought sitting on a greasy pole – best suits were left at home. Contestants had to hold on with one hand and grab the pillow with the other. Some assailants thrashed their opponents so hard that it was not unknown for pillows to burst and feathers flutter to the earth like a plucked chicken.

The pillows, of course, were not quality. Silk or satin was never seen; few residents possessed these luxuries anyway. The pillows used were often home spun, made from hessian. And in the past, when grudges were borne, they'd been stuffed, not with down, but rough sand and pebbles so that the toppled loser also went home bearing bruises in the nether regions. And boasters and the overweight were invariably the first to fall.

Today, the contestants included Toby, the landlord of the Diving Duck, who faced Richard Coningsby from Upsy-Daisy. Young Harry Prescott, whose family had a cottage in Down Daisy, tackled his classmate Bernard, who lived in a council house in Daisy Hill; and Fred the postman faced Malcolm, principal cornet player in the local brass band.

An unusual match, one to be watched, was between Josephine, the beauty from the caravan site, and Markie who had borrowed £10 from her and didn't seem willing to pay it back.

The intercom spluttered. 'I have it on good authority that in this next pillow fight a personal issue is at stake.'

The contestants sat rigid for a moment and listened.

'One of them owes the other a tenner. Which can it be?'

'You had no right mentioning that,' Markie grumbled.

'I've said nothing,' Josephine assured him, 'but I've a good idea who has.'

Earlier that morning Miss Primm had approached her. 'I'm sorry to trouble you, Jo. But I suddenly find I'm short of cash until the bank opens on Monday. Could you be a dear and lend me £10?'

'I'm so sorry, Miss Primm, but I'm well and truly skint. I lent Markie £10 a few days ago. He promised to repay me within the week, then Richard borrowed my last few coppers to get some postage stamps this morning. I'm broke. Sorry.'

Miss Primm went away, grumbling and angry. Mainly angry at Markie who had borrowed money off her and it had still not been repaid. 'The man deserves to be shown up,' she muttered.

And that is exactly what she did.

'I borrowed it in confidence,' muttered Markie. 'I'll tell you what, if I win, we'll call it quits.'

He didn't ask, he made an assumption.

'You cheeky blighter,' Jo said.

'On your marks,' called the announcer. 'Ready, steady… go!'

Each of the contenders had a grudge to bear. In Markie's case it was also an embarrassment. They lunged at each other and pillows thwacked in mid-air. Markie grabbed the bar, greasy though it was, and Josephine, sitting upright, arched her back. Both remained erect.

Throughout that week, Josephine had practised on a swivel chair, twirling and lifting her feet off the ground. And that very morning had had a rehearsal with Richard, learning to duck.

Also that morning, prior to the day's events, Markie – almost certainly using Josephine's £10 note, or somebody else's – had spent a happy hour in the Diving Duck.

Each of them swung again. Markie caught Jo on the elbow and she wobbled somewhat. Then Jo twirled her pillowcase like a weighty lasso, brought it round half a circle and caught Markie on the side of his unshaven face. He toppled down to the ground, landing on his piles, accompanied by a mighty cheer.

As he fell, Mrs Marks, who'd fumed like a boiling kettle when she learnt that Markie was insolvent once again, grabbed him by the earlobe and hauled him away. Josephine was half-heartedly repaid that evening.

The egg-throwing contest was the most recent addition to the Daisy Fete. Instead of teams, the competitors paired off into couples. One person threw the egg and their partner, hovering some eighty yards away, caught it – if they were any good at it! If they failed to catch it, they finished with yolk slithering down their countenance because all thrown eggs were raw. Indeed some were a bit 'off'. Then, the idiom 'egg on his face' becomes a yolk on a fathead as the catcher walks around like an underdone custard.

Prizes were awarded to the pair – invariably the cleanest – who were able to produce the most unbroken eggs. Young Charlie Wrigley currently excelled at this diversion, and some folk wondered if the Olympics would foster the sport.

That day, Charlie was awarded first prize, which illustrated that not all interesting projects are located in the classroom. Later in the day, Charlie would carry out an unscripted finale.

'This is my squire,' announced Major Merryweather.

The Professor bowed, quite willing to be introduced as such.

Bob, the trombonist, ignorant in history or military warfare, frowned and nodded curtly. 'Your squire!' He said it with distaste, as though the noun were a remedy for teetotalism.

'Yes. My squire. Professor Sparrow.'

'Sparrow!' echoed Bob. 'That's a funny name.'

'Why is it funny?' questioned the Major. 'I know a chappie called Bull. I've an acquaintance named Fox. I know a Nightingale, a Lamb – and so forth.'

'You know a person called Soforth?' said Bob incredulously.

'No, you chump,' snorted the Major.

Bob understood chump. He had been so dubbed many times. 'Don't you call me a chump. I'll remember that when we're on our bikes.'

The last event on Daisy Fete's Programme was the tournament. Two contestants were selected, one from each of two villages. This year it was the turn of Upsy-Daisy and Daisy Hill. When it was known that Bob had been chosen, the caravan coterie realised they had to nominate, from their own group, someone of equal calibre. Major Merryweather had, naturally, been flattered.

'Bikes!' scoffed the Major. 'Huh, had it been left to me, we would be charging on horses, like we used to do.'

Professor Sparrow looked at his 'knight' quizzically. He couldn't recall the Major pleading for a horse.

In the past, the Daisy Fete had used horses, but too many accidents had occurred, so bikes had been introduced instead.

'Bikes or horses, I'll still beat you,' boasted Bob.

'Beat me! You couldn't beat a carpet.'

Bob, beginning to get angry, took a step forward.

'Steady now, Bob,' said a bandsman called Brendan. 'Save your anger for the tournament.' He placed a placating hand on Bob's shoulder.

The contestants and their assistants were in the robing tent, where they had changed into medieval costume, or partial thereof because Major Merryweather insisted on wearing his officer's hat accompanied with his beribboned medals. Bob had served in no military campaigns, so he wore a string of beer bottle tops strung round his neck; and getting his history and his apparel mixed up, he proudly wore a codpiece.

Over the Tannoy they heard their introduction.

'Now for our final entertainment of the afternoon. Will you please welcome the contestants for the jousting.'

To a surge of rapturous delight and yells of encouragement the valiant challengers trundled their two-wheeled steeds into the arena. As they emerged, noise from the spectators grew louder. And if the contestants had been willing to admit it, their nervousness, perhaps even fear, multiplied.

As the crowd cheered, a gang of forgotten lads at the far end of the field began their own entertainment by throwing raw eggs at each other, with a view to scoring rather than catching. The eggs were the remains of the ammunition from the egg-throwing competition which had ended forty minutes earlier; and these leftover eggs were due to be fed to Farmer Bradshaw's Saddleback pigs, who could gobble them up fresh or foul. But tomorrow's breakfast was currently being squandered by Daisy louts.

As the tournament contestants took up positions, one either end of the field, their assistants walked beside them like mourners.

The tournament track had been earlier laid by an amalgamated gang of Daisyites, strewing sand, sawdust and fine gravel inside the enclosure, giving the track an appearance of a poverty-stricken race course.

The sun beamed strongly on the southern end of the field, causing Major Merryweather to sweat. Brassy Bob, at the northern end, felt an itch and began to scratch his codpiece.

Now, the Major clambered onto his sit-up-and-beg bike. Then he adjusted his officer's hat. Bob, his opponent, cocked a leg over his crossbar then revamped his codpiece which he believed made him appear not only more medieval but positively sensual.

On his head he wore an air raid warden's helmet which had belonged to his father in the '39–'45 war.

The referee, who happened to be the Reverend Miriam Peach, strode across the grass to the centre of the arena holding high a white flag, and placed to her lips a whistle – the Thunderer, the implement of many a flat race. She looked both north and south, blew the whistle and brought down the flag like a guillotine.

The fight began.

The contestants pushed with their feet and were away. Both of them pedalled hard, gripping the handlebars with one white knuckle and holding a lance with the other. The lances were made from broom handles with a large wet mop at the end – a mop which, according to rules, was soaked by their squire prior to pedalling away. As they approached each other, the crowd yelled with unreserved volume, encouraging various comments.

'Come on, Major, put your bloody back into it,' which was difficult for Merryweather who was concentrating on his legs.

'Move it, Bob, you dozy bugger. Lift your lance higher…'

'… Otherwise you'll jab him in the balls.'

'And why not,' encouraged another.

'Kick him in the codpiece, Major.'

These erudite remarks were greeted with fervent roars of delight by Daisy supporters from all sides. Prior to the match, bets were placed enthusiastically, encouraged by the Vicar, who intended to circulate with a bucket for the church appeal.

This brace of contestants now pedalled furiously towards each other and suddenly seemed to collide, but at the last moment swerved, causing each rider to fall off. The crowd loved it and encouraged them to remount. They clambered back onto their legless steeds and, moving away from each other, began a circuit of the track, feeling like charioteers.

On this second circuit the riders were obviously beginning to pant. Bob the Gob had neglected to blow his nose earlier on and he felt his nostrils were blocked. Major Merryweather had forgotten to trim his moustache and his top lip was starting to tickle. They had, however, entered the competition with eyes wide open, even though they were both a little short-sighted, so complaints were out of the question.

'Faster,' roared the crowd. But speed was in short supply. Their legs were like petrol tanks doused with sugar. But on they rode as brave as they could. Now they achingly approached each other for a second time and, as though they had received a personal signal, each one lunged with his lance.

It was now the brightest part of the day, one of those days when the sun looms from behind an innocent white cloud to roast everything on earth. As the sun flared, eggs were dispatched – unexpected missiles in an unpredicted attack. Young Charlie Wrigley from Down Daisy was the champion.

The contestants were now fifty yards from each other. The mob urged them on. Lances were raised and two hearts raced. They were now mere yards apart. Suddenly the sun came out strongly like a searchlight. Charlie lobbed his remaining grenade. The sun dazzled Bob, causing temporary blindness. The egg arched down and smacked the Major full in the face, making his moustache look as though it had kissed a large custard pie. Both contestants crashed into each other, causing them to collapse from their mounts where they lay exhausted as if they had run a marathon. The referee walked calmly across and waved her white flag over them like an emblem of defeat. It was certainly Wally who cried, 'Get up, you dozy buggers, it's not bedtime.'

TEN

Every year, Daisy Hill Brass Band organised a coach outing. To augment the cost anybody was permitted to attend, whether they were band supporters or not. Just cough up your cash and you were part of the bash. This year it was a mystery tour. Even the driver wasn't sure of the destination. All he knew was: they'd finish up at a pub.

Big Bill Ramsbottom, the band's factotum, and manager of the Co-op, was also the B-flat bass player; he now stood on the pavement. 'Come on now, don't dally.'

Someone started to sing, 'Don't dilly dally on the way.'

Wally was on the front seat sitting next to the Vicar. 'If he's singing now, there'll be no stopping him when he's had a few.'

'Do you recognise that voice?' Reverend Miriam Peach asked.

'Oh aye. It's Dave. Young Charlie Wrigley's dad.'

The Wrigleys stowed their two instruments in the hold, watched by Big Bill as though they might chip the paintwork. 'Neatly does it,' said Bill. 'Good lad.' He ruffled Charlie's hair as the Wrigley trio climbed on board. Bill stepped up behind them. 'I suggest you lot sit on the back seat.'

'Us lot?' echoed Dave. 'There're only three of us.'

Young Charlie was already on the back seat, kneeling up to gape through the back window. Next came his great-granddad followed by Dave, his dad.

'Now then, young fellow, keep your mucky shoes off the seats.'

'I cleaned my shoes this morning,' the lad retorted.

'If we need a sermon,' said Dave, 'the Vicar is here.'

But Big Bill was known to expect the last word. 'I'm sorry, Granddad, but you can't smoke that pipe in here.'

The old chap nodded and smiled. 'Very good,' he said, continuing to chuff on his briar.

Big Bill frowned. 'What does he mean, "Very good"?'

'He can't hear you,' said Dave Wrigley.

Young Charlie swivelled round. ''Cos he's deaf.'

As this chatter continued, the old man continued to discharge clouds of pipe smoke towards the front of the bus.

'Well *you'll* have to explain to him,' Bill pursued.

'He's on holiday, Bill,' a voice called. 'What do you expect?'

'He's turned ninety,' another voice added. 'He's earned his pleasure.'

Somebody laughed. 'It's his pipe what's kept him going.'

Only Mavis, percussion player, seemed to object by vigorously fanning her face with a magazine. The banter encouraged further titters, causing Big Bill to stamp along the aisle to the driver. 'I'm sorry, but there's an old guy at the back smoking.'

The driver removed his Woodbine, and coughed. 'He'll have a rest eventually.'

Exasperated, Bill stepped down from the bus like a circus elephant stepping down from a tub. He noticed the tenor horn section – Iona, Mona and Shona – clustered round the luggage hold. 'Stack your instruments carefully, girls, then the others can get theirs in.'

'I thought this was the driver's job,' said Mona.

'The driver's occupied,' added Shona.

'Yeah, he's having a fag,' observed Iona.

'Let me put mine in,' said Mona.

'As the curate said to the waitress.'

All three girls whirled round to find Bob Dyke grinning and eyeing them. They glanced daggers at him, shot each other knowing looks, then climbed aboard. They squeezed together on a two-seater, muttering.

'If that creep starts his touching tactics today, I'll stab him with a sharp pencil,' threatened Mona.

It was spoken slightly louder than intended, and Wally and the Reverend Miriam, on adjacent seats, exchanged stunned glances.

On the back seat, the Wrigley contingent were sprawled out. Great-Granddad puffed contentedly on his pipe, Dave was fiddling with his mobile and young Charlie pulled a notebook and chewed pencil from his pocket. He flipped open the notebook to reveal lists of numbers. Great-Granddad turned to look and, using his pipe stem as a pointer, tapped the booklet.

'What's all that lot?'

'They're car numbers,' said Charlie. 'It's my 'obby. I collect 'em.' And he emphasised by miming driving a car.

'Oh, right.' Information digested, the heedless ancient coughed phlegmatically, replaced his pipe and sent out a few smoke signals.

Two seats further on, Big Bill shook his thick mane and grumbled. Working in the Co-op as a shop manager, and being a long-standing member of the band, he expected all and sundry to carry out his instructions. Now the last two passengers boarded the bus: Bob Dyke and Chalkie White. Chalkie sat across the aisle from Bill.

'I trust you've brought your mouth organ, Chalkie?'

'I certainly have, Bill.' Chalkie patted his pocket. 'It's always with me. But it's really a harmonica. It's an instrument in its own right, you know.'

Bob Dyke shunted down the aisle and all but leered at the young tenor horn players as he passed them. They, acquainted with his peccadillos, stared him out.

Iona leaned closer to her colleagues. 'If that creepy sod starts his tricks as he usually does, I cannot be held responsible for what I'll do.' She assumed she was whispering, but Wally and the Vicar heard every warning word.

The others nodded understandingly. The girls were dressed identically. They wore light blue pullovers, tightly stretched across their ripe, pear-shaped breasts. Sheathing their slim legs they wore new jeans, each garment slashed at the knees, which peeped through like inquisitive ferrets. Identical earrings like curtain rings dangled from their pink lobes. And for the first time, metal rings were fastened to their noses like fickle young bullocks. According to band members, whether their septum piercings were trashy or cute was a matter of opinion.

'I hope I'm around when you skewer him,' tittered Mona.

'He should really have his balls tattooed,' added Shona.

Their wisecracks were uttered carelessly and were inevitably heard by the Reverend Peach and Wally, who leaned in to her and whispered, 'Items for your next sermon, perhaps?' She nudged him playfully with a sharp elbow. But Wally couldn't 'shush'. 'It's like being in a confessional sitting here.'

The coach driver flicked his fag out of the window, turned the ignition, and they were away.

'At last,' grumbled Big Bill. 'I thought the engine had seized up.' They moved off into the countryside and the day seemed to promise calmness and tranquillity.

The next overheard titbit was normal, day-to-day – boring. 'What do you do for a living, Norman?' asked Mavis.

'I'm a peripatetic brass teacher.'

'What does peripatetic mean?'

'Well, instead of teaching in the same school all the time, I travel about from school to school,' he said, laying it on with a trowel.

'I see.' Mavis seemed to analyse his reply, inspect the info, then weigh up the value. 'That sounds like a secure job.' Married life had taught Mavis to value security.

On the seat in front, the Reverend Miriam turned her head and whispered to Wally, 'That's Mavis. She plays percussion. Not long ago, she lost her husband.'

Wally chuckled. 'It sounds as though she's fishing for another.'

He was rewarded with another sharp nudge.

'Secure!' Norman exclaimed. 'I've never thought of it like that before.'

In front, the Reverend Miriam muttered, 'I feel as though I'm eavesdropping.'

Wally placed a large hand over hers. 'We are. It's up to them to talk quieter.'

Then they heard Mavis say, 'Do you have many friends outside the band and your work?'

Norman, reserved by nature, shook his head and pushed his spectacles further along his nose. 'Friends! Well, not really. This band, and my teaching job, more or less dominate my life. Mind you, I'm not complaining.'

'You really do need acquaintances,' she persisted. She gently tapped his arm. 'If ever you fancy a change, you're welcome to call on me.'

'Call?'

'Yes. Phone.'

Norman, never really comfortable with females, apart from pupils, experienced an unusual sense of fellow feeling.

The two passengers sitting in front of them, unwittingly hearing all that was said, exchanged more knowing looks.

The coach moved quietly and rhythmically through the countryside and a yellow sun appeared on the horizon. A tractor driver steered his steel leviathan nearer the kerbside to let the daytrippers through, and a few passengers waved their comradely approval. Ten minutes later, the coach driver eased his speed slightly then pulled into the car park of a country pub, appropriately called, Travellers' Rest.

'Well, here we are,' the driver said, his voice tinny over the mic. 'We'll pull up for about forty minutes. The toilets are a bit primitive, so I suggest the ladies go first, to, er, well, go first.' He pressed a red button and the door slid open with a hiss.

But first off the bus was young Charlie, clutching his notebook. He trotted fifty yards then plonked himself on a milestone and at once began to record car numbers as the vehicles sped past. Chalkie White walked a few paces behind the youngster and as he approached he said, 'You'll catch piles sitting there, Charlie.'

'Oh, that's cool, but I've got piles already, and I've lots more pages left.'

Chalkie smiled and walked on. Then he took his harmonica from his top pocket and began to play 'Roll Out the Barrel'. A group of small village girls dancing with a skipping rope pranced along with Chalkie as he passed. He could play most simple melodies at first try; this was because he practised daily in his signal box on the railway, while awaiting each train.

Sitting on his stone-cold stool, young Charlie heard the tune and pricked up his musical ears. 'Cool,' he muttered, and rose from his observance seat. He'd been learning the cornet for six months, and through sympathetic motives, and because his dad was a band member, Charlie had been admitted into the Daisy Hill Brass Band, third cornet section, which only tootled at every lamppost. He shoved his notebook back into his pocket and fell in beside the rope dancers and Chalkie, who had changed the tune to 'Colonel Bogey'.

'That's a nice tune, Chalkie,' Charlie said, striding out to keep in step, 'I wish I could play like that.'

Chalkie paused his playing. 'You will if you practise regularly. But to be really good, it takes years. The best thing you can do is continue with your cornet then when you've mastered that you can buy a harmonica. But to learn two instruments at a time is very difficult.' He stopped and looked at his pocket watch, a precise timepiece, used to confirm the punctuality of locomotives. 'It's time we were getting back to the pub, before all the cakes get scoffed.'

'Cakes!' echoed the lad. 'I didn't know there were cakes.' And he at once turned about and shot back along the pavement. He entered the pub to find the Reverend Miriam Peach holding a tray of sweetmeats.

'Will you have a cake, Charlie?'

'Aye, I will that, but not one with currants in.'

'I see. Dried fruit is good for you, you know. Don't you like currants and raisins?'

'No fear,' said the lad. 'They remind me of my rabbits.'

Those who heard him smiled at the youngster's colourful explanation.

Wally loomed over the Vicar. 'Where've you been, Charlie? We've been waiting for you.'

With his mouth full of chocolate cake, the youngster muttered, 'I've been writing down car numbers.' And to prove his point he fished out his notebook and pencil stub.

'Good gracious,' exclaimed Miriam. 'Is that the only pencil you have?'

Charlie nodded as his mouth was full.

'Then you had better take this.' And she produced from her handbag a new pencil with a sharp point.

'Cool! I've never had a new pencil.'

Just at that point the Daisy group were joined by another visiting group, and Big Bill's deep voice announced, 'Well, well, if it isn't the Sally Army.'

Half a dozen Salvationists had arrived. Two of them handed out leaflets, the other four carried brass instruments. Obviously with the landlord's permission, they began to tune up.

'I think this might be described as carrying coal to Newcastle,' Wally said.

Miriam smiled and added, 'But it's nice to see them keeping up their good work. Quite a few dropouts rely on the good old Sally for help.'

The quartet struck up with 'Onward, Christian Soldiers', and, on his harmonica, Chalkie White quickly found the key and joined in. The leaflets handed round had the words of the hymn printed on one side, and a tale of an unfortunate individual on the other. The Daisy group joined in the singing with gusto, and in many cases the gusto was enhanced by inebriation. When the singing was over, the Sally's major addressed them briefly.

'Thank you and God bless you for joining in. Today's charity is for a young person whose picture you'll find on the sheet. Through no fault of her own she is experiencing hardship. But by your generosity and in the name of Jesus we can all help her. Please contribute generously. Thank you and God bless.'

The collecting bowls were soon filled with silver coins and a few treasury notes. On the other side of Wally sat Bob Dyke, staring at the leaflet. When the first hymn had concluded, those near him heard him moan, 'Huh, I don't swallow all this Jesus lark. I don't believe in it. It encourages layabouts to be idle.'

Young Charlie, standing near him, became quite perturbed. 'You don't believe in Jesus?' It was in reality a rebuke and coming from a youngster seemed dire.

'I've just said so, haven't I?'

Charlie looked up into the Reverend Peach's face as pain was etched upon his own features. She stepped towards him and placed a friendly arm about his young, broad shoulders.

'Don't worry about it, Charlie. Remarks like that happen all the time… By the way, when we were singing I heard your voice soaring above the rest of us. You obviously like singing.'

'Music is his best subject,' said Norman, the peripatetic brass teacher.

She smiled at Norman. 'Of course, you teach at Charlie's school.'

Norman gulped at his shandy then nodded. 'Yes. And young Chucky here is noted for his singing voice.'

'How about you joining our church choir, Charlie?'

'Oh, I dunno. I usually go fishing with me dad on Sundays.'

'I see.' She ruffled his hair. 'And does he pay you for that?'

Surprise sprang into his eyes like a sudden torchlight. 'Pay me? Well, no. I just sort of, er, stand around.'

'Ah. Well, we pay our choristers, our choirboys. And all they have to do is sing. We give them pocket money for attending twice on Sundays. Sometimes they only attend once.'

'That sounds like easy money, Charlie,' said Wally grinning.

This was augmented by Norman. 'I didn't know that. It's unusual, isn't it?'

'Not all that unusual,' said Miriam. 'Many years ago, a wealthy member of our church bequeathed a legacy to us so good young choristers would be encouraged to sing,' she exclaimed.

Charlie looked at his brass tutor, obviously hoping for further comment. 'There you go, Charlie. That's really cool.' And he winked conspiratorially.

The youngster turned back to the Vicar; his face radiated a smile. Praise from a pedagogue was obviously something new. 'Cool,' he said. 'I'll join.' Then, like small boys do who have quaffed too much lemonade, he clutched his crotch. 'I'll have to go.' And like a dancer on points he made for the gents.

Bob Dyke had taken all this in. For unascertained reasons, he resented the Vicar getting chummy with the boy, perhaps because she wasn't directly connected with the Daisy Hill Brass Band. Or simply because – as some folk swore – he was odd! Furthermore, Bob wasn't too keen on being regaled as a 'mean sod' by band members. Perhaps his attitude was due to some primeval reasoning, or simply supping too much too early. But his immature disposition caused him to mutter, 'That little sod's to blame.' So he decided, accidentally on purpose, to clip him behind the ear, just as his generation were clipped years ago. So he followed Charlie to the gents.

At the far end of the passageway the three horn players, Iona, Mona and Shona, were just forsaking the sanctuary of the ladies' loo, where they had left face powder on the floor and false eyelashes in the lav. They now walked – slightly tipsy and very giggly

– back along the narrow corridor, where many a lass had been touched up. Coming towards them, young Charlie suddenly remembered an item he needed to scribble in his notebook and began to scrawl with his new, sharp pencil. Lurking behind Charlie, Bob Dyke was poised to make Charlie a whipping boy for the perceived slights of some band members. All four suddenly collided as a scrum against the stationary, scribbling youngster. Dyke became lustful at the sight of the girls' tight-fitting apparel.

'Excuse me, ladies, if I may pass…' But he didn't. He lingered, as did his fingers around the luscious, well-formed undercarriage of the shapely Iona.

'You touching us up again, are you?' And she grabbed Charlie's pencil and stabbed Bob's unfettered paw. Bob yelped. Blood spurted. And Charlie found the pencil thrust back into his hand. The females walked on, giggling.

Bob scuttled into a toilet and held his bleeding hand under the cold tap. Young Charlie relieved himself, washed his hands and returned to the bar area, and was disconcerted to find two policemen asking questions. He became suspicious, nervous even. Had he done something wrong? He halted.

'Ah! Young Charlie might know something,' Chalkie said. 'He was collecting car numbers.'

All eyes swivelled towards the boy. He frowned. 'I know nothing.' He was well versed in defence monologue. He clutched his notebook and slipped his new pencil into his pocket. 'It's private. I've done nowt.'

'We know that,' said the Vicar. 'But I personally am asking you to help the police. A small child has been injured. You can help… Only you.'

The police sergeant who had been talking approached the boy who, uncertain, like a lamb needing its mother, moved closer to the Vicar. If his mother *had* been there, she would have stood no nonsense. 'Dad!' he called, looking round the room, but he could see neither his father nor his great-granddad.

'Your dad has taken your great-granddad back to the coach. He needed a lie down,' the Vicar said.

Charlie looked up at her. She smiled and nodded encouragingly. So he opened up his notebook, which was very personal to him, and the police sergeant looked down at it, noting the unexpected remarks pencilled in beside some of the numbers.

'You've written that this car was going very fast.'

'Aye. Like a bomb. It were right cool.'

'What does this sentence say?' asked the sergeant, pointing.

'It says grey, with black snakes painted on it.'

Constable Cole, standing near the bar, called across, 'It will be that pop group, Serge. They're called Anaconda.'

Charlie arched his head well back. The police sergeant now seemed to be tall and vigilant rather than looming over him. 'Well done, young fellow.' He patted the lad's head. 'You're a hero.' He tossed a £2 coin onto the bar counter. 'Get this young man some crisps and lemonade.' And without more ado, the cops left the pub.

The departing police were soon followed by a grateful Sally Army sextet who had relieved the Daisy Hill band of a quantity of cash in a casual but well-meaning exercise, worthy of dedicated salespeople.

Now Big Bill lumbered to his feet. 'Well, it's time we were off again. We have a performance to fulfil for which we'll receive a very good meal. So finish your drinks and visit the lavs if need be.' Within minutes they were away.

It transpired that the band had been engaged to perform for a Methodist church who were as hard up as many members of Daisy Hill, but the church needed the wherewithal to stop their premises from leaking and pay looming gas and electricity bills. So ye olde barter system had been practised: they would produce an entertainment for a paying audience. The band would receive payment in kind, a nourishing meal with the ingredients, vegetables and meat provided by, and cooked by, church members, i.e. a potato pie supper with apple strudel and fresh cream to follow. Many Methodists were teetotal, so the beverages would be tasty herb beer and homemade non-alcoholic wine. The band committee had settled for that unanimously.

Contentment descended on the passengers. The driver drove smoothly and his charges were lulled into silence. Some snoozed and others took crafty slurps from the bottles they had smuggled from the Travellers' Rest. Even the brassy horn players were quieter than usual. Then, after an hour and twenty minutes, and almost secretly, the coach pulled into a small car park shared by a Methodist church and its schoolroom.

Sleepily and reluctantly, they all piled out.

The schoolroom had been built in 1895. No one could dispute this because the date was carved into the brickwork over the door. The players lugged their instruments inside, where a reasonable-sized stage had been furnished with hardback chairs. Band members erected their music stands before their own chair, and Colin, the conductor, placed his rostrum nearer to the edge of the stage.

The floor area was wide, having once been a day school, and the bleached smell of recently mopped woodwork caused the room to seem uncommonly clean. Two long tables had been erected with a wide gap between them. The audience would sit on the dining chairs, side on, to save having to remove furniture prior to and after the concert.

The first chore, as with any visiting group, was a trip to the loo. This time, Methodism proved more exclusive than the Travellers' Rest, for the lavs were separated in olde worlde style: ladies on one side of the room, gents on the other. Then the band squashed into the vestry to place their valuable brass instruments on the floor. Bob Dyke, his pierced hand still wrapped in a hanky, kept well away from the horn trio.

'Listen up,' called Big Bill, his voice bouncing from one wall to the other, 'because we have an efficient coach driver, we arrived here about fifty minutes early, which gives us a bit more leisure time… There is a suggestion that we visit the Methodists' museum just down the road. It costs £1 to go in and that entrance fee I believe goes to this church. The alternative is to sit here or trudge up and down the high street.'

At that point Bill took a breath, which allowed Petra Moody to say, 'We're not likely to catch germs in there, are we?'

A man, who turned out to be the church caretaker, said, quite strongly, 'No, you will not catch germs. Everything about these Methodist premises is quite clean.'

'I'm not being personal,' she countered, with the whine of a delicate person in her voice, 'but…'

Her reasoning, however, was thrust to one side, as Chalkie White clarified. 'I was once sent to this area to monitor a new signal box. While I was here I visited this museum. It's really just a terraced cottage, but you'll find it interesting.' He chuckled. 'It makes me laugh when I think about it. And… I never caught any germs.'

'That settles it then,' said Big Bill. 'If it was good enough for Chalkie it's good enough for me. Come on, off we go.' And without further discussion he swung away and everyone followed him.

They shuffled after him, some of them muttering.

'A museum?' said Mona, scorn colouring her voice. 'It sounds like school.'

'Do we have to go?' grumbled Shona.

'Sounds boring,' added Iona.

'You'll probably see something interesting,' said a voice behind them. They turned to find the Reverend

Miriam and Wally walking side by side. The Vicar was careful not to say *learn something*.

'How else will you get the time over?' asked Wally.

'Walking round the shops,' chirruped one of the girls.

'I'll tell you what,' said Wally, 'have a look at this place. If you don't like it at all, I'll pay your entrance fee.'

'You'll get a laugh when you go in,' Chalkie assured them.

They all trudged along for ten minutes and arrived at the venue, which, as Chalkie had assured them, was a small terraced cottage. They paid their admittance fee and trouped in. Years ago somebody had decided to earn a bit of extra cash, but instead of tolerating a lodger had decided to turn part of their home into a museum... of sorts. Around the walls were mottos: 'Do unto others before they do it unto you'. The motto for Islington was: 'We serve' (someone had added, 'Mine's a Guinness'). Orkney's motto was: 'The North our home, the sea our friend...' with the addition: 'The lav our relief'.

Then came the exhibits. Under a glass case was displayed a length of shingle. In the centre was compressed a beetle-shaped fossil, gathered from the Jurassic Coast. This was reputed to be 'The First Creature Born on Earth'.

'Look,' said young Charlie, 'a baby dinosaur.'

Behind him stood Wally. 'Yeah. Unfortunately it didn't get chance to grow.'

Next came a tatty and de-plumaged arrow with

the caption: 'The arrow that killed King Harold at the Battle of Hastings'.

'I think they're having us on,' said Norman.

'Ah, but you have to prove it isn't so,' Chalkie pointed out. 'Now this next exhibit could be true.'

They gaped at a large champion conker, threaded on a string: 'This conker has been used to shatter a thousand other conkers'.

Under a glass display case was an old-style leather football, almost deflated. Attached to it was a label on which was printed: 'The last football Sir Stanley Matthews kicked. Career: 1936–1965'.

'Well, at least they've got the date right,' said Big Bill, laughing. 'I bet none of you youngsters have heard of him.'

'I've heard of Bernard Matthews,' said Mona.

'He was the turkey breeder,' replied Shona.

'They could have shown a picture of him in here,' added Iona.

This caused the girls to giggle. 'They're laughing,' the Vicar said to Wally. 'You won't need to pay for them now.'

Next on the list of wondrous sights was a pair of bootlaces. They had been spread out and shaped into a swastika and were reputed to have belonged to Adolf Hitler.

But the final item caused the most fuss: 'This medium-sized pebble is the missile with which David killed Goliath'.

'That's the type of testimony every vicar should include in their sermon,' said Wally.

'Come on, let's go back,' said Big Bill. 'I can't take any more.'

※

Back in the vestry, the band changed into their jackets – light blue with faded epaulettes. The jackets were years old. Some fitted, some didn't. They tuned up in the vestry, and one or two players wondered why they didn't tune up before every rehearsal and assumed it never crossed Colin's mind. Patrons would be surprised to learn that tuning took place once a year before the Christmas concert in church, and whichever event seemed important to Colin. This occurrence prompted the comment that Colin was a poseur.

Whilst the band waited in the vestry, thinking more about their potato pie supper than the concert, the audience arrived in dribs and drabs and settled on the dining chairs aligned alongside the long tables. Most folk eased their chair forward to sit beside their companion. Naturally they chatted whilst waiting.

'I reckon that museum would be suitable for a visit on the first of April,' Wally said.

'It's certainly a rum place,' replied Miriam.

In the vestry young Charlie complained, 'I'm hungry, I am.'

'It won't be long now, kiddo,' Chalkie assured him.

'Not too much noise, please,' said Colin. He had acquired the conductor's job because the previous four conductors had resigned due to deplorable attendances by the band in general. Big Bob had warned them, 'Not turning up could break up this band that has flourished along for ninety years.' 'Lurched along' would have been more accurate.

Colin was accepted as conductor on the recommendation of his girlfriend, Phyllis, who struggled to play third cornet. (But she badly wanted a man.) His experience amounted to directing the junior ensemble of a rival band a few miles from Daisy Hill. But Colin couldn't play a brass instrument, therefore couldn't advise a brass player on performance technique.

To provide himself with some substance he stood on an upturned box. This gave him some confidence. His baton technique was questionable. It was not unknown for him to waggle his stick and include an unwritten beat... or was it? Newer players weren't sure. Experienced players ignored him. He often used his left hand to augment his right, which clutched the stick. And his means of expression was indicated like a floundering swimmer performing the breaststroke.

'Let's go,' he said. This bit he got right.

The band marched from the vestry to an explosion of applause, which intensified when the roly-poly conductor bounced on. They began with the hymn tune, 'Crimond', a favourite with Methodists.

Standing beside the Vicar, Wally muttered, 'I see Chalkie's not playing.' Which was true. The experienced musician just sat, nursing his cornet.

Miriam whispered into Wally's adjacent ear, 'Chalkie refuses to play hymns because Colin spoils them by conducting too slowly.'

Then they played an arrangement of 'Dashing Away with the Smoothing Iron' and Colin appeared to be signalling semaphore.

'What's he doing,' muttered Wally, 'practising to be a goalkeeper?' Miriam nudged him with her elbow.

The next item was a gentle piece. However, just before it began, a reverberating cough rattled round the room. Every head turned towards the gents, where Great-Granddad Wrigley sat puffing on his pipe. Someone shushed him. Another said, 'He shouldn't be smoking,' which prompted an official to remove this smouldering item. But the old guy wasn't having this and pushed the upstart official to his backside. No lasting damage was done, nobody wanted interruptions, so the official was left to perch embarrassingly back on his buttocks.

The kitchen was situated beside the ladies' toilet. A waitress emerged from the kitchen, went on stage and handed Colin a note, then she retreated. Colin read the note then announced, 'The meal is ready, ladies and gentlemen.' He rocked his beefy face as if he'd done everyone a favour. 'So we'll skip the interval and play the last two items. First a dance by our lovely tenor horn trio.'

Iona, Mona and Shona jettisoned their jackets, revealing white shirts with frills, and stepped elegantly down the stage steps. The band stuck up with the 'Hokey Cokey', and the fetching young women danced this corny hoof number like it had never been danced before. It later transpired that in earlier days they had attended the same dancing school, and only lack of funds had prevented them from enrolling at an established dance academy. They wore tap dancing shoes and could execute quite complicated steps, particularly when the band occasioned tacet, and during these brief silences their clever footwork encouraged extra applause. Then the band broke into a cha-cha-cha and the girls danced a roundelay, which was traditionally a slow medieval dance, but this trio increased the tempo, and as they circled they threw up the hems of their dresses in can-can style. This, of course, encouraged wolf whistles – even from the Methodists.

To follow this was going to be challenging, but the band rose to the occasion. Charlie's dad was seen to vacate his cornet and join the percussion section, of which there was only one player: Mavis. The musical item proved to be an arrangement of 'Pack Up Your Troubles', 'I Love a Lassie' and 'Auld Lang Syne'.

Yet these casual, innocent items brought the house down.

Dave, Charlie's dad, had simple items to play. First he shook the tambourine then pinged a triangle. Next, during a quiet passage, he beat chords on three chime bars. Then as the music swelled, the audience gained confidence, and the climax beckoned them. Colin's enthusiasm became demented and his gestures exaggerated. On the very last chord he threw his baton at Dave who gave the cymbal some welly.

Colin missed his footing and fell off his box. A great cheer rang through the hall and the audience rose to its feet.

Even as the food was being served, the laughter hadn't subsided. Band members suggested Colin should go on a diet. Some said he needed his eyes testing. Fortunately he sat at one end of the long tables so didn't hear Chalkie, who was sitting across from Miriam.

'Well, he certainly made us laugh,' she said. 'Has he got a wife or a girlfriend?'

'Supposed to have one, Phyllis,' echoed Chalkie. 'But I reckon if he had castanets in his underpants he still wouldn't click.'

The Wrigley trio – young Charlie, Dave and owd Sam – sat almost opposite Wally and the Vicar, but slightly further along. Great-Granddad Sam had forsaken his pipe for cutlery, which he handled like spanners. Young Charlie had piled his plate like a harvest festival, and Dave forked out red cabbage from a jar until it squeaked for mercy.

Wally leant closer to Miriam. 'What does Dave do for a living?'

'He's a pickle packer.'

Wally grinned as he glanced again at the gourmet. 'He's a pickle un-packer if that red cabbage is anything to go by. Seriously, what does he do?'

'I've told you: he's a pickle packer at Daisy Hill pickle factory.' Wally all but choked on his laughter.

Chalkie White was sitting next to Wally and immediately opposite young Charlie. 'You've worked hard today, Charlie, what with your cornet playing and collecting car numbers.'

Charlie nodded, his mouth crammed with potato pie and gravy dribbling down his chin.

'Mmm. It's been dead cool,' he spluttered.

'You'll be able to rest tomorrow.'

'No, I'll not.' Gobble, gobble. 'Important, tomorrow.' Munch, munch. He stuffed more pie into his mouth. His words became unintelligible. 'Tomorrow doing…' Chomp chomp.

The adults within earshot sat up. Frowned.

'What was that?' asked Chalkie. 'Did you say it's sex tomorrow?'

Charlie nodded. 'Yes.' And continued to scoff his grub.

The diners looked at each other. But Great-Granddad continued to fork into his nourishment, like the stoker he had been during the war. And Dave, Charlie's dad, still delved his fork into the red cabbage.

'And where is this sex happening?' asked Chalkie.

Charlie swallowed and drank some water. 'In t' barn.'

Diners had stopped eating, except the Wrigleys.

'So… you're, er, involved in sex tomorrow?' Chalkie pursued.

'I am that. Early morning.'

Dave joined in. 'I've told him, he has to check these secks for holes, otherwise the little potatoes will drop through.'

Eventually it was all over and the band piled back onto the coach. But there was an encore for one young shaver. When the Wrigleys closed their front door and Great-Granddad had spread himself in front of the fire, the little woman, who was a bit rounder than she used to be, presented Charlie with a large envelope. 'Open it carefully,' she said.

Charlie did as advised and withdrew from it a wide envelope, and inside was a large piece of embossed paper.

'A policeman brought it,' she said. 'It's a certificate for being an outstanding citizen this morning.' All the family applauded. 'So I've made you some chips for being a good boy.'

'Oh…! Cool.'

ELEVEN

Josephine stepped down from her caravan just as Dreen Dewhurst was passing, pushing little Andrew James in his pram. 'Morning,' called the child's mother.

'Oh, hello, Dreen. Going somewhere nice?' She stepped towards them to gaze at the youngster.

'Well, we're just off to the weekly baby clinic. I suppose you could call that nice. It's peaceful. You're welcome to join us if you fancy a walk.'

'Oh, lovely. Just give me a minute.'

Jo was in and out the van in a flash, dressed appropriately for the weatherman's promised fine day. She was keen to spend time with babies, as she was herself feeling broody.

The two young women stepped out smartly, pushing baby Andrew James in turn.

'I don't suppose you'll be attending the Co-op Dance?' said Jo. 'Not with two youngsters to look after.'

'No. You have to alter your lifestyle when the little ones come along. It doesn't bother me though. Not like it would have as a teenager. You couldn't drag me off the dance floor in those days. Are you and Richard going?'

'Yes. We've been told it's worth attending. A good old-style band and very friendly and all that.'

Behind them a gentle breeze from the North Sea cooled their casual expedition and they soon arrived at the crossroads leading to Daisy Hill.

'This is a weekly trek for you, I suppose?' Josephine enquired.

'Yes. But it is pleasanter when the weather's nice. Well, most of it is pleasant. Personally, I'm not too keen on Dr Mackistry.' She laughed lightly at this.

'MacWhiskey, they call him,' said Jo, with a chuckle in her voice. 'Though many people like him.'

'I've no doubt he's a good doctor, but he always reeks of the hard stuff.'

At the crossroads they turned right and headed for the Co-op hall which was hired out for various activities. Today it was designated 'The Clinic', and was already busy. Before they went in, however, a cheeky voice called, 'A nice day for baby business.'

They looked up. Wally was on a ladder clipping the privet hedges. 'Hello, Wally,' they called in unison. 'Working hard?' said Jo.

'No. The council don't allow that.'

'Why is that?' asked Dreen, laughing. 'Are you all Bolshevics?'

'Not yet. Just socialists.' He came down from his ladder. 'Let's have a gander at my favourite godson.'

He stood tall, staring into the pram. 'By heck, he's growing. Make sure MacWhiskey doesn't put him on the wrong bottle.' Then he scrambled up his ladder again.

Dr Mackistry was holding his fort behind drawn curtains where his moonshine could be enjoyed impromptu, between each baby's performance. The paediatric clinic was usually held in an anteroom, but today that room was the store for a jumble sale to benefit the running of the hall. As well as the Doctor, two nurses swanned around, augmented by two volunteers, one of whom was the Reverend Miriam Peach.

'Good morning, ladies. I expect you are ready for light refreshments after your little journey.'

'Oh, thank you, Vicar,' said Jo. 'That would be most kind.'

Miriam leaned over the pram and looked with pleasure on the little child she had recently baptised in the open air. 'He's still sleeping soundly,' she said.

'For a while,' Dreen assured her. 'But when he wakes we'll all know about it.'

The Reverend Miriam made tea and served refreshments for various clients of the clinic, most of them young mothers or expectant parents, and washed the pots. Many of the patrons were regulars but not the young woman who now entered the building: Mavis, who, along with Norman had sat behind Miriam during the coach trip.

Curiosity invaded the Vicar's features as she noticed the newcomer settle herself on a chair situated near the curtain serving as the Doctor's temporary paediatric clinic. She and Walter had not been able to avoid the conversations between the obviously gullible Norman and his rather cocky companion; and the Vicar felt a concern for the young man. But she felt she needed some authentication before she could assess what seemed an uncomfortable situation. She kept her eyes on Mavis for the rest of the morning.

'I'll go and have this rascal weighed,' Dreen said.

'Yes, you do that and I'll take away your cups,' said the Vicar. She walked into the kitchen then turned casually, just in time to see Mavis enter the makeshift paediatric clinic. She quickly made the Doctor's coffee and placed two biscuits on a plate. She approached the swinging curtain, cautiously, then hesitated outside, listening. When she heard the attendant nurse say, 'Have you brought your sample, Mavis?' and then heard Mavis reply, 'Yes, it's here,' the Vicar, completely contrary to etiquette, coughed loudly and said, 'Here's your coffee, Doctor. I'm sorry I'm not able to knock.'

'Come in, Vicar. We're all pals here.'

Miriam entered, placed the Doctor's tray on the table and noticed the specimen bottle on the table. It was secured with a red top... red being positive.

'There you are, Dr Mackistry. I'll collect your cup and plate later.'

As she exited through the curtain again, she felt her face go red and an angry feeling invaded her being. She suddenly felt ashamed. She'd no right poking her nose in someone else's business. She needed somebody to explain her feelings to. If she was a Catholic she could speak to her priest. Then, after mulling it over, she knew who would listen.

She went into the kitchen and brewed a large, strong mug of tea, ideal for a thirsty workman. When she'd brewed it she heaped a plate with biscuits and went outside. Wally was up his ladder, clipping away.

'Here you are, Walter. I reckon you'll be ready for a drink.'

'Oh, thanks, love. Just what I need.'

As he gulped the hot tea, she said, in a castigating voice, 'I've just done a dreadful thing.' He waited... 'I've just found out that Mavis is pregnant.'

'Ah.' He paused, holding the large mug aloft like a winner's cup, leaning on his ladder. 'Well, we suspected as much. That poor lad Norman is going to get let in. I shouldn't think that trick is all that common.'

She became calm, having expected a roasting. 'Is there anything we can do?'

He shrugged, drained his mug. 'We'll think of summat. But it's a new 'un on me.'

'I shouldn't have been so curious,' she said. 'I mean, it's really none of my business.'

He shook his head, emptied the cup and replaced it on the tray.

'Look, it bothers you, because it is your business. Y' know, you were a soldier, a lorry driver in the army. You've entered enemy territory to find out what's what. So you've just done something similar: you have invaded enemy territory to assess the situation.

Now you've withdrawn to weigh up the info. I don't think you've done owt wrong.'

She picked up the tray to return indoors. 'Wally, whatever would I do without you?'

TWELVE

I t was Friday morning. In the Comfy Café in Down Daisy, Richard Coningsby was handing over his weekly collections to Vic Venables.

'I suppose you'll be well settled on that site now,' said Vic.

Dick shrugged. 'Well, partially. The wife's gone all broody and would like to start a family in a house, but of course we haven't got the wherewithal to buy our own property, and renting is far too high.'

Vic placed the paper money in his wallet and the coins in his shoulder bag. 'Even in this day and age, there are still some folk who couldn't manage to buy new clothes or insurance or nick-nacks without getting it on tick, you know.'

'I know. Youngsters should be taught how to handle money at school.'

'Righty-ho. Cash collections all correct,' said

Venables, standing and sliding back his chair. 'Thank you, Shirley, see you next week.'

The waitress waved to them as they walked from the café.

Outside, Richard compared his tatty van with the smart Vauxhall Venables drove, and wondered how his nonchalant boss, often devious, cheeky with the women, managed to pocket enough boodle to live the life of Riley.

'What was it you were saying about wanting a house, Dick?'

Richard became suddenly alert and moved a metre nearer this go-getter. He shrugged, as though the subject didn't really interest him. 'It's the wife,' he said. 'Jo... Josephine. She's sort of gone all broody and doesn't want to bring up a child in a caravan. She wants a house, but we don't have the wherewithal.'

'Right. I get it. Well, you know the geography of Daisy Hill by now?'

Richard nodded. 'Oh yes. I'm familiar with the streets, I know all the shops, the Co-op, the pub, the little nooks and crannies. There's not a little cottage for sale, is there?'

Venables lit a cigarette. Richard, non-smoker, stepped back apace.

'There might be. But if you're not flush with the readies, say for a deposit, renting is your best bet. And that's often a hit-and-miss business.' He drew on his fag and sent twin twirls of smoke down his nostrils. 'I'll ask you this: are you religious, Richard?'

To sanctify the chit-chat a little, Venables used his colleague's Christian name.

Richard was somewhat taken aback by the question, particularly from a seeming quack like Venables. 'Well, no, not really.'

'Is your lady wife's faith greater than yours? I mean, is she a believer?'

Richard mulled the question over. Josephine sometimes took flowers to the graveyard and placed them on her Great-Auntie Polly's plot. And she often attended funerals of people she hardly knew, to make up the numbers, he believed.

'Er, yes. I reckon she has a casual interest in religion.'

'Good.' Venables drew on his fag again. This time he pursed his lips as though preparing for a big kiss with a child. This time, however, the exhaust came from his embouchure and ended in a cleverly created smoke ring. 'So – you know that little chapel in Daisy Hill? Opposite the children's playground?'

Puzzled, Richard frowned deeply, bringing his black brows together.

Venables climbed into his car, inclined his head through the window and twisted the key in the ignition. 'Well, go there on Sunday.' He grinned, displaying nicotine-stained choppers, like teeny gravestones. 'You'll meet somebody you know. Don't mention houses for a week or so, then bring the subject up casually.'

He winked, then, like the victor he knew he was, Venables shot off like a speedway driver who is late for a date.

For a while Richard stood wondering if it was the first of April, then, deciding it wasn't, he drove home with the puzzle buzzing in his head, the riddle being: Venables had only recounted half a story. Was there a catch? Would the venture be expensive? Would he be tested on difficult questions? He shunted his van into the caravan site's car park then walked, still pondering, to his house on wheels, the home Jo wanted to vacate, because she felt broody. He looked at his caravan; it looked quite new and he – he personally – had no reason to leave it. But if he didn't at least follow up the advice Vic had given him, Richard felt that Venables would never again offer any suggestions.

As soon as he entered the van, the tantalising aroma of frying bacon perked up his senses like an agreeable remedy, a feeling that made him believe in Santa Claus.

'We've both timed it nicely,' Josephine said. 'I saw you chugging up the road so I put the frying pan on. Had a good day?'

'Yes, quite good. Plenty of collections and a bit of mysterious news from Vic that may pander to your aspirations.'

They sat down to eggs, bacon, mushrooms and sausage, cholesterol exactly as Richard liked it. And after a few delicious mouthfuls he spouted his story.

'I must say it seems like a poor reason for attending church,' she said.

'Oh, I don't know, if you attend church and some good comes from it, surely that proves that, er, religion, in that particular case, is genuine. I think experiencing something good is what going to church is all about. I think we should go.' Was this an edict, a command from on high?

So Sunday found them driving down to Daisy Hill where, anticipating a confrontation, they shunted their chariot into the car park belonging to the church, which was called The Sanctuary Meeting House.

'I reckon it's a chapel,' Richard said, 'not a church in the traditional sense.'

'I don't care if it's an Anglo Whatsit,' Jo replied with pagan-like truth, 'as long as it leads me towards bricks, slate and woodwork.'

But the building itself was smaller than they expected, and they had poshed themselves up expecting a classic, traditional-style church. Richard wore a navy blue suit that had togged its way into many a wedding. And Josephine, who looked attractive wearing anything – or even nothing – was today dressed in a swish black and white costume she wore for funerals. Hand in hand, they strolled through the well-kept gardens, breathing in the scent of the various flowers. At the church door they were warmly greeted by a handsome young man with a mulatto complexion.

'Welcome to The Sanctuary.' He smiled, displaying beautiful teeth deserving of an advert for dentistry, and handed them an information sheet and a booklet of hymns, containing words only. 'There are no reserve seats. Sit where you will.'

They chose places in the middle of the third row, then looked about them. Many of the congregation appeared to be foreigners. Josephine leaned towards Dick. 'This is where the care workers and field labourers come on Sunday.' Shortly, a keyboard player, drummer and guitarist traipsed onto the platform. This was no parish church organist about to play Handel's 'Largo'. They kicked off – well, the drummer did, literally – with a jazz number more suitable to a disco than a church, but everyone enjoyed it. Then, from a side door, obviously the vestry, a young lady entered, ascended the pulpit and intoned, 'Let us pray.' And pray she did. Without actually mentioning any names, she all but prayed for everyone in the United Kingdom. In fact, when she finished, a few ancients in the congregation could actually be heard snoring, and were gently brought round with... *Smelling salts!* thought Josephine. It was obviously an expected routine.

Now the young woman announced, 'Let us sing fifty-four.'

Dick was thrown for a moment, thinking she said 'sing fifty-four hymns'. He recovered as she said, 'Shine, Jesus, Shine.' In fact everybody shone – the congregation, the ushers, the band, and especially the drummer, whose rhythmic drumming was a broad hint that rock and roll was next on the list. The hymn, a song really, was known by all, even the Coningsby duo, and when concluded all were glad to flop down.

On the front row, still standing, was a member with a broad back; you couldn't see his face, but he was a Humpty Dumpty. Now he ascended the pulpit and turned his chubby chops towards the congregation.

The Coningsby pair, as though prompted, expelled an audible gasp and Josephine sat forward in surprise. 'Mr Grimshaw!' She clasped a hand to her mouth. It was truly him, the roly-poly plonker from the council offices.

At once Richard twigged why Venables had advised him to join this congregation. Mr Grimshaw was not really grim, he was a saviour to this congregation who were friends indeed; even the young chap on the door had said, 'Welcome to The Sanctuary.'

Richard wondered, *Is he in on it, too? But what did Grimshaw gain? Members! Why?* He argued with himself, and answered his own question: to swell his congregation, of course. Rightly or wrongly, priests, vicars, preachers all have an ego. They want acolytes, they need followers. And to a puzzled Josephine he muttered, 'I'll be an acolyte then. See if it works.'

'Are you alright?' she whispered.

'I'm not sure if I'm as pleased as Punch or as sick as a parrot.'

And Mr Grimshaw preached. Again, he wasn't grim. His sermon wasn't as grim as his name. He told them about heaven and how they would make out when they got there. To Richard it was like being on a coach trip, but with the knowledge that you wouldn't be coming back.

Jo felt equally ambivalent. Was she downcast or delighted? She wasn't sure. But if attending this church nudged her towards the front of the queue in acquiring a council house, she reckoned it was a small price to pay. At least, every Sunday she'd be able to wear nice clothes instead of slopping about in an apron.

'So, praise the Lord,' hollered Mr Grimshaw, whose phrase was taken up by half the congregation. 'Praise him for saving us...'

'... A council house,' added Jo.

Then came three more hymns accompanied by jumping up and down and much clapping. Next came coffee and cakes served with chatter. Then Richard and Josephine made sure Mr Grimshaw knew who they were; but, guided by Venables, they never mentioned houses. When he spoke to them his lazy eye remained indolent, but the healthy orb seemed to peer round the pews, as though checking up on the occupants.

Richard sensed it was time to decamp, and as they withdrew he repeated his name and trusted they'd be remembered next week. They drove home, entertaining each other with the entertainment they'd experienced.

'If attending that little gospel hall will cover our heads with bricks and mortar,' said Jo, 'I think we can tolerate attending, for a while.'

'And I think "for a while" has to be the slogan,' said Dick.

THIRTEEN

'But can you dance or not, Walter?'

'Well, I can wiggle about a bit, especially after a few bevies.'

'Look, I've been given two free tickets and it's not fair to waste them just to – your phrase – bugger about a bit. They could go to somebody who can't afford a night out.'

Wally was now used to the Vicar's unrestrained army talk if she became exasperated.

'Neither do I expect to be accompanied by a perverted private…'

'Corporal. I was a perverted corporal.'

'Whatever. But don't expect to get sloshed when you're out with me, sonny Jim.'

'I'll remember that, padre,' his voice coloured by a chuckle.

'Be serious. If you're not keen, we could just go to the pub.'

This conversation occurred as they walked towards the town hall, which was much less posh than its legend. Tonight, the auspicious building – circa 1925 – was the venue for the annual dance of the Co-operative Society.

They entered the hall, to be welcomed by Big Bill Ramsbottom, factotum of the Daisy Hill's brass band and manager of the local Co-op. He was big, boisterous and kind. His staff enjoyed working for him.

'Oh, I'm so pleased you managed to get here, Vicar. And you, Mr Watson. Your presence will keep them, er, subdued.'

'I hope not, Bill. Tonight, I'm here to dance.'

'I suppose she'll find a partner,' Wally said.

She stood on his toes and Big Bill smiled and gestured cordial submission with a shrug of his sturdy shoulders.

'There's a table reserved for you on the other side,' said Bill. 'Enjoy yourselves.'

The Vicar and her escort walked round the dance floor and located their table as the band began to tune up. As they sat, Wally nodded towards the foyer. 'Look who's arrived.'

Miriam looked up as Iona, Mona and Shona arrived, seeming to shimmer into the hall. They were dressed identically from their glittering tall heels to the pendulous earrings. They each wore a tight-fitting red dress made all the more tighter with a broad black belt. Their stylish wardrobe was made available by their employer – the Co-op – but the

Co-op didn't know that. The attire was borrowed from the firm and carefully returned to the costume department. Mr Ramsbottom wasn't aware of this facility as he was in charge of grocery, alcohol, detergents and accounts. After the unauthorised loan, the clothes were checked for damages, repaired if necessary and returned to their cellophane protection. Their peers wondered how they always arrived so well dressed.

They always attended the Co-op Dance because Mr Ramsbottom managed to wangle three complimentary tickets on condition the girls helped to serve drinks at the interval, thus saving the Society from hiring waiters.

'Oh, look who's over there,' crooned Iona, and waved to the Vicar and her escort. 'They seem very close, these days.'

'Well, she is nice,' added Mona.

Shona sniggered. 'I wonder if they've got as far as nooky, yet?'

'I bet they have,' said Iona. 'Look, he's got muscles up to his eyebrows.'

'He's from the Upsy-Daisy caravan site. Wally Watson,' Mona told them.

From across the dance floor, Wally returned the girls' greetings. 'They remind me of the Beverley Sisters.'

The band began their first number and the playing was not at all bad. Several couples got up and began to shake a leg to the quickstep. Big Bill walked by their table carrying a tray of drinks.

'Are you not going to trip the light fantastic? The band like to see people on the floor.' He moved on.

'Come on then,' she said. 'And don't step on my toes.'

Magically, Wally seemed to alter. He transformed himself from labourer to dandy, holding his partner appropriately as would a maestro, and they tripped round the dance floor confidently.

'You can dance!' Miriam exclaimed. 'You never said.'

'You never mentioned it,' Wally responded, all but whispering in her left ear.

'Yes, but… How did you learn to dance like this?'

'My mum's cousin – Aunty Sue, I called her – ran a dancing school, but she was always short of the male species. So I was recruited, after which she paid for me go to the pictures.'

'Pictures!' she queried.

'Aye. Y' know, the cinema. So obviously I had to learn to dance and got lots o' practice in. It's been very handy for picking up the lassies.'

She thumped him on his shoulder. 'Trust you.'

'But I got weary of it and when I was eighteen I volunteered for the army.'

The music came to an end and the couples vacated the floor. Just as the music ended, a couple entered the ballroom.

'Here they come,' said Iona. 'She said she wasn't sure she'd be attending.'

'Who?' asked Mona.

'Lady Muck, of course,' and she pointed towards the

corner of the ballroom. 'But she got a complimentary too, so she'd have to attend, if only to wait on.'

'Oh, Mavis,' Shona said. 'Yeah, I can spot her. Hey, she's wearing that yellow dress. I hope she remembers to put it back, otherwise Ramsbum will go scatty. I see she's managed to drag Norman along.'

'Two odd bods together, if you ask me,' Iona said.

That Mavis and Norman were now an item was not in doubt. But to the purist's eye, the unexpected affair was dubious. During the band practice following the coach trip Mavis had mentioned the upcoming Co-operative Society's annual dance – an important event in the area. Norman responded that he wasn't much of a dancer and that she'd enjoy the occasion better with someone less likely to fall over their own feet.

'Norman, I get more pleasure being with you than anyone else I've ever met.'

This comment caused the reticent Norman's disposition to lift like unexpected sunshine on a dull day. Since being a child he'd always been shy with girls; yet here was a member of the opposite sex actually flattering him. So to decline this date, even in a half-hearted way, he needed a better excuse.

'I don't have transport to get to Daisy Hill, particularly as I've had to get spruced up. There's no bus service, y' know.'

'What about your peripatetic teaching job? Surely you must use transport for that?'

'I use a bike. I only have to carry a cornet in me carrier bag. And when it rains I wear wellies.'

A gleam hardened Mavis's experienced eyes, a gleam worthy of any checkmate; the king was under attack and unable to escape. 'Then you need a car.'

'I'm quite aware of that. But I haven't got one.'

'I have. And it's yours if you'll use it.'

And within three weeks he was driving, under the firm but considerate instruction of his pursuer. Furthermore, traffic police were thin on the ground in that part of Blighty.

(When Mavis's husband had died, he had been driving the self-same bubble car that was now an inducement for the toy boy, now within her sights.)

The patrons were now coming through the doors quite consistently and two teenage motorcyclists decided to join them. The cyclists smelled strongly of drink.

'If you're thinking of coming in here,' said Bill, 'you'll have to remove your helmets, but I don't think this is your scene.'

'Summat wrong wi' our money then?' said one cyclist, belligerently.

'I'm just saying it's for respectable folk.' Bill folded his thick arms and looked down at what were louts to him.

'Hear that, kiddo?' said the boozy spokesman. 'This twat reckons we're not respectable.'

At that Bill lost his patience. He suddenly thought about all the stroppy customers he'd had to deal with in the Co-op. He grabbed the kiddo lout and bundled him outside. The other, noting Bill's broad back, decided to skedaddle.

'And if you know what's good for you,' called Bill, 'don't come back.'

During the next interval a young couple from Upsy-Daisy sauntered in, walked round the perimeter of the ballroom searching for a space and strolled by the Vicar's table.

'Hello,' called Miriam. 'If you don't find a vacant table, draw two chairs up and join us.'

The couple walked a few paces then returned as the ballroom was becoming crowded. They commandeered two chairs and accepted Miriam's invitation.

'You're sure you don't mind?' Richard asked.

'Not at all,' Wally said. 'Plonk your chairs under the table and I'll order some liquid glory.'

'We've not finished these,' Miriam pointed out.

'All the more reason to get our reserves in.' Wally clicked his fingers as Bill walked by, carrying a tray. 'Mr Ramsbottom, could you top us up?' Bill nodded and the newcomers settled themselves in. Wally inclined his head, smiled at Miriam, winked at their guests. 'This is Josephine and Richard on Sundays – and Jo and Dick during the week.'

Richard stretched out a hand. 'And you're Miriam.'

'Oh, she knows that,' interrupted Wally. ''Cos Miriam was the sober one when we wet the baby's head.'

'How do you put up with him?' quipped Jo.

'Easy. He pays for the drinks,' joked Miriam. All four grinned, making a silly toothpaste picture. 'I've seen you since then,' she added, 'at the clinic with Doreen, or Dreen, as Wally Whatsit here calls her.'

Their waiter arrived, looking plump and posh in his large bow tie, and each of them gave their order. Big Bill registered their requirements in his best Co-op scribble.

Dick had earlier noticed the four-piece band. 'Have you noticed what the drummer is drinking?'

'He drinks bitter shandy,' Bill confided, as though it was hush-hush. 'I'll bring you one for him.'

'I didn't expect it to be so full, tonight,' said Jo. 'It's obviously very popular.'

'Oh yes. It's always popular.' Miriam nodded. 'Although the Co-operative Society doesn't present this dance to make money, it gives them some good publicity.'

'Obviously,' said Jo. 'It's more than the supermarkets offer.'

'Can you imagine Mrs Marks organising a dance up at the site?' Dick said.

'I can imagine Markie organising the beer,' Wally added.

'The residents up there seem to get on well with each other, don't they?' Miriam remarked.

'Well, Major Merryweather is quite sociable if you let him think he's in charge,' Dick replied.

'And Professor Sparrow will help you out if you tell him wildlife is more important than community life,' said Wally.

'And Markie is your friend for life if you suggest that pub life is better than any other life,' added Josephine. As they chuckled, Big Bill arrived with their drinks.

'This is the bitter shandy for yon drummer.'

Dick picked it up. 'I won't be long,' he assured them and walked towards the stage. 'Hello, Malc. We're enjoying the music... I've brought you a shandy.'

'Ta,' Malcolm said, expressing his style of *sheer* gratitude, and took several gulps. He raised his pint glass. (Dick expected a toast.) 'Cops on the prowl, y' see. Looking for subscribers for their Drink Driving campaign.'

'And if Brother Grimshaw hears about our little tea party,' chipped in the keyboard player, 'he'll stop lending us the drum kit.'

'Huh, if he does, he'll have to pray for his next drummer,' added Malc, flippantly, then tipped his glass and drained it, and drew a bare arm across his mouth to wipe away the froth.

'I didn't realise you played for dancing as well as for the chapel,' Dick said.

Malcolm's voice took on a little intolerance. 'Huh. Chapel is a voluntary job. But Grimmy lends me the drum kit, provided I play for him too.' He gestured towards the drums which, to Dick's unpractised eyes, seemed an expensive outfit.

'Oh, these are not your drums then!'

'Nah!' Malcolm drawled. 'There's 'undreds of quids' worth there. Not many of the rattle and thump brigade could afford summat like that.'

'So they belong to Mr Grimshaw then?'

'Yeah, Grimmy. They're his. Mind you, he gets me for free on Sundays. So he can't complain.'

'I suppose you play drums at other places during the week?'

'Have to. Else I'm skint. But don't let on to Grimmy. He wouldn't like his drums being pounded in a pub. Have I seen you up at The Sanctuary?'

'Er, yeah. We have started going, me and Jo.' Dick pointed to their table.

'Right. That good-looking bird, eh? And what's your moniker?'

'Dick.' Then he felt a berk adding, 'But it's Richard at The, er, Sanctuary.' Then he noticed that the other musicians had left the stage, as it was now the interval.

'Naturally… I say, er, Dick. Do summat for me?'

'Sure. A drink?'

'No, no. Just look after the kit, Dick, while I go and check up on my dick.' And Malc sloped off to the bog.

Iona, Mona and Shona had now draped themselves in white overalls, and as Big Bill trundled a large tea trolley round the dance floor the girls poured drinks for the guests.

Richard walked to the rear of the stage to scrutinise the precious drum kit. Though no expert, he looked closely at the bass drum, and the side drum with its catgut wire stretched across the top, known as snares. Two beautiful brass cymbals reared up, one either side like cautious giraffes ready to leap away. In the middle of the kit, a steel triangle waited to be struck. Dick checked no one was watching then picked up the rigid beater and tapped this easy instrument. It gave out a lingering note, lasting so long that, a little embarrassed, he halted the vibrations with finger and thumb. Richard reckoned the whole kit was worth more than £2,000, and understood why Brother Grimshaw guarded it with such care.

He now stood at the front of the stage looking down the length of the hall currently being finely dusted with talcum powder by the caretaker, to help dancers move smoothly. Richard now looked up at the three walls onto which had been built a balcony of Columbian pine and with slight imagination resembled the hull of an ancient schooner, except the old wooden ships were made of oak.

Just as Dick was beginning to feel like a prize berk keeping guard over the drum kit, the keyboard player returned.

'What's happened to Malc?'

'Oh, he's gone outside for a fag.'

'The cheeky bugger. Here I am frittering me time away, watching that nobody starts tapping his drums and he's fugging up the foyer.'

'Aye. That's Malc for you,' the keyboard player said.

But just as exasperation began to cloud the evening, two motorcyclists drove into the hall and began revving their bikes and circling the ballroom. Big Bill turned on his heel and shouted, 'I've told you lot to hop it.'

One brazen rider rode past the drinks trolley and smacked Iona's bottom as he passed. Now all the guests were on their feet as the interlopers circled again. Wally left his group, grabbed the trolley and pushed it in front the circling motorcyclist who, now a little nervous, felt obliged to stop or at least slow down. As he hovered on the edge of the dance floor,

Mona said something to Shona before grabbing a hot spoon from the washing-up water and touching the driver's naked cheek. The action rather than the hot implement caused the driver to stop and yelp. In that instant Shona shot forward and snatched the ignition key from the ignition lock and slowly threw it to Miriam who dropped the key into her dress handbag. This left the driver stranded. Bill strode forward and poked the driver on his shoulder blade. It was an unrehearsed production number.

'I stopped you louts from barging in earlier. Now, if you don't leave I'll throw you out then call the Old Bill.'

'She nicked my keys,' shouted the lout who, at sniffing distance, smelled of strong drink.

The other driver, a little braver, drew alongside. 'Yeah! I saw her.' Now, obviously sweating, he removed his helmet. 'She's the religious bitch what married my cousin.'

'Watch your language,' snarled Wally, and cuffed the lad on his naked ear.

'Hoy. That's an assault, that is.' And with a futile and comic gesture he appealed to the audience of dancers. 'You lot saw him belt me.'

But no one had noticed anything amiss.

Braveheart came forward holding the key aloft. 'You'll get this key back,' said Miriam, 'when you and your crony have left the hall.'

The lout looked uncertain. The crowd was pressing forward. 'Clear off,' ordered a new voice. Others joined in. 'Move it.' 'Hop it.' 'Take your rubbish bike with you.'

This hurt him. His bike was his world. Both the louts dismounted and shuffled towards the exit, followed by a posse of angry patrons.

'Pass this to him, Walter.' And Miriam gave him the key.

'They're obviously blotto,' Wally said, then followed them to the exit and handed over the key. 'I suggest you keep well away from this area,' he advised them, 'otherwise the cops will confiscate your bikes.' He watched them mount and ride away, but wondered if there'd be payback.

Back in the hall the event had created a talking point. 'They didn't even have the brains to blot out their number plates,' said Dick, who had now rejoined his pals.

'I've made a note of their numbers,' added Bill, grimly. He turned to his assistants. 'If ever they come near the Co-op, you must lock the doors and phone for the police.'

Soon, order was restored and a couple of guards placed at the main door.

Back at their corner table Norman and Mavis were finishing their drinks. 'I've been coming here for years,' said Mavis, 'but I've never experienced anything like that before. It's made me feel quite afraid.'

'They won't bother us again,' Norman assured her as he slyly fondled her breasts.

'Maybe.' She pressed herself closer. 'But I'm nervous when anything like that happens.'

By nature Norman wasn't a knight in shining armour but he felt he had to show a teeny-weeny bit of bravado. 'Don't worry, pet. I'll look after you.'

'Oh, Norman, I feel so safe with you. Will you stay with me tonight?'

That was a shock to his system. It took him back to the time when his music teacher told him he was a natural cornet player. The second shock she delivered was when Mavis said, 'I'll give you the time of your life.'

And she did!

In between the warm sheets Mavis demonstrated all the intimacy she had learned as a married woman. Had there been a prize for a wooing contest, Mavis would have won it that night. She gave Norman thrills he had never imagined existed.

And they both slept like proverbial logs.

The following morning, whilst they were still holding each other, they spoke of this, that, then the other, which went:

'Norman, love, I hope you don't mind my saying, but when I kiss you, your lips taste dreadfully salty. Perhaps you should try a better quality toothpaste. I'll get you some from the Co-op.'

He frowned. 'Perhaps I've eaten too many crisps and salted peanuts.'

These innocent remarks became a devastating prologue.

FOURTEEN

The spring sunshine shed benevolent light over Daisy Hill – but not over the parish church on this particular day. Many village folk donned their best togs and sauntered towards the sole tolling bell. The interior alterations had been completed satisfactorily but scaffold still ugly-fied much of the outside, ancient stonework.

The Reverend Miriam Peach left her vicarage and trod the pebbled path that skirted the main door and ended at the high road. Miriam casually hummed one of the hymns she had carefully chosen for matins. As she walked along the path she admired the spring flowers bordering the path. Since several parishioners now assisted with gardening jobs, patches of snowdrops peeped through the black soil, and green daffodil tips braved the early morning to make an appearance.

Just as she approached the porch, one of the sections still not quite complete, she paused. Something was not quite in order. A tarpaulin covered the roof, which was being retiled with new wooden tiles. And the ground surrounding the porch was also covered with a tarpaulin under which the new tiles waited their turn to be fixed in place. This section was flat.

But it shouldn't be!

The Vicar stood and concentrated on this area, on the ground, which was flat.

'Flat! Why? It should be in rows, up and down like a ploughed field.' She muttered this to herself. She looked up at the porch where the 'tarp' – as the builders called it – protected the roof. Then looked down at the tarp on the ground protecting the tiles awaiting... She stooped and lifted one edge of the tarp. 'Nothing!' she exclaimed. She retraced her steps and raised the tarpaulin every few feet. All the wooden tiles were missing.

'Nicked! Well, I'm damned.'

Morning service was due to begin in ten minutes. Members of the congregation were arriving, so she hadn't time to investigate further.

'Something wrong, Vicar?'

She straightened up. A member of the choir stood facing her.

'Have you got your mobile with you, Eric?'

He felt in his pocket and conjured out a phone.

'I haven't time to return to the vicarage. May I borrow it, please?'

'Of course you can. Return it to me after the service.' And this conscientious church member, realising something was amiss, handed it over and walked away.

She dialled.

'Walter, sorry, but I didn't wake you up, did I?'

'No, but it's a bit late for me to pedal down there and play the organ. Apart from the fact that I haven't started having lessons yet. So...'

'Wally! I'm in a hurry. Please listen. The building material outside the church has been nicked.'

'Strewth! What material?'

'The tiles. The wooden tiles reserved for the porch. Look, I'm due to take a service in...' She glanced at her watch. '... Six minutes. Will you please phone or pedal on your bike to the police station, and leave a message for Sergeant Forester? Then afterwards come to the vicarage, have lunch here and tell me what they said.' Her voice sounded cracked as though she was about to burst into tears.

'Don't worry, pet. I'll see you later.'

At the same time as the C of E drama unfolded in Daisy Hill, a rather more comic production unfolded in Paradise, not the one in Hereafter, but that little pile of bricks and mortar in Down Daisy; and among the chequered clique were two struggling believers from Upsy-Daisy.

Richard and Josephine Coningsby entered the little chapel with rather more confidence than previously. Today was their fourth appearance. Earlier, Richard had proposed 'a day off'.

'No, my love,' said Josephine. 'Not yet anyway. I

already feel guilty at using my membership to maybe – still only maybe – acquire a council house. Let's be as sincere as we can.' (What she didn't mention was the fact that she wanted to wear the nice blue dress bought for her birthday by Auntie Maggie.) 'And when we get there, try to be moved!'

So here they were, in the 'Portals of Paradise', as Mr Grimshaw sometimes referred to his Free Church, but also called 'Yon heap of rubble' by greedy speculators.

Today the service began by – warbling is the best word – raising the leaky roof with three tuneless yet rhythmic hymns. The last song – perhaps to make it seem modern – was accompanied by jumping up and down in a river, as the ditty mentioned the River Jordan, the old original Jordan, because these days, that stretch of water is a muddy stream polluted by plastic cups. And one must be fair to the keyboard player who, the previous day, had played for the Co-op Dance; the Paradise performance was his party piece as he had jazzed it up.

Then, after what seemed like sentry duty, they all flopped onto their second-hand chairs while a well-meaning but over-imaginative lady recited her miracle of the Co-op. There she had lost her purse, and as she was about to return home minus brass or groceries, the item had been found by a young shop assistant called Shona who was roundly rewarded with a bar of chocolate. And, perhaps because of this miracle, the witness was now treated to a hearty hand clap, augmented by several solos of 'Yes, Lord' and a strong 'Hallelujah'.

Next, the younger members of Paradise were persuaded/coerced into providing youthful praise. And they sang – supplemented by the congregation – about Noah's Ark. Each child was nominated an animal. One child refused point blank to become a zebra. 'I don't like the stripes,' he cried. So he became yet another elephant and joined lustily in the singing.

This musical praise complete, Brother Grimshaw cruised from the ark into the quieter haven of the pulpit.

'Oh gawd,' groaned Dick, 'more punishment.' And he received a nudge in the ribs from Jo.

'Concentrate,' she ordered.

But he couldn't. His mind wandered to the previous evening's experience at the town hall. And when he recalled how that teenage tart from the Co-op had seared the motorcyclist's cheek with a hot spoon, Dick had to smother a giggle by breaking into a coughing fit. Indeed, an ally in the congregation came to his aid with a cough sweet. Eventually all ordeals were ended for disinterested oafs, such as Dick, as they were rescued by the final hymn. The caravan dwellers contributed towards the collection, then, as they made for the exit, Josephine was waylaid by Brother Grimshaw, and she thought, *Oh, not a council house so quickly.*

She was right – it wasn't.

'Could I have a brief word, Sister Josephine? I was wondering,' he said, his odd eye rolling from side to side like a lost billiard ball, 'do you think you could hand out the hymn books next week? It's a very important job.'

Wally mounted his bike and pedalled first to the parish church to examine the evidence of a burglary, and affirmation there was aplenty. He raised the tarpaulin in front of the porch and saw, as Miriam had done earlier, the imprints where the tiles should have been. He took out his mobile and phoned for police – as against fire and ambulance – but nothing was available, certainly not immediately. So he decided to pedal the extra two miles to the rozzers' residence. He smiled to himself, recalling his Cockney mates in the army who referred to 'Redcaps', military police, as rozzers… There was now no urgency, so he cycled at a leisurely pace.

Shortly, Wally entered the police station, panting only slightly from the exertion.

'Morning, Constable. Is Sergeant Forester likely to arrive this morning?'

'No, sir. It's his day off. And I cannot interrupt his leisure time for anything less than a rebellion. And more to the point, I'd lose my overtime. But can I help you with anything?'

The constable was about twenty-two, fresh-faced and amiable.

Wally explained about the – as yet apparent – burglary, or removal of the wooden tiles.

'I see. Well, I'm on my own for a couple of hours, and I can't leave the desk just yet.'

'It's Constable Cole, isn't it?' The policeman nodded. 'What is it?' asked Wally. 'Clarence, Cuthbert?'

'No. It's Colin,' the police officer said.

'Well, you've jotted down the details I gave you,' Wally said, 'so if you would leave the gist of the complaint for Sergeant Forester, I'm sure he'll call at the vicarage tomorrow. I know the Reverend Peach would like him to deal with it, if he can.'

'I'm just going to make a cup of coffee. Would you like one?'

'Oh, yes please, Colin. I usually have one on a Sunday round about this time.'

As the constable rattled the cups and boiled the kettle, Wally shuffled round the small station reading the various posters and pictures pinned up. Within about eight minutes the constable returned with drinks and a tin of biscuits.

'Here you are, sir. One coffee without sugar, and biscuits to while away the time. You say the Vicar prefers Sergeant Forester?' Wally nodded.

'I think it's a bit odd for a woman like that to be a priest,' the constable said, with youthful immaturity.

'A woman like what?' Wally almost bridled.

'A good-looking bird like her being a vicar! And she's tall with it.'

Wally smiled inwardly. 'She used to be a professional soldier, you know.' Unwittingly, he said it proudly.

'Never!' The young constable was so surprised, he paused with the mug of coffee halfway to his mouth. 'Well, I'd never have thought it. I suppose she was a padre?'

'No. Basically, she was a lorry driver. She's seen action in Afghanistan, you know.'

'I am surprised. Mind you, my girlfriend is religious, y' know. She's a Sunday school teacher.'

'Is she?' said Wally. 'You'll have to keep your hands to yourself then.'

'You can say that again. I won't get me leg over until we're wed. Apart from that her mam would kill me, as would my own ma.'

Wally realised the young copper spoke a little too freely, so being inquisitive he pumped him. 'I suppose you have to curb your language too?'

'You can say that again, as does her dad. He's a scaffolder. Instead of bugger, we have to say sugar. For cunt we say punt. If we need to refer to some twat as a dirty old sod, we say dirty old cod. He laughs about it, does her dad.'

'He's not religious then?' said Wally.

'Not him!' The young copper laughed. 'He's an atheist.'

Wally drained his coffee cup and placed it on the counter. 'Thanks for the drink. I must be off.' Then out of sheer devilment said, 'Suppose you were really angry and wanted to be decidedly profane, what would you say for coitus interruptus?'

'I think it's "three Hail Marys".'

Wally was still laughing when he mounted his bike. As he pedalled, various thoughts jostled for attention. The force were obviously short of staff to rely on just one copper to respond to the public, but the young bobby seemed glad to talk to somebody.

He obviously knew about Miriam too. *Funny,* thought Wally, *the way he referred to her.*

Hey, he told himself, *if the copper thinks that way, others must do the same.* Suddenly he chuckled. *I bet all Upsy-Daisy think I'm courtin' the Vicar.* An unfamiliar, but not disagreeable feeling permeated his torso as he urged his roadster along.

He and Miriam had become accidental friends by casual events throwing them together. Perhaps their separate association with the army had cemented that. What had young Colin said?

'A good-looking bird like her being a vicar!'

Wally had not been without female company during his life, before, during or after the army. Since his demob, he'd never encouraged a woman to shack up with him because he'd had very little money. But now, working for the council and with his army pension, he was better off.

I wonder what she'd think if…

He had arrived at the church and dismounted his bike.

The church of St Aidan and the vicarage, along with two acres of land, were surrounded by a red brick wall, about six feet in height. The top of the wall was embedded with pieces of metalwork. And metalwork was also embedded in the sides of the seven-foot red brick uprights of the gate. The gate itself had disappeared along with the floral metalwork. In 1941, all unnecessary metalwork had been removed – sawn off – to provide scrap iron for the steel industry during World War II. After the war, the decorative metalwork had never been replaced as promised.

So on the residential side of the wall, a seven-foot high privet bush now grew and over sixty years had become impregnable. The whole of the church premises were built in 1925.

Wally leaned his bike on an established sycamore tree and rang the doorbell. His arrival was acknowledged within a minute, and Miriam smiled as she opened the door.

Wally hesitated on the threshold. 'By heck, what a welcoming smell.' He sniffed the aroma like a Bisto boy.

'Come in and wash your hands,' she said, 'then draw up to the table,' uttering a phrase any dismounting cyclist would welcome.

He did precisely as instructed and realised he had never been in the dining room before.

'There's wine on the table,' the Reverend Miriam said, 'and beer on the sideboard behind you, if you prefer it.'

He opened a can of bitter. 'I didn't realise vicars could afford so much wet stuff.'

'We can't. But parishioners present us with bottles as presents, and I happen to have nearly a cellarful.' She quickly laid out the table with succulent fare, and served him with a bowl of onion soup, the like of which Wally had never tasted before.

'This is fantastic,' he said, and briefly thought about the canned consommé he bought from the Co-op. 'I never realised homemade soup could be so good.'

She appreciated his artless opinion as she watched him tuck in. 'Before I joined the army, I was an apprentice chef with The George, on the Strand in London.'

'By heck, that sounds posh.'

'It was. And it was also flippin' hard work.'

From force of habit she spooned her soup in forward strokes as Wally scooped his up like he had during free dinners at school.

'Don't eat so much bread with your soup, you'll have no room for the roast lamb.'

'Want to bet,' he said. And made room, not only for the lamb, but also for the parsnips, roast potatoes, delicious string beans; and made particular room for Spotted Dick and hot custard, his favourite sweet. When offered coffee he said, 'I'll have another beer if you don't mind.'

Finally she asked about his errand to the police station.

'It was Constable Colin Cole on duty. The same young copper we met on the coach trip. He said he'd ask Sergeant Forester to call here tomorrow, but it's Forester's day off today.'

She sipped her red wine and Wally whacked back his beer. 'I've never been in this room before,' he said. 'Is it all your furniture?'

'I presume it is, now. But it belonged to the previous incumbent.'

'Ah, a bit before my time,' said Wally. 'He obviously shot off somewhere else.'

'He truly did. He scarpered, alright, and took a young parishioner with him.'

'Oh dear.' He took a long pull at his beer. 'Was she very young?'

'She was a he and all I really know is, the young bloke's name was Clive.'

'I see. So the elders thought, *Next time, we'll have one of the fairer sex.*'

She laughed. 'I hope they were satisfied.'

'Well, that young copper, Cole, thinks you're a bit of alright.'

She laughed again and poured herself more wine. 'Well, that can't be all bad.'

'Well, Miriam, thank you for that delicious meal. So, why did you give up cooking to drive an army lorry?'

'A handsome young soldier came into the restaurant one day and asked to see the cook. He said he was surprised the chef was a young female. Then he asked me out on a date. I was twenty, and like most young women thought about boyfriends now and then. We fell in love. I was so bowled over by him I enlisted in the same regiment. We saw each other quite a few times. Then he was killed by a landmine in Kabul.'

The Reverend Miriam stopped talking for a while and Walter could tell she was looking back into the past – a routine he'd followed himself, many times. Then with little more than a sigh, she continued.

'When I was demobbed I decided to work at something that would, hopefully, keep me away from young men, keep me in fact away from many people, because I was so sad – preferably something where I might do some good. You see, there was no one I could blame for my boyfriend's death – except the enemy – and I didn't know the individual who'd planted the bomb. I couldn't blame God for allowing it to happen, it could have happened to anyone. I wanted to live in a cocoon, I needed something celibate. So I applied to be a priest.'

'Aye. I can see why. And have you no regrets?'

'Not really. When events, such as accidents, happen, and there's really no one else to blame, you just have to get on with life.'

'Well, after hearing all that, I really am stuck for words. I'd best have another beer.' He quickly grabbed another can, in case it might be forbidden and took a few deep gulps.

Wally and the Vicar had become acquainted by causal events which had thrown them together. Perhaps their separate associations with the army had cemented this. He thought about what the young copper had said:

'A good-looking bird like her being a vicar.' He tried to stifle a laugh and some beer went down his gullet the wrong way.

'What are you laughing at?'

'A thought *you* might not appreciate.'

'Huh. Well, I'll have to go upstairs and get ready for this evening's service.' She placed her hand on the stair rail and lingered for a second like a ballerina, pausing. 'Ah. Before I go, do you ever read the parish magazine?'

'No. It's too racy for me.'

'Well, look at next week's edition. It contains an advertisement that you must reply to.'

Just as she reached the top of the stairs, the door knocker banged.

'I'll see who it is,' Wally said, and answered the door. 'Oh, we didn't expect you. Come in.' He called upstairs, 'A bloke has called to take down your particulars.'

She came back down. 'Oh, well Sunday is as good as any other day. Good evening, Sergeant Forester. I thought you were coming tomorrow.'

'Yes, I would have done. But I have a young nephew with me who's desperate to see inside a nick, as he calls it. While we were there, young Cole told me about your problem.'

'Excuse me,' said Wally. 'While you are talking about this theft, I'll cycle home, get changed.'

'Put a tie on,' she called, as Wally banged the door shut.

FIFTEEN

Norman sat upright and determined in the gym, without shirt, pumping weights. A couple of members walked past and called out, 'Pull that stomach in, Norman.' He took the quip seriously, and, puffing like a hopeful champion, and certain his colleagues were watching, he held the dumbbells longer than he intended then gasped as he eased them to the floor. As they passed, one crony muttered, 'Sitting there bollock naked, he thinks he's Tarzan.'

'More like the ape, I'd say,' his mate tittered.

Apart from his job as a peripatetic brass instrument teacher, and his membership of the Daisy Hill Brass Band, weight training was his abiding interest. At school he had never shone as an athlete, did not play football for the school team and cricket bored him. He had taken up trumpet playing instead, then changed to the soprano cornet when he joined the band. And when he began teaching, he found he had a little dosh to spare, so he joined the gym.

Norman picked up the weights again, exercised seven more times then placed them down.

'Don't overdo it, Norman,' the supervisor said, walking by, inspecting the equipment.

'Right, Bernard. I won't.'

'And put a bloody shirt on.'

But as soon as Bernard was out of sight, Norman placed the dumbbells on one side, not to don a shirt – as per regulations – but to scrabble in his pocket, from which he extracted a small box of pills. He quickly and furtively looked about, then under the guise of only drinking from his water bottle, he swallowed a couple of pills.

Time and time again, members of the gym were lectured about resorting to anabolic steroids to bulk up their bodies, but mindless aspirants like Norman ignored the advice, in the fragile and mistaken hope that the drug's malign constitution would have no adverse effect on them.

❀

The inhabitants of Down Daisy did not have much to boast about, but swagger they did about the recently erected complex comprising a new dentistry, cheek by jowl to a new clinic. And denizens who had neglected their molars for years suddenly decided to buy toothpaste and brushes. A few even chanced an appointment with Mr Clegg, a tooth quack of great extraction, and known to local urchins as Crusher Cleggy. His well-upholstered assistant, Stella Sudworth, was also the secretary of the Daisy Hill Brass Band.

Stella tapped her computer and a name appeared. 'Your next patient is Norman Tattersall.'

'You said that as if you know him.'

'I do.' She sighed intolerantly as she spoke. 'He's in the band.'

'Really. Well, hold the fort while I indulge in a quick squirt. I drank too much coffee at lunchtime.' And off he shot to the loo. 'Go inside, Mr Tattersall. I won't be a minute.'

Norman ambled in. 'Oh, hello. It's Stella, isn't it?'

Stella glanced at herself in the large mirror. 'Good gracious, so it is.' Before peering at Norm's face she scanned his jug ears, the bane of his youth. 'What's up – toothache?'

'No. Halitosis.' It sounded like a boast.

'I see,' she said slowly. Now she spoke to his ears again. 'You said that with pride.'

'Did I…? So you work here then?'

'No, I just turn up for me wages.'

A timorous smile flickered over Norm's face, unsure if the band's fat pen pusher was pulling his pisser. He ignored her, settled in the dentist's chair and examined the ceiling.

Mr Clegg returned and frowned at his patient. Then he advanced, leaned forward and sniffed, identifying a specific odour. 'So, one of your problems is halitosis.'

'Yes.' Norman sounded surprised. 'How do you know?'

'I can tell. Experience. You need a doctor. Fortunately there are two or three next door.'

Norman thought, *A doctor for halitosis? Surely not?*

'First, I'll scale then clean your teeth, then we'll proceed from there.'

The procedure was painless and Norman closed his eyes until, after ten minutes, the unaccountably bitchy Stella suddenly squirted mouthwash into the languid cornet player's now scrubbed and gaping gob, causing instant vigilance.

He thought, *What's up with the clumsy cow?*

She bundled him out of the chair as Crusher Clegg said, 'I'm going to phone the clinic next door, Mr Tattersall. You need to see a doctor. So wait here in reception for a minute.'

In a half daze, Norman shuffled into the waiting room while the dentist phoned. Then Clegg turned to Stella. 'So that patient is in the band?'

'Yes.' She all but snapped even that word. 'He plays soprano cornet. But he's not good enough for it.'

'Oh! Really?'

'My brother Bengie should be playing soprano.'

'I see,' said Cleggy, but thought, *Hence the peevish performance.* He then stepped into the waiting room. 'Dr Mackistry will see you in ten minutes, if you'll step into the clinic.'

The popular Paddy MacWhiskey, having done doctoring in the Merchant Navy, was well aware of young men's sexual proclivities. And could, by brief questioning and close examination, identify a person's present or even past lifestyle.

'Ah, come in, Mr Tattersall. It's nearly the end of my day, so it is, so let us not be circumspect. You've just seen Mr Clegg about halitosis, I believe?' Norman nodded. 'Will you remove your shirt, please?' While the patient tugged at his attire, the easy-going Paddy tossed off some liquid gold from the tumbler behind his telephone.

'Now, Mr Tattersall, tell me what sort of a lifestyle do ye have?'

'Lifestyle?' echoed Norman, sounding puzzled.

'Job, to begin with. Or jobs, if you've had a few. Incidentally you wear too many clothes.'

Norman described his employment since leaving school. 'I started at the steelworks because my father was still working there.'

'I see.' Dr Paddy slid his stethoscope along the patient's back then his chest, bid Norman sit down and took his blood pressure. 'The nurse has just gone home, lucky lass, so I'll do a blood test as well, so I will.' He gave Norman a titer test, gently inserting a needle. Then he took the syringe behind the screen and carried out the blood test.

'Was it hot, working in the steelworks?'

'Dreadfully! At times we had to rest in the cool room and drink salt water.'

'Remove your undervest, please.'

Norman did as requested and slung his old-style vest over the back of the chair.

'How long did you work at the steelworks?'

'Five and a half years. I left that to teach brass instruments in schools.'

'Do you exercise?' Norm nodded. 'You need to diet as well.' He took a step back and pointed to the patient's chest with his stethoscope. 'These are known as man boobs. Medically, they are gynecomastia.' He ran his Anglo-Irish eyes over Norman's pink body and sniffed at his open mouth. 'Answer me honestly: do the management of the gym allow you to take anabolic steroids to bulk up your body?'

Norman didn't answer.

'Well?' Now he was schoolmasterish. 'I need to know.'

'No.' The reply was husky. Norm realised he'd been rumbled.

The medico studied his patient and hummed, 'By Killarney's Lakes and Fells'. 'OK, lie on the bunk and remove your kecks which, incidentally, are far too tight. You should be wearing boxer shorts.' Norman obliged. 'Now open your legs… Ah! You've got a rash around your testicles.'

'I know. I put cream on.'

'I suggest you've had this rash quite a while. I'm afraid, young man, all the evidence you have displayed suggests male infertility. Are you married?'

Norman mumbled into the covering of the couch. 'No.'

'In your condition you could not father a child. Right, get dressed.'

Norman felt wretched. He sat on the chair again. 'Will I always be like this?'

'Not if you take my advice. I may have to send you to hospital as an outpatient. I'll have you right in six months, so I will.'

🌳

It was a mild Monday morning and Fred the postman was delivering his last letter and thinking about the Irish coffee he would enjoy at the Diving Duck. He lifted out the last letter, which was addressed to Professor Septimus Jack Sparrow, and walked towards the Prof's caravan and noticed the door was open. The letter seemed official, as it bore a cellophane window; so rather than call his customer's name and chuck it in the doorway – a lazy habit of Fred's – he called out, 'Hello! Professor Sparrow. Are you there?' But no Prof appeared.

He was now desperate for his coffee, with a drop of the hard stuff, as only Toby the landlord could make it. He was becoming irritable. Fred trudged round the side of the caravan. This was a part of the job that he detested, even worse than difficult dogs, for Fred, a one-time full-back, had put many a hound to flight with a well-planted penalty kick. He hated wasting time like this through no fault of his own.

He got to the rear of the van, looked about him, like a twerp peering into a mist, then suddenly saw his quarry thirty yards away, halfway up a ladder that was leaning against a tree. Fred decided not to call out in case the old guy responded by taking a tumble and falling from his perch. He walked quietly up to him. The Prof was peeping into the branches of the tree and cooing to one of his feathered friends.

'Come along now. No need to be afraid, my beauty.' He stretched out both his arms to the fledgling; this caused him to lean slightly back, and in doing so he tumbled from the ladder, and like a trainee acrobat without a net, old Sep fell to terra firma with as much force as his meagre frame could muster. The pigeon, faithful to the last, flew away.

Fred stood looking down at his client. The old man not only looked like a scarecrow, but he lay as still as one. His eyes were closed and his white beard was in need of a trim. Fred knelt down and peered closely at the ancient. The postie looked about him for help. But it was lunchtime – dinnertime in the North – so naturally the meagre population was busy – and hungry; so was Fred. He leaned closer to the pensioner and sniffed, wondering if the rascal had sampled a skinful earlier. But the Prof was as sober as a choirboy and no alcoholic tang lingered. He shook him gently. 'Sep. Can you hear me?' Fred had heard that you slap people to bring them round. But the postie hadn't the heart to do this. So he prodded him twice. Result: Fred two, Professor Sparrow nil. That coffee with its golden glow was badly needed now.

'Septimus, time to get up.' But Sep remained blotto and Fred would have to propel him home. The postie raised up the Prof. He wasn't heavy – hollow would be more accurate. Fred placed an arm about the wrinkly, although when their faces touched, Fred realised that Jack Sparrow was no wrinkly. He gathered an arm around the casualty and together they struggled back to the caravan like two heroes retreating back to the trenches (a rerun as far as the comatose twitcher was concerned).

Fred heaved the Prof into the van and laid him on a bunk. 'What next?' he puffed. The caravan site seemed deserted. So... who could take over immediately?

'Mrs Marks, I reckon.'

He left his post office van, and, now tired, plodded back across the site and tortoise-like entered Upsy-Daisy's only emporium. 'I need your help.' He explained the incident. 'If you could kindly tend him, I'll call in on the Doctor.'

The grumpiness within a reluctant Mrs Marks vied with her natural nosiness. Nosiness won.

They trudged back across the site and went into the ancient's caravan, where Professor Septimus Jack Sparrow lay on his bunk, just as Fred had left him. Mrs Marks advanced confidently, having washed and tidied many a diseased prior to an undertaker's responsibility. She bent over Sep, her brow wrinkled, perhaps suspicious. She sniffed. 'He's not sozzled, is he?'

'No. He's either copped it or he's in some sort of stupor.'

'He usually was... I must say, he's very still.' She poked him with a stiff finger. 'I don't like this,' she complained. She looked round the van but couldn't see what she sought, so took a dekko round his sink unit, as though seeking treasure trove, and excavated a shaving mirror thick with muck. 'Huh, full of dust.'

'Well it will be. He doesn't use one. Never shaved.' Fred could have made a detective had he been taller.

She didn't bother to wipe the glass, but held it in front of the bewhiskered, log-like Septimus.

Nothing!

'He ain't breathing,' she said.

'I don't like this,' Fred said.

'Well, I'm not making whoopee. He owes me for last week's bread and milk.'

'I thought it was No Tick The Clock Has Stopped,' Fred quoted.

'It is. And him and Markie settle up after ludo. But they didn't play last week 'cos Markie went pubbin'.'

'Make a note of what he owes you,' Fred advised. 'Meanwhile I'll shunt off and tell Paddy. He'll sort it all out. He's a damn good doctor.'

Without more ado, Fred swung into his PO van and drove to the surgery, leaving Mrs Marks to reflect; but she didn't contemplate, she rummaged. For ten minutes she ransacked every drawer and each nook and cranny, but there was nothing except bumph about birds: a leaflet on lapwings, pamphlets on pigeons, blurb about barn owls and a framed photo of a falcon. Books on birds were stacked about the caravan like coloured gravestones.

But no spondulicks of any denomination.

Eventually, she pootled off home and on the way she met Josephine. 'The Professor is dead.'

'Oh, I'm so sorry. Mind you, he was an elderly gentleman.'

Jo told Richard, who saw Wally wheeling his bike round the site.

'Have you heard about the Professor?'

'No, I've heard nothing.'

'He's died,' Richard said. 'Mrs Marks found him dead in bed when she delivered his bread, this morning.'

'Oh, poor bugger.'

Richard shrugged. 'Well, he lived a long life. I believe he was in his nineties.'

'He was a nice old guy,' Wally said. 'So, who's going to arrange the funeral?'

'I suppose it's down to us. Nobody ever visited him, from outside, I mean. Would you have a word with your friend, the Vicar?'

'Yeah, course. I'll go and see her today.'

There was little else to do or say, so they both went their separate ways. Wally pedalled down the slope of the site and when he arrived outside he phoned the council. 'Something's come up. I'll be an hour later starting work today. I'll explain why when I come in.'

He then pushed his bike under the sycamore trees at the front of the house, and banged the large door knocker.

'Hello, Wally, I was wondering if you might call. I'm sorry, I got involved in an emergency committee meeting after the service on Sunday, and by the time it finished you'd gone.'

'What did Sergeant Forester have to say?' Wally asked.

'Come in, don't stand there.'

Wally wiped his feet and accepted a cup of strong tea and a shortcake biscuit.

'He examined outside and said everything, that is the burglary, was done tidily as though it was well planned beforehand. When I suggested it might have been those lads who barged in the dance hall on their motorcycles, he didn't agree. He said he would get one of his detective constables to come and investigate. So, for the time being that's it. We'll probably never find out.'

Wally placed his empty mug on the sideboard. 'Well, I'm actually on my way to work, but I've called to say the old guy up at the caravan site, Septimus Jack Sparrow, has passed away so we'll need your assistance as to what to do. I suppose Richard Coningsby and myself will be responsible for organising things. But we'll need some guidance. Anyway I must be off.' And as he turned to go she did what she'd never done before… she kissed him on the cheek.

Norman checked his watch: just one more pupil, then he'd finished for the day. A knock came at the door. 'Come in, Charlie.'

Young Charlie Wrigley entered, carrying his cornet case. He looked round the small rehearsal room and wiped his finger over the seat of the only remaining chair. 'It's dusty in here. I've got some new trousers on and if I get 'em mucky me mam will kill me.'

'I doubt if she'll be so drastic, Charlie. Anyway, get your cornet out and let's start.'

'These cleaners are not what they used to be,' said the pupil, echoing his ma and retrieving his instrument from its box.

'Oh! Who says so?'

'Me mam. Her should know, 'cos her's a cleaner.'

'Really! Does she clean at a school?

'Not now. Her did. But her cleans the village hall and for yon Vicar.'

'Very good. Right, now let us try the major scale of B-flat which caused you some trouble last week. Right, off you go.'

Charlie attempted to play the scale but had to complete it with three breaths.

'Right. Now I want you to play just one note. Play the note of C without any fingering. Play it in one breath: ta ta ta ta ta ta taa, ta ta ta ta ta ta taa… Next, up and down the scale taking only one breath.'

Charlie did as he was instructed then waited for the next requirement.

Norman took an implement from his case. He pressed the tiny switch which caused the implement to produce a ticking noise. 'This is called a metronome. Your job is to play and keep in time with the tick-tock. Listen to what I do.'

Norman took a breath and in time with the metronome played the scale he was teaching Charlie.

Then he turned the clock face of the metronome and it 'ticked' slightly quicker, and he played the scale at a faster pace.

'Now, I could use this gadget to get quicker and quicker. But the main thing is to play the scale accurately. Right? Now, do you remember the name of this scale?'

'I've forgot, Norman.' The fact is, as Norman played, Charlie had watched and noticed, for the first time, Norman's protruding ears like a pair of red sea shells; he was entranced, and his concentration left him like a puppy leaves an empty bowl.

The teacher paused. 'It's B-flat. And I've told you before, Charlie, when we are in school, I am sir. When we are at the band practice I am Norman. Got it?'

'Oh, sorry, N... er, Sir Norman.'

Norman looked at his watch. 'Anyway, we'll leave it for this afternoon, it's nearly half past three. So put your instrument away.'

The pupil placed his cornet carefully in its case and stood to leave.

'Now, go straight home without dallying, and when you arrive home, the first thing I'd like you to do is play this scale and write down what it is called. Play it steadily four times.'

'I'm not going straight home today, N... er, sir. I have to go and collect a pram.'

'A pram, Charlie! What, a doll's pram or a...'

'No, a babby's pram. Our Lily is preggers, and somebody has give her a pram.'

'Preggers!' echoed Norman.

'Yeah. She's having a babby, so she needs a pram. Somebody from t' babby clinic said she could have it.'

Norman packed away his instrument, his music stand and the music he carried. 'I see. So you will be Uncle Charlie?'

'Aye. I know. Only me in our class will be an uncle.'

Norman pushed the chairs under the table. 'And where is this baby clinic then?'

'It's on t' main road. In t' Co-op hall.'

'Ah yes, I know. Two hundred yards up from the church. I didn't know it was hired out for a baby clinic.'

'Oh aye. Lot's of women go,' said Charlie, knowingly. 'But they have to be preggers. So our Lily goes. And whatsername goes too. Y' know, her what plays percussion.'

'Percussion!' Norman froze. 'Do you mean Mavis, who plays in the band?'

'Aye. That's her. She leaves t' Co-op where she works and goes to t' preggers clinic.'

Norman leant on the table and broke out into a sudden, prickly sweat. 'Right,' he said, huskily. 'Close the door after you, Charlie.'

Now he was on his own again, he began to think more clearly, but the progress was slow.

For some time, something had bothered him about Mavis but he hadn't been able to put his finger on it. Now reality was beginning to dawn, like an unexpected sunrise on a misty day. She had treated him favourably these last few weeks. She had let him into her bed. In spite of his inexperience, he was sure most women didn't do that. She had loaned him – in fact given him – the bubble car to save him pedalling from school to school. Whatever he mentioned, she gave him. His shell-like ear turned red as he realised: she had seduced him. But soon, he'd have no liberty. But in reality, everything was being angled towards what she wanted.

He was being ensnared!

Norman became suddenly angry. He snatched up his luggage, marched to the car park and drove haphazardly from the school.

Within ten minutes he was in front of the Co-op. He sprang from the car and stormed through the door.

'We're just going to close,' called Mona.

He ignored her and strode to the cooked meats stall. Mavis looked up in surprise.

'Oh, Norman!'

'Yes, Norman indeed.' He glanced down at her white smock. Now he saw quite clearly: the swelling. 'Did you get on alright at the baby clinic this morning?'

Nearer the shop door, Iona casually left her counter and tiptoed behind the shelves fronting the cooked meat stall where Mavis served. She peeped between a stack of baked beans and listened to every word.

'I, er, intended to tell you tonight about this,' said Mavis, encircling her hands around the bump.

Norman's voice had altered. His usually muted tone, habitually boring, had become harsh and rasping like glass-paper scrubbed onto coarse timber.

'What were you going to tell me, that I…'

'That you were going to become a dad,' she said, trailing her voice away, lamely.

'But that wouldn't be true, would it?' Norman croaked. He leant forward, touching the glass counter. 'Because it's not mine.' He pointed to the swollen evidence. 'That child is the offspring of your late husband.' She gave a brief gasp and clasped a hand over her mouth. 'I have visited Dr MacWhiskey,' Norman said, without mentioning the reason for his visit, 'I'm aware what your game was.'

He placed the keys to the little car on the glass counter and marched from the shop.

SIXTEEN

The church of St Aidan fronted the main road at the junction of Daisy Hill, Down Daisy and Upsy-Daisy. Behind the church stood the vicarage, roomy and imposing. And concealing the vicarage was a large, red brick wall. After the war the metal spikes had never been replaced. The area inside this high wall was quite private, and made somewhat exclusive by a thick privet hedge growing on the inside of the wall. The road outside the wall was known as Aidan Street.

Today, it was Wally's job, as the council's arborist, to trim the privets. Walter Watson had been sent, by the council, on a tree surgeon's course, a job at which he was now an expert. He erected a scaffold close to the wall in Aidan Street and laid his tools along the planks of the scaffold. On the pavement below him, he placed red and white cones so that if a pedestrian did walk on the wall side of the road, they would, seeing the cones, walk round them, avoiding the scaffold. His principal job was to clip the tops of the privet bush, and to make sure he could reach across the width he had raised the scaffold slightly lower than the top of the wall so that his knees, bound in thick material, just touched the top of the wall, otherwise scraped knees was the outcome.

He started at the end of the wall that was almost the end of Aidan Street. His mechanical shears were a fantastic improvement on the hand-held clippers of earlier years, and within two hours he'd finished clipping the privets belonging to the vicarage and, under council instructions, began to clip the privets of the neighbouring property without knowing who owned it. Because the privets were not the same thickness all along, he could sometimes see through them, noting what lay beyond.

As he moved along, stopping to resite his scaffold further along the pavement, he noticed the buildings, the stuff, and how the bits and bobs on the other side of the wall changed. The vicarage land was, on the whole, neat, tidy, uncluttered. This neighbouring property was neglected, with one or two old sheds, a dilapidated greenhouse and a rusty concrete mixer. Then, snipping and cutting away, peering through the bushes, he saw what seemed to be windows – a low bungalow, perhaps. He stopped work, laid down his shears and peered through the twigs and branches at a bus, a coach actually. And inside, the seats and passageway were piled with tiles. Wearing his helmet and goggles, he pushed his face into the privet. Wooden tiles!

'Wooden tiles!' he told himself. Then he realised what they were. He glanced at his watch; it was almost dinnertime (dinner in the North and lunch in the South). He climbed from the scaffold, taking his tools with him, and walked to the end of Aidan Street, and round to the main road and the church. He knocked. The door of the vicarage opened and Miriam popped her head out.

'I was just going to call you. I've made some soup.'

'I'm ready for it. And I've something to tell you later.'

He removed his boots, washed his hands and sat at the table. An unexpected thought entered his head: this setup reminded him of home, in the Pennines, on those days when he chopped logs then came in for a meal. He was comfortable then. *And I'm comfortable now,* he mused.

'What's this soup?' he asked. 'It's jolly tasty.'

'Spring vegetable. I told you, I almost became a chef. But after the army, I couldn't seem to tolerate working with groups of people. Too many memories.'

He dipped his bread in the vegetable soup, just as he did wherever he felt at home. Now, replete, he eased back in his dining chair and drank tea from a pint mug.

'What's this item you have to show me?' Miriam asked.

'You'll need to put your wellingtons on and some overalls, if you have any. Oh, and a firm hat, to prevent getting scratched.'

'Sounds mysterious,' she said, pushing away from the table. 'I'll get changed then.'

He put his boots back on and waited in the porch until she appeared. 'This way.'

She followed, six feet behind. 'More mystery?' But Wally didn't reply.

They followed the twisting path and walked round the side of the house.

'You've clipped those privets lovely and straight,' she said.

'Thanks. Do you know, if they were clipped from the inside, you'd get an account from the district council. But because I clipped them from the other side of the wall, the council foot the bill.'

Following the path, they turned right and arrived at the side of the house. Wally took a few more paces then stopped as they were confronted by a tall fence.

'Oh no! I'm not expected to climb that, am I?'

'Thankfully, no.' From his narrow side pocket in his trousers, the ruler pocket, he extracted a jemmy. 'You didn't know I was a part-time burglar, did you?'

The fencing facing them was the inside section, the portion clarifying that the fence belonged to the vicarage. Wally jammed the thin, blade-sharp edge of the jemmy between a spar and one length of the seven-foot-tall planking of the fence. He eased the jemmy like a lever and the planking began to come away.

'I hope you know what you're doing, Wally. These neighbours will go mad.'

'Eventually they will, but not because I'm dismantling a section of fencing, because this is your fencing. The person who lived here originally erected it, and because the spars are on your side, it's your property.' He thrust the plank away and it fell to the ground on the other side. The fence was screened by ivy, camouflaging and hiding items. He now prised away a second plank, demonstrating there was now enough space to climb through. 'Come on,' he said, and stepped over the bottom spar and entered the neighbouring property. He held her hand as she climbed through.

'I'm not sure about this. Aren't we trespassing?'

He grinned, nodded and placed a finger over his lips. 'Whose land is this?'

'That fellow who plays in Daisy Hill Brass Band.'

He stopped in his tracks. 'Well, well. Why am I not surprised?' He walked on a few paces and came to the construction he had earlier assumed – because of the windows – to be a bungalow. The passenger steps were, fortunately, on their side, away from the line of privet. He stood on the steps and looked through the filthy windows, overhanging with privet and ivy. Then he stepped down from… the coach.

'Now you look.'

She climbed up, went a step higher than Wally. Then she gasped.

'The tiles! The wooden tiles belonging to the porch! But how have they got here? They must have been lifted over the fence.'

'They weren't lifted over the fence. The planks in the fence were removed just as I removed them.

Our friend Bob Dyke removed them from outside the church porch and wheeled them down here. To prevent tyre marks being impressed into the garden path, he laid a plank that the tilers use on the path. When he came to the end of the plank, wheeling the barrow, he lifted up the plank – they're not heavy – then pushed the barrow back on, and wheeled it along.'

'Then he prised the lengths of planking off the fence.'

'Got it,' he said. 'To get the wheelbarrow over the bottom spar, he placed one plank on one side, covering half the spar, and placed another plank, perhaps a shorter one, covering the other half of the spar. Then carefully he wheeled his barrow over the little pyramid and into his patch.'

'It must have taken a heck of a lot of time,' she said.

'I would say about twelve barrows. Five minutes each. That makes it an hour, plus time loading up in front of the church porch, then time emptying at this end. Another hour all together.'

'The nerve of the man.'

'And each time he arrived at this end, he was hidden by greenery. Shall I cycle off to Sergeant Forester?'

For a moment, she stood silently, looking up into his face. 'No. I am curious to learn why he did it.'

'It happened the night of the dance, when we were all in bed. OK. If you're going to see him, I'll come with you.'

Mrs Marks and Markie were stacking tins of baked beans. The tins were dented because they had – as the cop-out has it – fallen off the back of a lorry, a strategy more in keeping with Markie's activities than his wife's. Markie thought his contribution qualified for recognition and, of course, reward.

'Later on, I wouldn't mind going for a snifter at the Diving Duck,' he said, 'after we've dealt with this lot, of course.'

Mrs Marks ignored the hint and kept on stacking.

'I said, I'd like to go…'

'I know what you said. OK. When you've finished, go.'

'Right. Good. But I'm skint.'

'Now why does that not surprise me?' She didn't allow him time to answer, but chuntered on, 'And the reason why you're skint is because you're always in the Diving Duck.'

When she drew a breath, Markie entered the fray – metaphorically – holding a balloon on a stick rather than a spear. 'But I…'

'You're always skint. You still owe me from last time.'

Markie sighed. The Diving Duck was his celestial city; he was quiet there. 'I'm gasping.' He changed the subject, chancing craftier tactics. 'So you didn't actually see old Septimus fall off the ladder?'

'No. Like I said, by the time I got to his caravan, Fred had laid him on the bunk. He was as white as chalk. Not you, clown! Sep.' She removed her grubby apron.

Marky felt squeamish. He sat down. 'Oh!'

'Not you, you clown! Sep.' She replaced her apron with a grubby dress. 'Fred should have seen a doctor by now, or the receptionist.'

Suddenly her mobile rang. 'Oh, hello, Doctor.'

She covered the mouthpiece.

'It's Paddy,' she mumbled to Markie.

'We were just talking about you. Who? Me and Markie.' Her voice rose half a tone. 'You're coming? In half an hour? Yes, I've got a key to Sep's van. OK. I will. See you shortly.'

She replaced her mobile.

'What was that about? "OK, I will?"' Markie asked.

'He said I'd have to be a witness. It'll make things quicker. Anyway, you'll have to come with me, 'cos I'll have to come back here. The bread man and milko get here by twelve. So let's get going.'

Markie thought, *So Paddy's coming. He always has a flask on him. I'll get a snifter then.*

They locked Upsy-Daisy's emporium, and set off across the caravan site like two kids visiting the fair, rather than adults attending a serious meeting. They did not have to wait long for Dr Patrick Mackistry, who arrived in a jalopy in need of a good scrubbing.

'Will it take long to sort this out, Doctor? 'Cos I've got to get back to the shop for the breadman.'

'No, my dear Colleen. No need to linger. Just explain what happened to auld Septimus, then you can vamoose. Then I'll give the certificate to Markie, so I will.'

'Thanks, Doc. I knew you wouldn't waste any time,' she said, knowing that Paddy was a world champion at procrastination.

She went through her role as the conscientious assistant to Fred the postman. Then apologetically explained how she felt obliged to search – ransack – Sep's drawers for insurance policies, but didn't find any. Then, excusing herself, she returned to the shop.

Paddy looked at Professor Septimus Jack Sparrow. 'Ah, well. He lived a long life, so he did. Thousands who've gone earlier would envy him.' He sat at the table and, to Markie's delight, took out his flask. He attempted to take a swig, then turned the drained container upside down. 'Bugger. It's empty.'

Markie's heart sank. Then he perked up. 'I used to play ludo with Sep, on Friday. And during the game he'd bring out a bottle.' He stopped and looked at Paddy who understood Markie's aspiration.

'And you know where the bottle is kept?' Markie nodded. 'Well,' said the doc, 'he won't need it now, will he?'

So Markie opened one of the long cupboard doors, a feature of caravans long before they were incorporated into cottage furniture. He brought out three bottles: one, vodka, one, whisky and a ginger ale.

'No wonder he lived to a great age,' said Paddy. 'He was pickled.'

Markie tittered. 'And what a way to go.' He went through to the back kitchen, rummaged in a cupboard and brought out two large glass tumblers. 'What'll you have, Paddy?'

'A whisky mac.'

Markie poured tumblers three quarters full of whisky then topped them up with ginger ale.

Paddy knocked his back, half emptying the glass. 'Jaysus, I needed that. I was out last night until half six this morning. I'm wrecked now.' He finished off the glass and picked up the vodka.

'Ossified, were ye?' said Markie, picking up the Irish from habit.

Dr Mackistry nodded. 'Fortunately, I'm off duty now, so I'll try a noggin of vodka.' And without so much as a by your leave, he topped up his own glass and handed the bottle to Markie, who followed suit.

'Have ye located any policies?' asked the Doctor.

'No. The wife has looked, but found nothing.'

The Doctor lit up his pipe and was soon chuffing away. 'Old Septimus thought about nothing but birds, you know.'

'Aye. Ornithology, they call it,' said Markie.

Thirty minutes later, a knock came to the door, and by the time Richard Coningsby walked in, the boozers were sloshed. 'Sorry if we appear ossified,' said Paddy, articulating like a Celt, 'we're celebrating the life of the old or… er, or…' He turned to Markie. 'What did you call the old guy?'

'Ornithologist,' said Markie. 'They gawp at birds, you know.'

'Twitchers, they're known as,' Richard said. 'Well, I've called to tell you that I hold the Professor's insurance policies, in case you were searching for them. 'But I can see you've had other things on your mind.' He wafted a hand and shook his head in dismay. 'I'll leave the door open', and he walked out.

When he got back home, Josephine asked, 'Have they got things organised?'

'Organised! It's doubtful if they know what day it is. If this funeral becomes a cock-up, I know who to blame.'

'Don't tell me Dr Mackistry is…'

'Sloshed,' Dick said. 'Completely blotto.'

❧

'Do you know where this Bob Dyke bloke lives?' asked Wally.

'Well, at the far end of Aidan Street there's a detached bungalow. I presume he lives there. People rarely walk down that street because it leads nowhere. But before we go, I'd like to get rid of this mucky overall and fortify myself with a cuppa and a cake.'

'Good idea,' he said. 'I'll join you in that too.'

They made their way back along the twisty footpath to the main door of the vicarage, and, while Miriam went upstairs to change, Wally brewed a pot of builder's tea, just as most ex-army types like it. Then he rummaged in the cupboard to find two packets of crisps and an unopened carton of Eccles cakes. He set everything on the table just as Miriam came downstairs. They sat at the table facing each other, comfortable and with growing familiarity.

'Why are you not contacting Sergeant Forester?'

'Because I want a reason or at least an excuse why Bob Dyke went to all that trouble to nick something he'll probably never use.'

Wally took a long pull at his tea. Looking over his cup, he again noticed her green eyes. Her eyes had been the initial attraction, an appeal enhanced by unusually long eyelashes. 'Well, it did take him a heck of a while to swipe those tiles. As a Redcap I once went to a lecture where a copper said a burglar only wants to be in a property for twenty minutes maximum. He wants to be in, grab the stuff then out.' He shook his head, perplexed. 'It's not as if he quickly sneaked an item off a shop counter.'

It was about three o'clock when they finished their snack. They left via the large gate on the main road, turned right, walked fifty yards and turned right again where the school bus turns round. At four fifty the kids became a rugby scrum as they pushed and shoved to board the bus. Conscientious drivers reprimanded them for swearing, but most drivers never bothered.

Now, the two pedestrians were on Aidan Street beside the long red brick wall. Wally noticed the privet poking an even nine inches above the wall; its green pruned appearance gave him a brief feeling of satisfaction. They passed Daisy Hill secondary school on the opposite side, and by this time the long wall had given way to a boundary of picket fence through which they could see rough, neglected land.

'This land must belong to Bob Dyke,' Wally said.

'I suppose it does. I only come along this street when I visit the secondary school about twice each year. They are not obliged to teach or even listen to religious education. And the current head is not that way inclined. And since ninety per cent of the pupils catch the school bus, very few come this opposite way.'

'So Bob Dyke sees only a few people at this end. What are you going to say to him?'

'Well, that depends on his answer to my opening gambit. I've deliberately omitted phoning him so I can spring a surprise. Is that nasty, do you think?'

'Miriam, this chap – whether you agree or not – has made himself your enemy. As an enemy, you're entitled to surprise him.'

'Here we are,' she said, as they approached the bungalow. At that moment a sudden commotion behind them caused them to turn round. The school gates were now unlocked and the youngsters surged forth and raced up the road towards the bus.

They went through a creaky gate and followed the path, overhung with trees, shrubs and sprigs. Wally banged the knocker, probably harder than required and Bob opened the door.

'Hello, Mr Dyke. Can we have a word with you, please?'

'Eh?' He sort of swayed on the step and looked much older than when she had last seen him. His hand was still bandaged, probably from when he'd been stabbed by a sharp pencil.

'Is it important?'

'I believe so,' she said. 'In fact I don't think you'd want anyone else to know about it.'

'So,' said Wally, making a long note of the vowel, 'if we stepped inside, briefly, it would keep things private.'

Bob could have indicated the isolation of the area, but he didn't have the presence of mind for this tactic, so he let them in.

An onion smell of recent cooking overwhelmed them and Miriam wondered if she'd be able to concentrate. Clattering dishes could be heard in the next room. Suddenly a noise like someone in pain cut through the rooms of the bungalow.

'Robert,' called a female voice, 'I have my hands full. Will you attend to Elijah?'

'I won't be a minute,' said Bob. And he left his visitors standing on the doormat.

They waited five minutes, which crept to seven. Then an obnoxious smell pervaded the hallway, a toilet was flushed and a garbled voice seemed to complain.

'Bloody hell,' whispered Wally, 'I can't stand this,' and he quietly opened the front door and stood on the step, taking deep, cautious breaths.

Miriam joined him. 'It must be Elijah,' she muttered, 'whoever he is, from the First Book of Kings.'

Wally looked at his watch. 'We've been here quarter of an hour.' Exasperation coloured his voice.

'It's obviously an emergency,' she said pacifically.

They stood looking at the shrubs and the weeds peeping through the soil. Then a movement was heard behind them, which prompted Wally to move from the step and pretend to examine a bush. 'I would say this is an ash tree,' he said. 'It'll look lovely in a few years.'

'Yes, if dieback doesn't destroy it,' she replied. 'That tree is actually a rowan tree. They flourish in Scotland, I believe.'

They then both turned to acknowledge the movement behind them, each receiving a shock. Bob stood just inside the hallway. In front of him was a wheelchair in which drooped a younger-looking Bob, with a lopsided head. He seemed to be about forty; phlegm hung from his pallid lips and his arms hung limply from him like thin branches on a sick tree.

It was difficult not to stare.

'So, this is, er, Elijah, I suppose,' said Wally lamely.

'Yes. He's a bit off colour today,' Bob explained.

'Oh, sorry to hear that,' said Miriam, realising she couldn't censure Bob now, as she'd intended to.

Elijah rolled his head around and produced a gurgling noise, to which his father responded, 'OK. I'll take you back in.' And Bob wheeled the contraption and its occupant back into the sombre kitchen.

The stench had gone so the callers stepped back inside and softly closed the door behind them.

Bob returned. 'It was too cold for him out here.'

Miriam felt all her zap had fizzled. She took a steady breath. 'I'll come to the point,' but she was aware it was a blunt point. 'I believe you took away the wooden tiles which had been stacked in front of the church porch.'

Momentarily, shock invaded Bob's face. 'Me!' he exclaimed. His monosyllable was neither admittance nor denial. He just stood there and stared.

Wally was losing patience. He reckoned Bob had played this game before, so he placed a hand inside his jacket and withdrew a tile. 'This is what they look like and your derelict bus is full of them.'

Miriam, now a little more inspired by Wally's speech, added, 'I've not been to the police since we found them. I thought I would first ask you why you did it.'

'Well, when we were on that coach trip a while back, our band members called me mean. That was your fault.' He pointed a stubby finger at her.

'Well, you are mean,' came his wife's voice from the kitchen.

Wally started chuckling and had to control himself.

'Oh! How do you make out it was my fault?' the Vicar said.

'Well, you put a fiver in their bucket,' Bob grumbled, his bulbous cheeks matching his grumpy voice.

'Give me strength,' muttered Wally.

But Miriam wanted to humour the blatant thief who obviously had unfair personal problems. 'I see.' She shrugged. 'Perhaps I was flush at the time and felt I could afford it. Anyway, the Sally Army said their collection was for an unfortunate young woman, who needed help.'

'Huh, she's not the only one who's unfortunate,' Bob complained.

Neither of the visitors could argue with that.

'Well, criticising somebody for giving to charity is a strange reason for nicking tiles,' said Wally, unexpectedly lamely. 'Are you sure there's nothing else?'

'And she,' Bob pointed to Miriam, 'persuaded young Charlie to join your church choir,' he said sulkily. 'That could cause him to leave our brass band. We can't afford to lose youngsters.'

'I didn't persuade him,' she said, uncertain whether she had or not. 'The small fee he gets persuaded him.'

'Well, it's all religious. I don't swallow that Jesus stuff.'

'That's exactly what you said in the pub, on the coach trip,' Wally said. 'Is that religious stuff another reason why you nicked the tiles?' Wally blew out his cheeks. The fruitless argument was beginning to weary him.

Now, getting entangled in his own odd reasoning, Bob said, 'We used to attend your church, you know.'

'Really? Why did you stop?' Miriam asked.

'Well, when we realised Elijah wouldn't be normal,' his voice almost became a whisper, 'we lost faith in a god who had treated us badly.'

'Well, I do understand that,' Miriam said, to his surprise, 'but God doesn't plan misfortune. He has given us free will, and that sometimes goes haywire.'

Wally's patience was wearing very thin, but he tried to be reasonable. He changed the subject. 'How long have you lived here, Bob?'

'I was born here. My dad – he was an Elijah too – was a haulier.'

Like a shot, a dish crashed to the floor in the kitchen and Elijah released a dreadful racket as though he were being tortured. 'Robert, you're needed in here, quick,' Mrs Dyke screamed. Then without warning, the lights went out.

'Time we went.' Wally lifted the catch on the front door and raised his voice. 'Any road, here's a suggestion: you return all those tiles within two days...' He left the remainder to Miriam.

'... and we won't go to the police.'

'Otherwise it's the chop.' And Wally stepped through the open door, smartly followed by the Vicar. As they walked back along Aidan Street, he said, 'What a strange fellow.'

'I'm not surprised,' she said, hurrying beside him. 'I'd go strange if I had to tolerate that impediment as my offspring.' Then she surprised and shocked him. 'Poor bugger.'

'You're too soft, you are. Bob just wanted to blame somebody for all his problems, so he took it out on you.'

'Well, it didn't cause me any personal pain.'

'Have you noticed,' Wally said, 'all the lights have gone out?' Every house was dark, like a wartime blackout. 'Huh, a power cut.' So they walked quickly and were soon at the vicarage. They were about to enter when Wally's mobile rang.

'Oh, hello, Dick. This is a pleasant surprise.'

He listened to Richard speaking, then Wally closed his phone, his jaw actually dropped and, rather shocked, he stared at Miriam.

'He reckons the Professor has come back to life!'

Miriam gasped and smothered her mouth with a nervous hand.

SEVENTEEN

'I'll have to get back to the site,' Wally said. 'Find out what it's all about.'

'I'll come with you. It's a rum do.'

'Have you got petrol in your car?'

'Yes,' she said. 'I filled up yesterday.'

At that moment the choirboys came out of the church.

'Hello, Charlie,' she called. 'You've finished early!'

'There's a power cut, miss. We couldn't read the music.'

'Ah, of course. Come with us then. I'll give you a lift home.'

The three of them piled into the Vicar's jalopy, an old but serviceable estate car. Naturally, they were soon talking about events at the caravan site in Upsy-Daisy.

'That's a turn-up for the books,' Wally said, momentarily forgetting their young passenger. 'I've never heard about a person coming back to life again, have you, Miriam?'

'It happened once in the army. A chap got a bullet in his chest. The MO examined him, listened to his chest, checked his pulse. Pronounced him dead. The squaddies lifted him into my truck and I drove for perhaps half a mile, when one of the stretcher-bearers said, "Hey, he's coming round." And sure enough the bloke recovered, and as far as I'm aware, he is still walking on terra firma.'

'That means the earth,' said young Charlie.

'Aye, aye. I'd forgotten little pigs have big ears,' Wally said.

'That's what my granddad says. Has somebody been shot up at the caravan site?'

The adults laughed. 'No,' Wally assured him. And he glanced at Miriam, who, anticipating his next remark, nodded her head. 'But somebody on the site has supposedly returned to life.'

'What, like Jesus?'

'That's what we're going to find out.'

'Cool,' the youngster said. 'Let me come too.'

'Well, I'm not sure,' Wally said.

'There is time,' said the youngster. 'I'm still supposed to be at choir practice.'

'Oh, look,' the Vicar announced. 'The lights are back on.'

'If I come with you,' Charlie urged, 'it will be a really cool subject for my next essay.'

His companions laughed, as the Reverend Miriam sat behind the steering wheel. Just before the passengers climbed aboard, Wally bent down and placed his lips next to Charlie's ear.

'Do you remember when I taught your class and we all had to walk round the caravan park?' Charlie nodded, recalling his bad manners. 'Why did we do it?' Wally continued.

'Because I farted,' Charlie admitted.

'Right! Well don't fart in this car, otherwise I'll turn you out. Understand?'

This time Charlie nodded with great solemnity.

The Reverend Miriam drove through the church gates, which were invariably open, then she turned left. The main road was a very gradual rise for a mile; to accommodate this incline she changed into a lower gear, but this didn't affect the traffic behind them, which already seemed to be queuing.

No one realised there was a problem ahead.

Fifty yards along was the Co-op, in front of which was a pull-in used for vehicles to unload goods. A few yards beyond that was a zebra crossing in front of the primary school. Just as they arrived at the pull-in, Miriam – because the road was becoming crowded – inched nearer the kerb and ran over what appeared to be a brown paper bag, which turned out to be a concrete brick that had fallen from a badly stacked lorry. The result was a terrific bang and a front wheel puncture.

'Oh God, no,' she wailed.

'Pull into this layby,' said Wally, which she did. He climbed out and rummaged in the car boot for the tool kit, then began to jack up the car to change the wheel. Young Charlie was about to follow him, but Miriam checked him.

'Stay here, Charlie, it's getting busy on the road.' The lad moaned a bit but did as he was bid. 'So you were sharing jokes in church when the lights went out?'

'Yeah. Some of the men know quite a lot.' He kept glancing at Wally, busy outside.

'OK,' she said. 'Tell me one. Tell me one of the choir members' jokes.'

'Oh. Right. Well, Lawrence told us this. The lady of the manor called Jeeves into her bedroom. "Jeeves, please unzip my dress." And he did so, but felt proper shy about it. "Now, Jeeves," she said, "take off my stockings." And he did and felt real stupid. "Now take off my underwear… and if I ever catch you wearing them again, you will be sacked."'

She chuckled. 'And Lawrence told you that, did he?'

'Yes, miss. But don't say owt.'

'Don't worry. I'll keep the joke to myself.'

Charlie turned and looked through the rear window. 'By heck, there are lots of cars behind us.'

Miriam glanced through her driving mirror. 'Good gracious, the traffic is piling up.'

Wally, having changed the wheel, climbed back into the car and the Vicar pulled very carefully away from the kerb and drove all of five miles an hour among the swelling traffic. She arrived at the zebra crossing and was obliged to apply her brakes as a group of youngsters marched across, the marching being perfect. As they crossed, the patrolman supervising them crossed with them, rather than stop halfway. On reaching the other side, a different group fell in under the obvious instruction of the patrolman – for it was certainly a male supervisor – and as he marched by the Vicar he saluted. Only two vehicles were allowed to cross in different directions, then the patrolman blew a whistle, held high his lollipop and marched another group across. He was actually heard to command, 'Squad, advance. Left, right, left, right.' When this group of eight children had marched smartly past, the guard – for he was certainly guarding the children – executed a smart about-turn and marched by again, wearing an officer's hat.

'Blimey,' Wally said, 'it's Major Merryweather.'

'Are you sure?' she said.

'Certain. Only a crackpot like him would perform like this.' They had inched forward again. Wally opened his passenger window. 'Hoy, Merryweather. Get a move on.' Cars were now honking, drivers were shouting. The Major continued the farce.

❦

As the marching continued near to the school, a more serious incident took place some two miles away.

When Miriam moved off through the open church gates, had she turned right instead of left, she would have arrived in Daisy Common, the smallest sector in the Daisy area. You know you've arrived there when you chance upon four lonely shops. One of these outlets is a general store. These outlets were built to serve an estate which has not yet been erected, so business is acquired by passing trade.

Cyril Pet, the proprietor of the general store, stacked his tins of rice pudding and, still behind his counter, stood back to view them. At that moment the shop door flew open and in barged two hooligans who, four days earlier, had decided to pay Cyril a visit and relieve him of his income. They made their intention clear when they entered the shop wearing face-covering balaclavas, with sockets for eyeholes.

Cyril was a small person, fiftyish, with a halo of ginger hair encircling a bald pate. Years earlier, working at the Co-op, he had experienced a robbery after which an alarm had been installed. But little Cyril was smarter than most folk, and had a secret camera fitted in his shop ceiling and a concealed button placed out of sight, near the till, before launching the business.

He spun round.

'OK. No need for violence. There's money in the till.'

The louts – for they were riff-raff rather than con men – looked surprised at each other and relaxed their arms, letting the rough cudgels dangle.

'No funny business,' one said, stepping towards the counter. 'Keep an eye on the door, Mervin.'

Cyril memorised the name.

The hooligan who considered himself the brains of the outfit stepped forward and looked into the drawer of the second-hand till.

'Not much in, is there?'

'Very little. No brass round here. Mainly passing trade.'

'Lucky *we* were passing, eh?' said Mervin, on lookout. 'Get some fags instead, Billy.'

Another name for me to remember, thought Cyril, who, under the eagle eye of the intelligentsia depressed an alarm button camouflaged as a sauce bottle.

A sudden shrieking noise exploded outside. The two hooligans stiffened and looked at each other. 'A bloody alarm,' shouted Mervin. 'The cops will be here.'

'You've set the alarm off, you bastard,' yelled Billy and made a grab for little Cyril who'd nipped behind the bacon slicer. The frustrated shoplifter grabbed some coins from the till, moronic Mervin grabbed a packet of boiled sweets hanging from the door and they fled from the premises.

They leapt onto their motorbike – Billy driving – and shot towards Daisy Hill.

At the far end of Daisy Common, half a mile away, Constable Colin Cole heard the alarm and saw it register on the station monitor. 'I'll go, guv,' he shouted and was fluttering down the steps and leaping into his car while Sergeant Forester was still on the phone.

Ignoring speed limits and enjoying every minute, the young copper shot towards Daisy Hill as though racing to the maternity ward.

In Daisy Hill, between the Co-op and the primary school, Major Merryweather was still commanding his contingents and dreaming of earlier days when his troops were much taller.

An irritated driver leant out of his car window and called, 'You dozy git. What are you playing at?'

But the Major was not accepting criticism. Using his lollipop sign as a lance, he advanced and lunged at the driver who was forced to duck back into his cab. The Major now produced a notebook and took the driver's number. 'I shall report you for insubordination and careless driving.' He then blew his whistle and marched another group of kids across. Once again the traffic was stopped so the sound of an approaching motorcycle was very clear. It weaved in and out of the stranded traffic and Major Merryweather looked up from his notebook. Quickly thinking of his platoon's safety, he ushered the primary schoolchildren back along the crossing to let the loony motorcyclists through. As soon as it was over the crossing it roared away; Constable Cole was left behind trying to manoeuvre his vehicle through the impasse.

Billy, the dunderhead driver, began to grin, believing he had once more put one over the Fuzz, and he scorched away from the traffic with Mervin clinging on for dear life, but risking a fisted farewell as they sped away.

Half a mile ahead of them, Taffy from the caravan site was doing a roadmender's job he liked best:

controlling signals, watching the traffic lights turn from green to amber to red. In his hand he held the reserve notice, the lollipop sign which read GO on one side and STOP on the other. This lollipop was Taffy's reserve staff in case the traffic lights went wonky, as they occasionally did. He twisted his hand signal to STOP and glanced at the traffic lights, and saw with satisfaction that both signals matched. (This was a private game he dallied with on the job.)

Half the roadway – where he stood scratching his backside – was dug up and blocked. But the useful section was now the domain of an articulated lorry bearing down like an armoured tank. The reason for this was the driver was desperate to stop at the next garage and use the lav. So quickly did it race along that Taffy stepped back a few paces.

Billy Bonehead, recklessly forcing his bike along, suddenly saw a signal ahead; so quickly had it appeared that he thought it had been craftily planted there. Normally the obstruction would have bothered Billy not at all he would have driven through it and enjoyed the audacity. But today, death was looming, and looming quickly in the shape of an articulated lorry. And it gave him warning, for the driver blasted his horn, a looming threat. There was nowhere to turn. On Billy's left was the scooped-out road littered with red cones. On his right loomed a high kerb like a cliff edge. Just beyond the kerb stood the front gardens of peaceable houses surrounded by stout railings.

The articulated lorry screamed its existence.

Billy did what any other mastermind would do: he reduced speed, turned about and shot back the way he came. He knew he would have to slither over the zebra crossing again, but he'd worry about that when he got there. Although the lorry blasted him with its horn again, it now lay further behind.

Major Merryweather breathed a sigh of relief and allowed two vehicles either way to cross his territory. The pedestrians he'd ordered to retreat were now commanded to advance.

Then without warning, the roaring motorcycle bore down on them again, this time in the opposite direction and travelling a little slower as he was among the traffic. This was more than the Major could tolerate. The louts on the bike were now the enemy. As they rolled over the crossing, Merryweather raised his lollipop like a spear, pikestaff first. He brought back his arm and threw his weapon at the rear wheel of the bike; as a throw it would have been applauded at the Highland Games. The spokes of the wheel were shattered, the cycle collapsed and the riders fell off, sprawling over the crossing like floppy scarecrows.

Wally was out of his vehicle in a flash. Without a second thought he sat on the driver and pinned him to the road. The schoolkids followed his example and flung themselves on the passenger. There they all sat, with seemingly nowhere to go.

Constable Cole had vacated his vehicle several cars back. He now whipped out his handcuffs and shackled the culprits together.

Wally identified his captives. 'Blimey, these are the same hoodlums who tried to bugger up the dance at the town hall.'

At that point Sergeant Forester arrived. 'Well done, everybody. You'll hear more about this. Constable Cole, you escort one prisoner to your car and cuff him, and I'll take charge of the other.'

When the detainees had been confined, Forester phoned for extra assistance and within a few minutes the crossing was cleared of traffic and Major Merryweather was welcomed into Miriam's car. She pulled away, with the Major as her extra passenger in the rear seat with young Charlie, then he removed his officer's hat and placed it on his knee.

'I heard that Mrs Beesly, the crossing control, was unwell,' said the Vicar, 'and I heard the school had located a replacement but I didn't know it was you, Major.'

'It was all done in a hurry, you know, an emergency, of course.' But he couldn't refrain from adding, 'Still, I'm used to that.'

'Have you supervised a pedestrian crossing before, Major?' Wally asked.

'Oh no. But I've tackled several emergencies.'

En bloc, but silently, his audience hoped his previous predicaments, like his bald head, had a smoother outcome. After a pause, young Charlie suddenly said, 'You heard my last joke, didn't you, Vicar?'

'I hope so,' she said. 'The choir were exchanging jokes in the church because the electricity went off,' she explained.

'Ah, jokes, eh! That's how we kept our spirits up, years ago,' the Major told them.

'You can have a turn if you want, Major,' the youngster said.

'What! Er, well: two old diggers were renewing old acquaintances at the Anzac reunion, when one said, "Was it you or your brother who got killed in New Guinea?"' The Major then chortled away at his own wit. Charlie sat, puzzled, and the Vicar tactfully said, 'Well done, Major.'

Before Charlie could top the Major's effort, Wally said, 'It was a pleasant surprise to learn Septimus, er, recovered.'

'Yes,' the Major responded, 'an unusual business, that. Apparently he'd been severely concussed. I'm dashed surprised Dr Paddy Whatshisname didn't spot that.'

'Was anyone with the Doctor?' Miriam asked.

'Markie, I believe.'

'Say no more,' Wally muttered.

They turned right for the incline to the site, and because several vehicles seemed to be parked, Miriam drove to the top end. Quite a crowd had gathered and many were enjoying a barbecue.

'If this is a wake,' the Vicar said, 'it's the jolliest I've ever seen.'

'Well, there was a power cut,' the Major said, 'as I'm sure you know, and the manager of the Co-op gave the caravaners the produce rather than have it go to waste.'

'It doesn't take long to go off,' Wally confirmed.

They alighted from the car and joined what was obviously a party. Young Charlie spotted some of his school chums and shot off before anyone could stop him. The Major walked down to his caravan to change and Wally bumped into Richard Coningsby.

'Hi, Dick. Sorry I couldn't get back to you on the phone, I'll explain later. This is an odd setup. What's been happening?'

Richard sighed deeply and explained the events earlier in the day. 'When I saw Markie and Doc Do-nothing, this morning, I knew things would go off half cock.'

'You guessed that?' said Wally.

'No, I didn't guess, I expected it. They were...' he almost said pissed, but respecting the Vicar, said, 'three parts sloshed then. Later, when the Prof came round from a severe bump on the head, I hared down to the surgery, but the gallant Doctor had done a bunk. And Markie was out to the world.'

'The Doctor is always sober at the baby clinic,' Miriam said.

'Ah, there are no customers there,' Richard said. 'It's when he gets with like-minded folk he's apt to surrender. Mind you, it's not surprising, he was in the Merchant Navy years ago.'

'Say no more,' Wally said. 'Matelots, like onions, are more congenial when pickled.'

Someone had erected fairy lights, which came on suddenly and a wild cheer went up. A group of merry mourners gathered round the sizzling barbecue and a voice called out, 'Three cheers for Jack Sparrow.'

The Reverend Peach wrinkled her brow. 'Who's Jack Sparrow?'

'The Professor,' said Wally. 'Septimus Jack Sparrow.'

The three of them approached the barbecue and joined in the toast to the resurrected, as some revellers insisted on describing the Prof. Three cheers were proclaimed and a voice called, 'Speech.'

'Tell us what it's like to die,' urged a thoughtless individual.

Fortunately this request was ignored. Miriam nudged Wally and indicated with a nod. He looked up and saw Dave – of Dave and Dreen prominence – walking and abstractedly scribbling in a dog-eared notebook. Wally smiled. 'P'raps he's taking minutes.' Then Dreen herself pushed through the growing crowd.

'Listen, everybody. My husband won't mention this…'

'Ooo, the naughty boy.'

'… but he's pretty talented at scribbling verses, and he's written something for Mr Sparrow.' She pushed him forward and, scanning the words, Dave began to read.

'Here's to Septimus,
Old Jack Sparrow.
He's a man worth knowing,
A real nice fellow.

Earlier today
He dropped down dead,
"He's a goner,"
So the doctor said.

But Sep fooled everyone,
Perhaps for a jest,
He wasn't deaded,
He just wanted a rest.

So raise your glass and drink a toast:
"This special veteran"
Because tonight, we celebrate
A resurrected man.'

Dave's literary contribution was followed by many genuine compliments and the usual cheers. Professor Septimus Jack Sparrow was slapped on the back until he looked exhausted, and was only rescued when the Reverend Miriam Peach went and placed her arm around him. Then a voice called, 'Well done, Dave.' A second voice added, 'The Poet Laureate of Upsy-Daisy.' Someone suggested, 'What we need is some music. Do you like pop music, Sep?'

'No fear,' the old man replied. 'I prefer songs like "Bird Songs at Eventide", and "O for the Wings of a Dove".'

One of the children pricked up his ears. For a few weeks the choir of St Aidan's had been rehearsing, by coincidence, Septimus's favourite song. So, without prompting, young Charlie Wrigley clambered onto a trestle table, and as a pale moon shed its early evening light, Charlie displayed his flute-like voice and sang, 'O for the wings, for the wings of a dove.'

EIGHTEEN

ally pulled the sheets back from his bunk bed to allow fresh air to freshen the clothes. Then he put the kettle on for breakfast. Whilst it boiled he noticed the leaflet on the doormat under the letterbox and picked it up. It proved to be the parish magazine, a free monthly publication advertising tradesmen, church services and a few letters about parochial events. He read the magazine while he ate his breakfast of oatmeal porridge, these days eaten without sugar or honey as he was trying to lose weight.

Then he spotted the item that Miriam had told him to look out for.

'Wanted: gardener handyman. Just a few hours each week are required from a fit person – male or female – to carry out general duties. In lieu of the small remuneration available, free lodgings are offered as a supplement. Apply, the Reverend Miriam Peach, St

Aidan's vicarage.' Wally smiled and continued with his toast and marmalade.

He read most of the remaining items in the magazine, then stopped and turned back to Miriam's ad. Now he remembered she had informed him to respond to it.

'I'm sure she did,' he told himself. 'I wonder why?' He read again: free lodgings. 'That's it. The crafty Clara. Blimey, she fancies me!' And he laughed out loud. 'I'll go today. Saturday is not usually busy.'

He spruced himself up, cleaned his teeth and cocked a leg over his bike. It was ten o'clock. 'I'll probably get morning coffee.' And he grinned. Twenty minutes later, as he passed the church door, he heard the choir rehearsing, and he noticed a tarpaulin covering something; then he knocked on the vicarage door.

Miriam was still in her dressing gown and wearing glasses when she answered his knock.

'Hello, love,' he said. 'Are you getting up or going to bed?'

'You cheeky monkey, I'll have you know I've been working, writing letters since seven o'clock. Anyway, come in, you're making the place look untidy.' She held the door slightly wider.

As he stepped through he said, 'I'll make a guess that your tiles have been returned.'

'They have indeed. Not a word of an apology, though.'

'No. You won't get one from a gobbin like that. But one has to sympathise. I shouldn't think many

302

folk have Bob Dyke's family problems. But I've come to solve one of yours.'

'Really? You're too kind you are, Wally Watson. So, to what do I owe this privilege?'

She removed her glasses and gave him a quizzical look, but feigned innocence.

He removed his woolly hat. 'I've called about that handyman's job, miss.'

'Have you now. I'll bet the print on the advert's not dry yet.'

'And, of course, yon room that's available.'

'I've not seen your woollen hat before.'

'Aye, well I needed summat to keep me lugholes warm when I'm cycling. Look.' He showed her the tab at the back. 'As you can see it says St David's, Wales. I once had a cycling holiday in Milford Haven and went to see that small cathedral. That's where I bought it.'

'So, you've come to view yon room,' she mimicked. 'You're sure you've not called for a coffee?'

'If you could spare a saucerful for a lonely traveller, that would be great.'

He stood further into the hall and as she closed the door she said, 'Well, as you know from the announcement in the parish magazine, I can't afford much in the way of legal or indeed illegal tender, that's why free lodgings is offered.'

'Fair enough, miss. Can I inspect the room?'

'Inspect! You're not an army officer now, you know.'

'I never was. One rainy day I did rise to the rank of corporal.'

'Right, inspection takes place upstairs, and no funny business. You don't need to remove your boots, but wiping them on the mat would help. Although I've not hoovered yet.'

'So I see.'

Wally followed her. He had been upstairs before to do minor jobs. It was a large room facing east and contained 1930s furniture: a single bed, in dark red mahogany veneer; a double wardrobe; and a tallboy.

'Blimey, this furniture is like my grandma's. It's certainly solid enough.'

The furniture was placed near the window. Nearer the opposite wall stood a leather settee, a table and two dining chairs. A beige carpet covered the floor.

'It looks very cosy,' he said.

'It's better with the light on,' she said, and depressed the switch. The room became suddenly golden like an old-style movie.

A knock sounded at the door and she made her way downstairs. 'I know who that will be.' She chuckled to herself. 'He's called for his money.' She opened the door and Wally heard her say, 'Hello, Charlie. Have you come for your money?'

'Not yet, miss. I've not quite finished. I've another twenty minutes to do. So will you tell me when my time is up?'

'I will, Charlie,' and she closed the door again. Wally had now come down. 'He came a little earlier to do a gardening job, before choir practice, and he's now finishing off. Obviously when I've installed my handyman, I won't need to hire casual labour.'

Wally stood in the hallway, not sure where to go or what to say next.

Miriam glanced at her watch. 'I will guess that you're ready for a coffee?'

'You are a prize winner and have guessed correctly.'

She went into the kitchen and dealt with the coffee maker. 'I've got some fresh scones if you fancy one,' she called.

'Wow. Yeah. I fancy all kinds of things in my prospective lodging house.'

She returned to the living room. 'Well, take the weight off your bunions, lodger.'

'So, I've got the job then, and the room, of course?'

'Well, no other dodger has applied to be lodger, so I would say the benefit is all yours. So long as your union doesn't start hinting about minimum wage and all that guff.'

'They wouldn't dare,' he said. 'By the way, the choir don't usually rehearse on Saturday, do they?'

'No,' she said. 'But because of the power cut the other day, they need to complete their music for a wedding they're performing at this afternoon.'

'Young Charlie made a good impression with his song the other day,' he said.

And as the name conjured up the person, a knock came to the door and Miriam answered.

'I've finished now, miss. Can I have a drink of water, please?'

'Certainly, Charlie. Come in. Wipe your feet. Would you prefer a glass of milk?'

'Oh, cool, miss. Cool. I'll have milk.'

'I see that ginger tom cat was helping you in the garden, Charlie.'

'Yeah. It was chasing leaves.'

'Do you like cats?' she asked.

'They're OK. But elephants are my favourite animal. What's your favourite animal, Wally?'

'A unicorn.'

'Oh, cool. I've never seen one.'

'Ah, that's because they only come out at night when a bloke is sloshed.'

She placed two mugs of coffee, a large tumbler of milk and three buttered scones, on plates, on the oak table. 'He's teasing you, Charlie… Now, let's see, you want exactly £2 from me as well.'

'Aye, er, yes please, miss.' Charlie sat at the table and took a long, noisy drink of the milk.

'£2, eh, Charlie? What are you going to do with that?' asked Wally.

'I'm saving up for summat.'

'Good lad. Well, you've earned two quid quite easily,' Wally commented.

Charlie took another gulp at his milk. 'Not as much as Harry Prescott gets.'

'How much does he get?' the Vicar enquired.

'He gets five quid. And all he has to do is hold two candles for Mr Grimshaw.'

The adults glanced at each other and both seemed perplexed.

'Are these candles lit?' asked Wally. 'Y' know, do they have flames on?'

'Oh aye. All he has to do is hold 'em and look at a picture.'

'Sounds a bit odd,' she said.

'Are you sure you've got the facts right?' Wally added.

'Oh aye. Only Harry says it's secret. So don't say owt, will you?'

All three were quiet for a while, the adults wondering where this was leading and Charlie wondering if he dare ask for another glass of milk. Miriam poured another coffee for her new handyman and one for herself. Then she poised the milk jug over Charlie's glass.

'Where does this, er, candle-holding job happen, Charlie?' To encourage him to answer, she poured another glass of milk.

Charlie sat thinking for a few seconds, then said, 'I've gor it now. It's called The Sanctuary.'

On hearing this, alarm briefly showed in her face.

'I think I'd best ger off now,' said Charlie. 'I have to get changed for the concert. Hey, I'll get paid for that, too.' Off he went and banged the door behind him.

When Charlie had gone, Wally said, 'What's up?' Miriam shrugged. 'Come on,' he insisted, 'I can see it in your face.'

Very slowly, she replied, 'Young Charlie's pal Harry Prescott is paid £5 for holding two candles for Mr Grimshaw.'

'He holds candles and looks at a picture,' Wally amended.

'Well, Grimshaw is the Pastor of The Sanctuary church.'

Wally nodded. 'Aye. I heard him say that. Well…'

She interrupted. 'On that day you did some emergency teaching for the school, I called in at the Co-op. This Grimshaw character was filling his shopping bag with candles.'

'Right. P'raps a bit unusual,' Wally said. 'But maybe Grimshaw is stocking up in case we have a power cut. We had one recently, remember. Or he's going to save on electricity bills.'

'Perhaps he is, perhaps he isn't,' she said. 'But I have a funny feeling about this, and don't know what to do.'

'And you're looking at me for inspiration.' He grinned, and his craggy features beamed and lit up a face which had encouraged many people to trust him. 'Well, at this point, I don't know what to do, either, but I'll think about it.'

His hands lay slack across the table. She closed her fingers round them.

'You're a gem,' she said. 'Meanwhile I'll make some more coffee,' and she rose from the table.

Wally looked round the room which was soon to become his home. He'd been here many times before but had never regarded it as permanent. It was a large room, suitable for the meetings needed, or at least arranged, for a member of the clergy. A large picture rail traversed the room and was hung with pictures of a previous era – *Stag at Bay* being one painting he recognised. There were also photographs of dignitaries whom Miriam didn't even know. The furniture was good, solid timber, much of it made by the Mouse Man, late of Yorkshire.

She returned with two steaming mugs of coffee and a packet of ginger biscuits.

'There we are,' she said, 'help yourself.' He did as instructed. 'What will you do with your caravan,' she asked, 'when you're holed up here?'

'I'll get Mrs Marks to rent it out for me. She does that for other folk now and then, provided she gets a cut.'

Miriam drank most of her coffee, then chanced a question she'd been reluctant to approach. 'I seem to recollect you mentioning you had a girlfriend once. What happened?'

'She died,' he said, focusing on the milk jug. 'We started to go out while still at school, when we were in the final year. Then when we were both eighteen, she contracted something called Berry's Aneurysm. A blood vessel split in her brain.'

'She seems very young for something like that.'

'It can happen at any age. She'd been having headaches for ages, on and off. Then she developed pains in other parts of her body. Her family sent for an ambulance, but she became unconscious during the journey and didn't make it to the hospital.'

'Oh. Wally, I'm so sorry.'

'I felt quite lonely after that and that's how I joined the army, basically. It seems a lifetime away now.'

They sat quietly munching biscuits; neither had anything to say. Then the grandfather clock in the hall struck two, and Wally decided it was time to return to the caravan site.

NINETEEN

'I hear you are leaving us, Wally,' Richard said.

'Aye. I shall leave my van here, though, and rent it out.'

Josephine came from their van and tipped rubbish into the dustbin. 'Hello, Wally. Keeping well?'

'Not too bad, Jose.'

She went back inside and returned with the ironing board and iron on a long flex and began to iron a shirt for Richard.

For want of something to say, Wally said, 'Do you like ironing, Jose?'

'No. Not even with tomato sauce.'

He smiled and trusted he understood.

'It's hot in the van,' Richard said. 'So I fastened an extension to the cable.' Then he added, 'Wally is leaving us.'

She straightened up in surprise. 'Really? I thought you were a fixture here. Have you got a house then?'

'Well, a flat. But it's a step nearer to bricks and mortar,' he said.

'That's what we are waiting for,' she said.

'Ah! On an agency list, are you?'

Richard released a deep sigh. 'Josephine! It's supposed to be confidential,' he said with the slightest reprimand in his voice.

'Ah, wheels within wheels,' Wally said, recognising a faux pas.

Husband and wife looked at each other, both waiting for their spouse to speak.

'Well, come on then,' Wally urged. 'Surely it can't be a state secret.'

Richard looked about him as though he might be heard. 'It's the housing manager from the council.'

'You mean Grimshaw?' Wally asked.

Josephine nodded, still ironing. 'He said he would try and get us further up the queue,' she said casually, finishing off the disclosure.

Wally tapped his nose. 'Say no more. If you have influential friends, use 'em! That's what I say.' And he walked on towards his own caravan.

Immediately he was inside his caravan, Wally began to prepare lunch and sliced some bread. All the while he thought about the revelation he and Miriam learned from young Charlie; the intimation that Charlie's school pal, Harry Prescott, was paid £5 for holding two candles for Grimshaw. It irked him.

'Summat odd there,' Wally told himself. 'I don't like it.'

He boiled a hard egg and a soft egg, made a pot of tea (not long ago he would have dropped a tea bag into a mug), buttered the bread and sat down to his lunch. He thought about Grimshaw who was now chief housing officer for the council, and therefore a man with influence. Wally wondered how he could make arrangements to talk to him.

Huh, the bugger won't remember me, not now he's been promoted.

But, he thought, *will talking achieve anything?* He suddenly decided against it. Instead: *I'll visit the Prescotts, and tread carefully.* He wasn't sure what he'd say, nevertheless, he'd go there. He glanced at his watch.

'One o'clock,' he murmured. The Co-op would still be open. Without more ado, he slipped into his cycling jacket, pulled on his bike clips, then his balaclava – he still didn't wear a helmet – clambered onto his machine and pedalled away. He was in the Co-op within fifteen minutes.

'Hello, Bill.'

'Ah! Wally. We don't see you often.'

'You will when I move to my new address.' He didn't wait for questions but carried on. 'I thought I would get a tin of pink salmon, y' know, just to have in.'

Big Bill, the Co-op manager, and B-flat bass player for Daisy Hill Brass Band, quickly located the commodity and placed it on the counter. 'Anything else, Wally?'

'I'll take a jar of fish sauce.'

'Not for this tinned salmon, surely?'

'No, no, just to have in.'

Bill strode over to the far counter again, where fish and fresh meats were served. As he came back, Wally asked, 'Are you on your own today, Bill?'

'Just for an hour. The girls, the triplets as I call 'em, have collectively gone to a dress shop. But Mavis has retired, or at least taken maternity leave. She's expecting a child, you know. They get paid for that these days. It's called benefits!' He snorted the word as though it was distasteful. 'They didn't have it when we were younger, but we managed.'

'Wasn't she involved with that young cornet player in the band, er…?'

'Norman. Aye,' Bill said. 'He's shot off too. Some sort of teaching job. But the child, it's not his, it's her late husband's. He died suddenly.'

'So you have a vacancy?' Wally asked.

'Yes. And it's a steady job. Well, owt else you need?'

'If you sell wine gums, I'll take half a pound. Put 'em in a strong bag, Bill.'

Next, he paid, then made as if to go. He stopped, mid-stride. 'Do you by any chance know where the Prescotts live? They have a lad called Harry.'

Bill flipped through an old-fashioned ledger. 'Here we are. They used to call their row of houses Boggart Row. Y' know, ghosts. Officially, it's Number 4, The Green, Down Daisy.'

Wally scribbled it down, bid good day and pedalled off. He was still uncertain about what he was going to say. It depended on whether young Harry was at home or not. He knocked and the door was answered by a young teenager.

'Hello,' Wally said. 'You must be Lily.'

She smiled and preened. She had good teeth, complemented by ruby lipstick. Her nascent breasts thrust against her fawn pullover like ripe pears. 'How do you know who I am?' She frowned very slightly. The crease in her brow made her look desirably older.

'I had the pleasure, or perhaps the pain, of teaching young Harry's class in an emergency, and your name came up.'

'My name!' Now slight concern was shown.

'Yes. If I remember rightly, Harry had his ninth birthday the day before. You put his sandwiches up and included a bar of chocolate. He was delighted about that.'

'Oh yes,' she said. 'I remember now. You must have a good memory.'

Wally smiled. There was a time he would have got off with her. 'Well, just average, I suppose. It's Harry I've come to see, actually.'

There was a loud cough then a stern female voice called, 'Who is it?'

'A man for our Harry.'

'Well, ask him in.'

Lily opened the door wider and Wally stepped immediately into a small living room. It was an older-style house without a hall or passageway. His first impression was like stepping into a second-hand shop.

Mrs Prescott was seated on a chair which provided the best view of the television.

'Hiya,' she said, squinting through cigarette smoke. 'I know you, don't I?'

'Very likely. I work for the council, trimming trees, sawing branches and so forth. Lots of folk pass the time of day.'

'Sit on the couch,' she commanded, but not severely. 'What can we do you for?' She expertly blew a plume of curly smoke across the table.

'It's Harry I've called to see.'

'Our Harry? He's not in. He's off playing football on t' rec. He goes every Saturday.'

Wally's gaze wandered round the room. The mantelpiece was cluttered with debris: a clock which had stopped, two off-white ornaments of female ballet dancers, a syrup tin marked 'Meter Money' and several dated cards, Christmas and birthday. On the wall above the clock flew three ornamental ducks. The whole of this area was sprinkled with dust as though a pepper pot had been shaken over it.

'These older houses have lots of charm,' he said.

'Lots of charm but no bath,' Lily said.

'We're supposed to be getting better lodgings,' Mrs Prescott added.

'They're not lodgings, mam. It's a proper council house.'

'Yeah! A bath and central heating – everything.'

'You've been on the council waiting list, have you?' Wally asked, artfully.

'Waiting list!' she echoed. 'I think we *are* the flamin' waiting list. That chap up at little chapel is supposed to be helping us.'

'Little chapel?' he queried, although he knew by now.

'She means The Sanctuary,' Lily explained.

A notion now lodged itself in Wally's mind. 'Oh yes. That's Mr Grimshaw, isn't it?'

'He likes to be called Pastor,' Lily explained.

'You attend there, do you?'

'We've just started,' said Mrs Prescott, wedging a new woodbine between her dry lips. 'But we tried to move for years. This was Dad's house. He tried. If my Dad was alive today, he'd be turning in his grave.'

Wally stood. 'Well, I'd best be going.' It struck him as odd that he hadn't been asked about his business with nine-year-old Harry. 'It's been nice meeting you.'

Mrs Prescott's farewell was a plume of tobacco smoke.

Wally pedalled towards the recreation ground where a game of junior football was being played. He laid his bike on the ground and watched the youngsters playing football. He spotted Harry straight away. In fact he recognised two or three kids he had taught that day on the caravan site.

Wally stood on the edge of the touchline admiring the expertise of these young players. They all appeared to be under ten years old, and Harry was one of the smallest but by no means the most timid. He jumped for the ball to head it even when it seemed out of reach; he hooked in a creditable corner kick, tackled courageously and ran rings round players much bigger than himself. Half time arrived and the players hung round drinking orange juice. Wally approached his prospect.

'Hiya, Harry. I see you're having a good game.'

'Oh! Hello, Mr Watson. Have you come to watch us?'

'Yeah, of course, you in particular.'

Some of the players trooped off to visit the loos. Harry watched them, obviously intending to follow suit.

'I'd like a quick word with you after the match, Harry.'

'After the match?' he echoed. 'I can't. I've got to go somewhere.'

'OK. I'll see you after you've been there.'

Slight anxiety crossed the youngster's face. 'Don't do that. It's, er, not allowed. Nobody can, er, enter the chapel on Saturday.'

'Oh, right. Who makes these rules, Harry?'

The youngster began to walk away. Over his shoulder he said, 'God.'

Wally had learned all he needed to know. Now he needed to see what occurred.

'All this for five quid,' he muttered.

He pushed his bike towards his destination, which lay at the top of the rise, still unsure of what to say. A hundred yards from The Sanctuary stood a coppice, which Wally had had to pollard two or three times. He went inside and leant his bike on a willow sapling to wait for Harry to appear. But before that occurred, the principal player himself arrived in his Vauxhall car. He drove into the chapel grounds and parked on the limited area. Grimshaw left his vehicle and let himself into The Sanctuary. Wally pulled his balaclava down his face and followed, unconcerned. He pushed his bike into the bushes surrounding the premises and stood pondering his next move. He turned round casually and saw a small boy approaching.

'Harry!' he breathed.

He elbowed his way into the bushes and waited, for what, he wasn't sure. The youngster walked up the path, knocked on the side door that Grimshaw had used, and was admitted.

Wally followed, tried the handle. Locked. He edged round the side of the chapel, using the hedges as a screen from the road. The hedges went round the back. Using his gloved hands, Wally thrust his way through and found himself at the rear wall of the building; eight feet high, in the wall, was a window. *How can I get through it?* he thought.

'The bike!'

He pushed his vehicle under the window. From his cycle carrier bag he extracted his comprehensive tool kit and took out the boy scout's friend: a multi-bladed knife. Although it lacked the implement for removing stones from horse's hooves, it held a glass cutter. Climbing onto the bike's crossbar, he stood, to be level with the window. The first cut he made was a vertical straight down the centre of the glass. Next he cut a horizontal at the top and one at the bottom. Ideally he needed a suction pad as used on car windscreens; failing this, with firm gloved fingers, he pressed the right-hand side at the top and near the bottom simultaneously. The window creaked, as though on a hinge, and skewed inward half an inch down the sides and split down the centre of the first cut also half an inch. He wriggled the right side of the glass out, and dropped it on the grass. It dropped on its edge and stuck into the grass like a crude sword. Now holding the left-hand piece of glass he wriggled it from the window ledge with a grating sound. This piece he threw further away. Next, he pulled on his balaclava, virtually covering his face.

Removing his leather jacket he draped it over the lower sill, and, arching his back, he slithered through the window, as he had done as a late-night teenager at home. He was now inside a toilet. He put his jacket on again. A door opposite was fractionally open. He crept up to it and was aghast at what he saw.

Young Harry Prescott stood stock still before a painting of naked angels and cherubs. Harry's bottom was also naked, his trousers round his ankles. He stood staring at the painting and holding a long candle in either hand. To Wally's left was a screen over which Grimshaw's ugly head could be seen. The jerking movements he made were indicative of a person masturbating.

Wally felt physically sick.

Almost without thinking, he barged through the door and shouted, 'What the hell do you think you're doing? You dirty bastard.'

Young Harry swivelled round and dropped his candles. Impulsively Wally stamped on them, extinguishing the flames. Grimshaw stepped back from the screen and adjusted his clothing.

'You could be prosecuted for this,' Wally bellowed. 'You,' he yelled at Harry. 'Get some clothes on.' He strode towards the screen. Grimshaw backed away. 'I ought to belt you one,' Wally shouted, his face concealed behind the balaclava.

'This is a private building,' Grimshaw bleated.

'Aye. And we can all see why.' He turned to Harry. 'Has he given you your £5?'

The boy nodded nervously. 'Give it to me,' Wally commanded. The boy did as he was bid.

'Now go straight home.' In a quieter voice he added, 'Say nothing to anyone and leave the rest to me.'

The boy trudged off, sobbing.

Wally swivelled. 'You, you cringing cunt, you can expect to hear more about this.' And with that he left the building. He had to leave otherwise he would have mutilated the pervert.

TWENTY

Wally had experienced most of the shocks that occur during a soldier's active service, but the behaviour he had just witnessed made him feel quite disgusted. Grimshaw was practising criminality on a grievous scale. He was obviously providing council houses for members of The Sanctuary and he was acting immorally towards the younger members of his congregation.

'I'll bet Harry Prescott's not his only prey.'

As he pedalled he racked his brains for what could be done.

'I could go to the cops, but Grimshaw would initially deny everything.'

Then he would have to rake in young Harry, who might also deny what happened – initially.

'It has to be summat tangible… but what?'

As he pedalled his way back to the site, he mulled over the events. He also thought of the broken window and the forced entry. He was in a situation where he could find himself in custody. By the same token, he could not ignore what he'd seen. Could he inform somebody? Involve somebody? Miriam was the first person he thought of.

'But I can't tell her about Grimshaw's wanking. I mean, God, she's a vicar.'

He knew she'd been an active soldier, mixing with the rough and the smooth, but not necessarily the vermin.

'Bloody hell. What a setup.'

He arrived at the crossroads, turned right for a few yards then left, to cycle slowly up the incline to the caravan site. The first thing he needed was a shower to swill away the depraved behaviour he'd witnessed, then a change of clothing to make him feel civilised.

Under the shower it came to him what had to be done. Grimshaw had to be marked, blemished permanently. Not branded, as such. Not tattooed.

'I can't bloody well do that. But…'

He knew what could be done. He'd seen it. Years ago. He smiled at the recollection. Initially, it would have to wait until Monday. Meanwhile, he needed, not so much advice, as bolstering, or in army jargon: reinforcements.

'I need a whatchermacallit… somebody who's canny. A wise individual who'll keep his gob shut.' He thought of all the locals but mentally crossed them off his list. Then slowly, it dawned. 'Miriam! I mean, she knows half the story, as trotted out by young Charlie. I'll phone first.' He searched for his mobile. 'It's me.

I've something to tell you and I need your advice. Are you in the middle of tomorrow's sermon? No? So I can come round? Thanks. I'll see you shortly.'

He had a snack then cleaned his teeth; he always felt more confident when his molars were brushed. Once again he mounted his bike and set off. He wasn't sure how much to tell her and he wasn't sure how much she would censure, but at least she wouldn't blab.

Miriam had the kettle on and some cakes on the table and her completed sermon pushed to one side. 'I suppose you've had your tea?'

'Course, but I didn't pack away any cake, 'cos I hadn't any.'

'Then you'd better scoff one of these, it'll help you with your sermon. Cakes always help me with mine.'

He did as suggested then he began his tale.

'You will recall what young Charlie told us about his pal Harry earning five quid by holding candles?' She nodded. 'Well, I visited the Prescotts today and learned a bit more. They've also been offered a council house, conditional on attending The Sanctuary.'

'Blimey.' (He'd never heard her say that before.) 'The rest of us can't compete with that.'

He then related the rest of the story. During the narrative they drank three cups of tea. Then he came to the nervous bit.

'I peered through the door, saw Julius Grimshaw behind a screen, he was actually trembling, as he...' Wally stopped searching for something refined. He didn't know many refined words. He told about the lad displaying his bum. He'd mentioned the picture of the cherubs and the naked angels. 'There he was…'

'Having a wank,' she said matter-of-factly.

Wally stopped. His jaw dropped.

'I suggest you keep your mouth closed, there's a fly in here. Well, I spent part of my life surrounded by men. Men with all kinds of proclivities.'

'You what?'

'Funny habits.' She smiled. 'Don't let it bother you.'

Slowly, he recovered. 'So, what happens next? What do I do?'

'Well, as Edmund Burke said: "For evil to flourish, it's only necessary for good men to do nothing." You've proved yourself to be a good man, Wally, apart from the breaking and entering, so I'm sure you have other ideas up your sleeve.'

'I once saw a dodge, years ago, that gives a lout a constant reminder to, er, watch his p's and q's. But in his case I've got to get him on his own.'

'Now steady on, Wally. It doesn't involve violence, does it?'

'No. I promise you he'll not get hurt, well, not physically. And he'll be reminded of his shortcomings for the rest of his days, I reckon.'

He then remained quiet; even when Miriam urged him to elucidate, he wouldn't. Now he added, 'Y' see, we cannot allow young Prescott's, er, boo-boo to leak out, he did it for the money. If it became common knowledge, it'd damage the rest of his life. As he grew, locals would jeer at him. But at the same time, the twat – sorry – who caused the grief musn't be allowed to scarper scot-free.'

'You say you've got to get him on his own.'

On the far corner of the table was a pile of leaflets; she leant over and took the top one. 'It so happens I'm inviting a group of people to a meeting. I could invite Julius Grimshaw. If towards the end of the meeting you found yourself within the vicinity of the Pastor, you could carry out your, er, shrewd plan... which I don't really wish to know about.'

Wally read the leaflet. 'Oh, learning new hymns.' He shrugged. 'I'm not sure he'll attend a meeting about that.'

'You are underestimating my letter writing. I'll alter one leaflet for his benefit only.'

Wally laughed. 'You're more devious than I am.'

'Well, we'll try it. If he attends, you've got your man. If he doesn't, you'll have to drum up something else.'

'OK. I'll go along with that.'

'I'll have to rewrite his invite now. I need to get these leaflets in the post by Monday.'

'OK, I'll buzz off then.'

On his way out she surprised him again by once more kissing his cheek.

On his way home, Wally thought about the lout who was dealt rough justice years ago.

In Walter's village lived a bully. He was known as Pete, his name, Peter Eaton; behind his back he was referred to as Pey Hey. At thirteen he was as big as a house, rather ugly, and because of his youth, his tormenting was sometimes seen as rough and tumble. Wally himself had been on the wrong end of a few smacks. If these assaults – for that is what they were – caught the large ears of Pete's parents, they – bigger than a row of houses – would, brawny cheek by jumbo jowl, drub the noggin of their thick-headed thug like two timpani players in a panto.

Not surprisingly, Pete believed this was the way to solve problems. And God help the next kid who stepped out of line.

Most of the village lads were boy scouts. By the age of seventeen, Pete was an explorer scout, in charge of others. His bullying got worse. The scoutmaster lectured him, but Pete was twice his size. One day Pete beat up Lenny, half his size. The lad ran home to tell his dad, who was also diminutive. The incident was mentioned to Wally's dad, and, along with others, they decided to act. Because Pete, now a teenage ogre, could clobber adults as well as fledglings, a quartet was enlisted: three to hold him down, one to do the deed. To preserve anonymity they wore balaclavas – back to front, with cut-out eye sockets. The scout hut was being creosoted, and a plan was hatched. Lenny was sent to summon Pete round the back of the hut.

In the past, villagers had appealed to Pete's parents to instil some chivalry into their defiant offspring, but they'd interpreted this as 'knock some sense into him'. And he, of course, had then knocked sense into others. The thought was, perhaps the tables should be turned on Bully Boy, then the Eatons, en masse, would learn there's more than one way to shear a sheep.

When Pete appeared round the back of the scout hut, he was pounced upon by four avenging paterfamilias. He was held down by wrestling holds; it was rough justice, of the kind often dished out in the craggy acres between Lancashire and Yorkshire – minus the red and white roses. Pete's scouting shorts were snatched off and his private parts doused with creosote which takes years to fade. As the creosote was applied, the painter intoned, 'A boy scout is trusty, loyal, helpful, friendly, courteous, kind, obedient, cheerful, thrifty, brave, clean, reverent. He is not a bully – you bloody gobbin.'

Another of the quartet said, 'This is called "an eye for an eye".'

Yet another said, 'Next time you smack a little 'un, recall what's happening to you.'

Pete never bullied anyone else.

❦

As Wally pedalled, reflecting the incident he had been aware of for years, and having known the individual concerned, he told himself, 'That's what I'll do to Pastor Grimshaw.'

TWENTY-ONE

J ulius Grimshaw picked up the letters from behind
the side door of The Sanctuary. The fact that letters
were delivered to his little chapel gave him great
satisfaction. It meant they were on the map. And the
fact that some letters were addressed personally to
The Pastor made him feel he'd been awarded a gold
medal. There were four letters: two begging letters
from – supposedly – established charities, another an
electricity bill and the third addressed to Mr Julius
Grimshaw, Pastor, The Sanctuary, Down Daisy. He
opened it carefully.

'Dear Pastor Grimshaw,

I know how keen you are to present the best and
most suitable music during your popular Sunday
services. So I thought you might be interested in
hearing new religious music written and composed
specifically to encourage your church members to
attend regularly. The business of motivating members

is, of course, a constant issue for religious leaders –
although I know you have better success than most of
us – so joining in to sing inspirational music must be
a buoyant venture for all congregations, particularly
younger members.

To this end, a forum has been arranged on Monday
the 14th instant. The new hymns will be accompanied
by the Daisy Hill Brass Band in their rehearsal rooms
at the Diving Duck tavern at 8pm.

An audience will also be in attendance to test
the singability of these new hymns. Complimentary
refreshments will also be provided. I look forward to
your eminent attendance.

Yours sincerely,

The Reverend Miriam Peach'

Julius read the letter a second time and decided
he ought to attend. He liked the way he had been
referred to in the letter. And though he would
never acknowledge it, his ego had been flattered;
and if the hymns were not to his liking, he could
always leave.

The incident he had experienced a few days ago
seemed to be fading. Nobody had come forward to
complain, so perhaps the boy had kept the occurrence
to himself; the lad couldn't really broadcast it. Julius
realised that to continue his inclination, a different
approach would be needed.

Miriam had been involved in organising this festival of new hymns for several weeks. Her final task had been to invite an audience, yet she didn't want a congregation, which would cause the event to seem too pious. In fact, many of these published hymns were hardly religious at all; these she would avoid.

The first person she had contacted was Father Byrne, the local Roman Catholic priest, a jolly man she often encountered in the Diving Duck. When he learned of the sing-along, he suggested she wrote to the choirmaster of his church, inviting this conductor along with his choir. This gave the Reverend Peach an idea, and she wrote to the choir trainer of the Methodist chapel too, and the Salvation Army, and concluded with some forty choir members of differing standards.

Quite casually she mentioned her project to the manager of the local Co-op, who was, of course, a mainstay of Daisy Hill Brass Band. Without troubling Miriam, he contacted the publishers and managed to hire the band accompaniments, and when he told her, she was obviously delighted, and knew now that the event was going to be successful.

TWENTY-TWO

arry, Lily and Mrs Prescott were trying to fly Harry's kite. They were keen but the wind wasn't keen enough. They'd launched it several times and young Pressy was getting tired and out of puff, tossing the framed dragon then running back and forth across the sheep-nibbled field to collect it; meanwhile, the canvas creature refused to co-operate and became tatty with failure.

'You'll have to chuck it higher,' Lily said, as her young brother came panting and puffing up to her yet again.

'I need a rest,' he gasped. 'Can't you chuck it up?'

'Me! I'll stretch my new jumper if I do that.' Then as her indoors, now out of doors, waddled up, Lily added, 'Do you fancy a go, Ma?'

Mrs Prescott sauntered towards her brood, lighting up the day's fourth fag. 'I'll have a go. When your dad comes back from t' pub, he might do some chucking.'

She took the kite from Harry as Lily wound the ball of string into a smaller sphere. As the trio fumbled, exchanging tasks, gunshots were heard in the distance.

'Somebody's shooting pigeons in yon Daisy Wood,' Mrs Prescott remarked.

'I hope they don't come any closer,' Lily declared.

'They're not allowed,' Harry stated with authority.

Mam took charge of the kite and examined it close up. 'Hey, it's a big 'un. Bigger 'n I thought. I mean, it should fly when t' wind gets under t' dragon's wings.'

'There's not enough wind, though,' Lily said, checking her new jumper. 'That's the problem.'

'Well, I'll do what I can,' said Ma, holding the kite aloft and walking away. As she sauntered she called, 'Gi' us more string, Lily, before I chuck this beast up.'

The marksman picked up the pigeon. It was neatly shot through its head with several pellets.

'Well, I've broke me duck,' said Julius Grimshaw. He smiled with surly satisfaction, displaying brown, chipped teeth. 'But I need another. A brace is more professional.'

He walked on and came to the edge of the wood to trudge towards the other arboreous section where he believed the fleeing pigeons had taken refuge. This modest knowledge gave Julius exaggerated pleasure. To reach the ancillary area of Daisy Hill Wood he must cross Five Acre Field, at the far end of which were a group of kite flyers.

'Huh, not enough wind for kite flying,' he muttered to himself, and accompanied his erudition by randomly rolling his weird-looking eye. Then, as all experienced marksmen do, he breached his shotgun, allowing the barrel to loll. To enter the far section of the wood, he had to pass close to the kite flyers, who had temporarily halted their amusement. As he trudged he heard one of them call out, 'Oh, look, it's Pastor Grimshaw.' And they moved towards him.

Julius recognised them. 'Dear God, it's that lad.' And he immediately began to double back the way he had come.

◈

'Let's speak to him,' said Mrs Prescott. 'We'll thank him for getting us the council house.' And she began to hurry towards their benefactor. 'Come on, Harry. Hurry up.'

The boy stood stock till. 'I'm staying here.' He remained rigid as though he'd taken root.

'Steady on,' Lily chided. 'This string has come untangled.' And by the time they had organised themselves, their peculiar patron had disappeared.

'This is useless,' Mrs Prescott exclaimed, 'and it's getting to teatime, so we'll go home.' Seeing apparent relief turn to presumed disappointment on the boy's face, she added, 'We'll come again when there's a bit more wind.'

They trudged across the field and climbed over the stile bringing them out on the main road.

'It's funny Pastor Grimshaw running off like that,' said Lily. 'I'm sure he saw us.'

'There's nowt so queer as folk,' said her mother.

Young Harry remained unusually quiet.

'Still,' said Ma Prescott, mumbling as she lit another fag, 'I don't care which way t' cat jumps, we flit into our new house next week.'

'Which cat is that?' Harry enquired.

'Any cat,' Lily scolded. 'It's just a whatsit – a saying.'

They walked along the lane towards home, Lily humming the latest pop craze, Mrs P chuffing on her fag and Harry kicking an empty can. In this manner they arrived at the small telephone exchange surrounded and stifled by mature trees and saplings. Placed in a semi-circle on the pavement were six roadside warnings and standing on a tall ladder was a workman trimming the overhanging trees. The Prescotts looked up. The workman looked down.

'Tread carefully,' Wally called.

'Oh, I've remembered your name,' Mrs Prescott replied. 'Still at it, Mr Watson?'

'Aye. No rest for the wicked. Been flying a kite, have you?'

'We tried,' Lily said. 'But there's not enough wind today.'

'What do you reckon,' said Mrs P, 'we're gerrin' a council house next week?'

Wally switched off his strimmer and stepped down from the ladder. 'Wow. That's great. Attending that little chapel paid off then.'

'But we haven't been often,' said Ma Prescott. 'That's the funny side of things.'

Young Harry simply stood there, hanging his head.

'I've just seen Mr Grimshaw drive past in his car,' Wally told them.

'He was shooting in the woods,' Lily explained.

'We tried to thank him for helping us,' said Mrs Prescott. 'But he ran off when he saw us.'

'Ah! He'd need to get home and pluck his pigeons,' Wally said with a sly glance at the boy, who had given no sign of recognition, as today, Wally wore his hard hat rather than his balaclava.

'You can call in for a cuppa any time you want,' Mrs Prescott told him.

As they walked away, Wally heard the boy say, 'Did me dad fly a kite when he was younger?'

'I expect so,' said his mother. 'As he got older he certainly had plenty of wind.'

As he climbed his ladder again, Wally thought, *That bloody Pastor ran off because he was embarrassed. The dirty bastard.*

※

The Reverend Miriam Peach ran her eye over the administration she had organised for the singing of the new hymns, scattered about her desk. Her eye rested on the excerpt she had extracted from her proposed address. It was discernible by a red cross to indicate its urgency. She was still uncertain whether to include it in her short speech or leave it out.

At that point the door knocker banged, a key wriggled in the lock, the door opened and Wally walked in. As a future lodger it was also his privilege to be a key holder. When he entered she walked across and pecked him on the cheek, a greeting that Wally now expected. It made him feel he had come up in the world.

He indicated the desk with a sweep of his arm. 'I can see you've been busy. Have all the singers you contacted agreed to attend?'

'Yes, every single one.'

'Great. At least it's not going to be karaoke.'

She smiled. 'Among the audience there'll be about forty experienced choristers, so it should be successful on that level.'

'Excellent. Is there anything you're *ever* unsure about?' It was said kindly with only the slightest hint of sarcasm.

'Yes. This!' She held up the extract. 'I don't know whether to include it in my concluding address.'

'Your concluding address!' He slit his throat with an index finger. 'Oh no!' He appealed to an imaginary crowd. 'She's going to preach to us.'

'No, I am not. Well, only a bit. I am unsure, as I often am.'

'OK then. Read it to me.'

This wasn't just a request or a suggestion. It sounded to her like a challenge.

'Well, this,' she waved it about, 'is just a paragraph taken from my closing remarks, which in themselves are quite brief. I speak – just a sentence – about youngsters being introduced to the great traditional hymns. Then I say: "As well as hymns that teach us to glorify the planet, and hymns that persuade us to have faith, there are hymns that suggest how we should behave towards others. Brotherly love, they call it. And brotherly love does not mean encouraging young people to become involved in lewdness. Oh yes, that's what I've heard recently. No names or pack drill, as they say in the army, but such lewdness has come to my notice recently; and if it occurs once more I shall go to the police."'

'Blimey. That's telling 'em. You sound like some old Catholic parish priest. But is it the right time and the right place?'

'I don't know, Wally. I still don't know. I've thought about nothing else recently.'

Wally glanced at his watch. 'Well, we have just two hours in which you can decide. Think carefully about it. Meanwhile, I'll make some tea. I've brought some nice cake from the Co-op.'

As Wally carried out his task, complete with pinafore, he thought about Miriam's attempt at retribution. He wasn't keen on it, personally, much preferring the remedy practised during his scouting days. 'She'd have kittens if she knew what I have in mind,' he muttered.

He went back into the room bearing a full tray and still wearing the pinafore.

She burst out laughing. 'Is that a waitress I see before me, or a Yorkshire puff?'

Miriam went to wash her hands while Wally set out the food, cutlery and crockery. The meal consisted of cream cheese on toast, angel cake and fresh fruit. As they ate they chatted about Miriam's hymnology production, then this topic found its way to Julius Grimshaw.

'He didn't have much of a start in life,' she said. 'So it isn't surprising he's become odd, as an adult.'

'Well, I know he's odd,' Wally agreed, 'but how do you know about his earlier life?'

'First of all, I booted up the computer and got online to the council where he works. Then I switched to Luton where his family originate from. I have already spoken to Big Bill in the Co-op who knew his family years ago. The upshot is, Grimshaw's father was placed in detention for mistreating children. What that mistreatment was I don't know. But, as a youngster Julius wasn't shown a good example.'

Wally mentioned about Grimshaw shooting pigeons in the wood, and his reluctance to talk to the Prescott family. Then Miriam, going awry, mentioned the various groups who had agreed to attend the hymn singing.

'Some of these new hymns are quite good,' she said, 'and I'm sure they'll become popular in time.' Further details were cut short as the phone rang and she answered it.

Wally heard mumbling then he heard, 'Oh no.' Then silence, as talking came from the caller. Now Miriam spoke again. Within a minute she was back in the room. 'That was Grimshaw. His car has conked out. He can't attend... so – and I'm dreadfully sorry about this – I told him I'd send a taxi.'

Wally shrugged. 'That'll cost you a few bob.'

'You're the taxi driver.'

'Ah, I can see why you said "sorry".' He shook his head in facetious resignation. 'Can you supply a taxi driver's cap with the job?'

For the very first time she went to him and placed her arms about him. The first thing he noticed was the fragrance of her perfume. 'You're a darling, Walter Watson.'

Wally was less amiable with women than most folk realised, so her action took him by surprise. Nevertheless he clung onto her encircling arms before she sat down at the table again.

'I'm so grateful to you for obliging me, Wally. I so much feel I have to, er...'

'Reprimand him?' he suggested.

'I have to. He's a right...'

'Bastard is the word you're obliged to avoid.'

After the meal they left the vicarage and walked to the Diving Duck just a few yards along the road. Then, after arranging the chairs in the band room, situated over the bar, Wally would double back and shunt Miriam's car out of the garage. Periodically he thought about how she had shown her gratitude by all but smothering him in her arms. In a word, he felt chuffed.

But the opportunity to carry out his penalty tactic on the scumbag Grimshaw had fallen into his lap. He would deal with him on his return trip as taxi driver.

First he went to his bike bag and retrieved his technician's holdall. In this were handcuffs, a can of creosote, a new, large paint brush, a balaclava with two holes in the back – this he wouldn't be using now, since he was a 'taxi driver'. He doubted Grimshaw would report him for what would be, to all intents and purposes, a physical assault; anyway, he believed the culprit would be too stupefied to know what day it was. To this end he tapped his top pocket to check the drugs were there. He carried the paraphernalia to the car and placed it in the boot.

Then he drove off. Miriam had told him to collect the passenger at The Sanctuary.

The journey took some fifteen minutes. He approached the venue via the straight road leading to The Sanctuary and reduced his speed, which meant he recognised young Harry Prescott walking along with an adult male whom he believed to be his dad. They were eating chips. Slightly further along he met mother and daughter ambling homewards. For some reason – and he could never say why – he pulled up and called to them.

'You seem to be enjoying them chips.'

They came towards the car. 'Help yourself,' said Lily, offering him the bag. He dipped in and took two. 'How's things?' he asked.

'Fine,' said Ma Prescott. 'On the way back from the chippy, we called at The Sanctuary, 'cos it were lit up. We wanted to thank the Pastor for gerrin' us a house. But he didn't answer. We know he was in. All the lights were lit up.'

'I shouldn't worry,' Wally said. 'You eat your supper and enjoy yourself.'

'Ta-ra,' she called, and belched as she moved off.

'Mam! Manners!'

'Better out than in.'

And Wally pulled away. He drove the remaining 200 yards and arrived at The Sanctuary. It looked even more poverty stricken in the dusk than it did in daylight. The Pastor's car was shunted to one side as though abandoned. Wally pulled up just inside the chapel boundary, climbed out and tried the side door entrance. Unexpectedly the door opened and Wally walked through. The last time he had entered the room, he'd done so from the rear, wearing a balaclava. Now he went in like an accustomed visitor. The place was eerily quiet. Nothing stirred, but a smell lingered, a stink he had choked over several times in the distant past.

He noticed the partition he'd seen last time and looked over the top.

Grimshaw lay on the floor, propped up by the wall. The barrel of his shotgun was still lodged in his mouth and a large hole gaped in the top of his head where he had blasted out his brains.

TWENTY-THREE

Wally Watson took out his mobile and dialled 999.
'Police, please. And this is urgent.'

Within seconds he was connected to Sergeant Forester. 'There's been an obvious suicide here, Sergeant.' Very accurately and without meandering, Wally gave details of his macabre discovery, explaining who the fatally injured person was, and agreed to stay where he was until the police arrived. Next, he pocketed his mobile and gazed round the room, which was much smaller and now grimmer than he had originally believed it to be.

Glancing about the place, he again noticed the old-fashioned painting of the angels and cherubs was still hanging on the wall. He thought he had smashed that. But at the time he was so angry with the situation, he couldn't think properly. He walked over and studied it. All the figures were naked; it was obviously this aspect that had given Grimshaw his kicks and caused him to bring the picture to life, as it were, by including a young, naked child. Wally shook his head in bewildered commiseration. In the army, Wally had met all kinds of individuals, some real loonies, but none quite so deluded as Grimshaw.

Now, studying the painting rather than glancing at it, he noticed that the bottom section was embellished with trees, but painted grey and white, rather than green and brown – vague trees, unearthly. Then he experienced the slightest element of unease, for curling round the lowest part of one tree, the bole of the tree trunk, was a snake. Was this supposed to be Satan? The artist had gone to a great deal of trouble to give the reptile a horrible facial expression, looking up ravenously at the cherubs. Did this represent the state of Grimshaw's mind? After all, he also had an ugly face and eyes that were out of alignment.

Wally pondered this: had people felt sorry for Grimshaw and been overly considerate towards him? Another thought entered Wally's mind: was Grimshaw married?

His mobile rang. 'Hello. Yes, I'm still here, Miriam. But there's a problem. No. Listen, I'll tell you all about it when I arrive. Grimshaw won't be coming. NO,' he almost shouted, 'I have done nothing wrong. I just carried out the job you asked me to do. You won't be able read out the reprimand you had hoped to do. So scrub it. And make a success of the main reason for your concert. OK. See you later.'

He heard what was certainly a police car pull into the small car park, and seconds later Forester and Constable Close came into the room. Wally explained why he had called at the little chapel, 'Which is called The Sanctuary, by the way.' Naturally, he said nothing about his earlier visit, neither did he mention young Harry Prescott or his family. And after ten minutes or so, the police allowed him to leave.

When Wally arrived back at St Aidan's church vicarage, the first thing he did was to remove the berating material from the car boot and replace it in his bike bag. He thought about the method of castigation he had intended to deal out on Julius, who was in effect his boss on the local council. And then touched his top pocket to feel the presence of the drug he'd intended to administer to Grimshaw.

'If she'd known about all this,' he muttered to himself, 'I'd be out of my new lodgings like the full throttle of a greasy turd.'

After he'd parked the car in the garage and hidden his felonious equipment, he walked round to the Diving Duck where the hymnology concert was coming to a close. Miriam had given her brief talk about the hymns, minus the passage intended for Grimshaw. Everyone, every drinker at any rate, hung around for liquid refreshment; brass players are noted for quenching a thirst after a concert – unless they play for the Salvation Army. All this time, Wally had refused to give an explanation for his absence.

Suddenly, everyone had gone, and Miriam and Wally went home.

Miriam sat him down in an easy chair. 'Well, what happened?'

'I'll come straight to the point. Grimshaw is dead. He shot himself.'

This information – blunt, unexpected – was like a blow below the belt. She sat down in an armchair, panting, as though she'd just run a marathon.

Wally sprang up and went over to her. He put an arm round her. 'Miriam! Are you alright?'

She nodded. 'It's just the shock. I wasn't expecting that… He shot himself!' she repeated, a belated echo. 'And I was going to denounce him.'

'Well, you won't need to bother about that now. At least he'll never molest any other kids.'

She looked up quickly. 'Is that what he did then?'

Wally shrugged. 'Well, I'm not sure. But he was lingering in that direction.' He kissed the top of her head and pointed upwards. 'Any road, he's got his comeuppance now, one way or another.'

She looked across to her lodger, and said, quite quietly, 'Wally, will you marry me?' And the Reverend Miriam proposed marriage to Wally, just like Queen Victoria proposed marriage to Albert.

For the second time that evening, Wally experienced a bolt from the blue, but this time the bolt was more like a bolster, a cushion, in fact, a cushion plump with love.

TWENTY-FOUR

Wally was stunned, as the vast majority of men would be. Here was a tall, attractive young woman, and she'd just proposed to him. He thought of several squaddies he had known and how they would envy his situation. He was obviously desired, but didn't believe he was up to it. He felt out of his depth, not good enough – and yet he wanted to be.

'Well? Lost your tongue?' she said.

'I reckon I have. It's just the surprise. The, er, stupi-whatsit.'

'Stupefaction… Once again, are you going to answer?'

'Yes. I mean, yes I'm going to answer and yes I'd love to marry you.'

He stood up. Though Miriam was tall, Wally stood several inches taller.

'And this occurrence is not for the tap room.'

'Right. More the bedroom, I'd say.'

'You appear to have a problem.' She looked up into his face, shaved quite close, as though for the occasion.

'Well, I don't feel good enough. I mean... you're a vicar.'

'Ah, you've noticed. If that bothers you, I can give it up. Vicars have feelings, you know. I've thought about you for some time, Wally. I fell in love with you some time ago. Do you think I want to marry you for your money?'

'Yes. I reckon you do. And if you find any, just let me know.' He then took her in his arms and kissed her. It was a long passionate kiss and when they broke apart she said, 'I've watched you solve problems for other people and I myself have experienced your help. Added to which, you're not a bad-looking old bugger.'

'Hey, vicars shouldn't say that.'

'That's why I said it, because I shouldn't. There are a lot of cretins in this job, you know.'

'Aye, I can believe that. Any road, where do we go from here?'

'Well, you now have a room here. You're the only one who answered my advert. That was part of my plan. But you're such a slow coach.'

'Ah! Well now I've got the green light, I'll speed up a bit.' And he kissed her again and this time stroked her bum.

She didn't resist his fondling, and this in itself gave him a thrill – that he was actually caressing the local vicar. They were still standing, and he brought a hand to the front and slid it gently between her thighs.

She pulled away. 'I fervently hope there'll be lots of that, Mr Watson, but meanwhile let's try to be practical.'

Although he had a hard-on, he knew what she said made sense. 'Right. We've both had a busy day in different ways, so I'll make a nightcap, Irish coffee, no less, and we'll talk tomorrow.'

The following day Miriam went to see Father Byrne, the well-respected Roman Catholic priest in Daisy Hill, and told him the news.

'So because I want to be married in my own church, Father, I'd like you to officiate at the ceremony.'

'I would be delighted, my dear. When do you propose to get married?'

'In three months' time.'

The priest wrote it in his personal diary. Then indulged in the main event of the day by insisting they celebrate the forthcoming occasion by enjoying a noggin of Irish whiskey, even though it was not yet 10am. 'How will you have the banns read out?' he asked.

'I shall ask the lay reader from my church to do it, on the first Sunday in the month beginning tomorrow.'

And in that manner, she began the necessary arrangements for her 'big day'.

Wally was also busy recruiting. The first person he contacted was Richard Coningsby from Upsy-Daisy. Dick was flabbergasted. 'You crafty old bugger. You kept that quiet. Yes, I'll be delighted to be your best man. You've heard about Grimshaw, I suppose? Bang goes our council house.'

Wally nodded. 'Summat else will turn up,' Wally assured him.

When Big Bill, the Co-op manager, heard about the unexpected betrothal, he immediately offered the brass band as a wedding present.

'I'm not sure there'd be enough room round the dining table for them all,' Wally said.

The wedding was the talk of the three villages. Invitations were sent to all and sundry.

They visited Miriam's sole relative, her father, Bryn. Miriam's mother died while she was still in the army. In the same year, her soldier boyfriend was killed in action. This double blow reduced her to perpetual torment. It was this experience that caused her to leave the army and seek solace by becoming a vicar, which partly succeeded in healing her mental state. Miriam's total recovery occurred when she became associated with Wally: Walter Watson.

Miriam had prompted Wally to say, 'I've come to ask for your daughter's hand in marriage,' and he'd joked that he wanted the legs as well. It was considered a rather old-fashioned request these days, but was a petition Miriam had set her heart on.

Her father, Bryn, having welcomed Wally warmly, had replied, 'All I ask is that you treat her well, and look after her, because this daughter of mine has had a very rough passage.'

The three of them walked round Winchester, went to the theatre and visited the cathedral, where Bryn was a professional chorister. Wally believed it was this aesthetic association itself that had persuaded Miriam to train for the Church of England. Bryn gave them his blessing before they left for home and promised to buy a new suit to give his daughter away.

Their next venture was a trip 'up North' to visit Wally's kindred, a completely different enterprise. Wally took three days' leave from his council job and Miriam made arrangements to be absent from church commitments, and they drove to Yorkshire. After five hours' leisurely driving, the Vicar found herself in rough moorland, west of Sheffield.

Miriam was greeted affectionately by Wally's parents, who, like their son, were tall and benevolent, an obvious family trait.

'This is my ma, Dorothy. Ma, this is Miriam, who on Sundays is the vicar.'

'You'll have to push him, if you want any jobs done,' Dorothy said.

Miriam disagreed but kept her counsel.

'This is the only dad I have, so he'll have to do. Dad, meet Miriam.' Introductions were without formalities but warm, like hay on the pasture. 'Dad can be referred to as "Hoy" or "Clem", and around these parts, clem means to starve yourself.'

'Pleased to meet you, Clem.'

'Keep your collections locked up, love,' he responded.

Late Saturday afternoon, all four of them visited a newly opened Bettys tea room, where they enjoyed traditional Yorkshire parkin.

Back home, Clements said, 'I presume we are invited to your wedding?' Where upon his wife poked him with a stiff finger.

'Only if you bring a pressie,' said Wally.

Miriam declined to go to church on Sunday, much to everyone's relief. On Monday the couple were shunted into Sheffield where the parents bought them a canteen of Sheffield cutlery.

'Now you'll allus have summat to pawn if you ever get stuck,' Clem assured them.

They returned to East Anglia on Tuesday morning, Miriam delighted with the family she was accepted into.

Miriam, like most prospective brides, wanted an elegant wedding. Elegance costs money; she had almost none. Her father, a card-carrying member of the set who invariably supplied the loot, had enough to keep himself solvent but little to spare. And Daughter would not embarrass him by mentioning it.

Furthermore, all her established female friends were well and truly married with children; and her recent female acquaintances were still in the army. She mentioned her problem to Wally.

'Well, most lassies will jump at being a bridesmaid, so we're not asking for summat unpleasant. They fancy wearing a nice frock, see.'

'And they expect – quite rightly – somebody else to pay for it, but dear Daddy doesn't have that sort of dosh.'

'Now, bridesmaids don't have to be clever, do they?'

She frowned, wondering where Wally was leading. 'Er, no… I suppose not.'

'But, they have to look attractive.'

This, she was uncertain about. 'Well, let's say presentable.'

He chuckled. 'But not as presentable as the bride!'

'Well, it is her day.'

'Right! Leave it with me then.'

She did, she hadn't much option, but she remained puzzled.

Wally then went to clip the privets near to the Co-op, knowing that the manager, Big Bill, kept an established and near sacred dinner hour. No one dare impose upon that sacrosanct period. Wally clipped and waited, waited and clipped. And no sooner had the manager left his emporium, the wily gardener entered and commandeered a counter. 'Afternoon, girls. Busy?'

'Not if we can dodge it,' Iona said.

'But we've always time for you, Mr Watson,' Mona added.

'Great 'cause I've something you will like.'

'Ooo, Wally, we've waited ages for this,' Shona claimed. 'What is it?'

'I need three lovely ladies, dolled up to the nines.'

Like a pop trio they sang, 'That's us.'

'Right, now, whenever you lovely lassies go gallivanting, you're always snazzy with it.'

The chicks had come together and they shared uncertain glances.

'When you were on the coach trip, you looked a million dollars. When you graced the annual dance, you lit up the room. I'd like a repeat performance.'

This was the language they loved. 'Oh, where?' tweeted Iona.

'Bridesmaids,' he breathed. 'Could you get wrapped up in that?'

Wally's words were magic. Like Christmas candles their eyes lit up: blue, green, hazel.

Iona, Mona, Shona: three sets of smiling peepers.

'Bridesmaids,' echoed Shona.

'And you want us?' said Mona.

'It's the Vicar's wedding, innit?' queried Iona.

'Right, on all three counts. Can you help out?'

'You couldn't stop us, now,' swaggered one confident voice.

'Three identical dresses?' he pleaded.

'Easy peasy,' muttered another.

'But can you keep shtum about it?' questioned Mona.

Wally nodded.

'We'll provide the flowers too,' Shona said. 'We have low-cost contacts.'

'Brilliant.' Wally was over the moon now. 'And one of you might catch the bouquet.

And at that point, the manager returned, the girls went back to work and Wally made himself scarce.

❦

News of the forthcoming wedding inspired all manner of folk to show their appreciation for the Reverend Miriam Peach. Since her arrival she had been a popular priest; and Wally, too, was noted as a villager who would lend a hand in an emergency or a day-to-day situation, often adding some light banter. Consequently, the pleasant attributes of the betrothed encouraged many villagers of the three Daisy villages to offer gifts, some of which were precious to the giver.

Major Merryweather presented them with a highly polished campaign medal. Professor Septimus Jack Sparrow gave them a book token for £30 which he'd recently received from a well-wisher. And Mrs Marks, known for refusing credit (No Tick The Clock Has Stopped), vowed to allow the betrothed deferred payment during their first year of marriage for any item bought in her shop. Big Bill, in his blurred capacity as chairman of the Daisy Hill Brass Band, urged the ensemble to offer their complimentary and collective services to the Vicar during the wedding breakfast. Bill had already insisted that Miriam should accept, as a small gift, the use of the Co-op hall for their after-wedding venue, which was skin off nobody's nose, as nobody owned the Co-op hall.

During one of his many trips to Upsy-Daisy to speak with Richard on best man business, Wally chanced upon David, of Dave and Dreen distinction, and Wally recalled Dave's ability at versification.

'Ah, just the gent I'm looking for,' he fibbed. 'I'll be despatching invites shortly about my wedding day. I insisted on inviting the best-looking couple in the district.'

'I'm flattered,' said Dave, accepting the patter courteously.

'And I was wondering if you could cobble together some light-hearted banter, to keep the natives quiet?'

Again, Dave said, 'I'm flattered. Can't guarantee it, but I'll try.'

Nothing quite like it had happened within the three villages for many a year, indeed longer if you included the war and the time the rickety ale wagon, with its plodding horse, dislodged two barrels of bitter beer, and everyone got merry. The big day went off with the proverbial bang, when one of the taxis pulled up at the church with two punctures. Chalkie White – who, between shifts as a railway signalman, worked in the local garage – rescued the situation. Donning one of Wally's large overalls, and to much applause, Chalkie repaired both punctures in record time and sent the taxi on to its next passenger.

Young Charlie Wrigley, at Miriam's request, sang 'Ave Maria'. By the time he'd finished there wasn't a dry eye in the church.

Later, in the church driveway, scores of photos were taken. On the high wall to the church entrance, a peacock claimed attention by preening itself. Miss Primm, recently returned from America, stared at the beautiful creature, and gesticulated with both hands. At that same moment, the bride was encouraged to fling the bouquet over her shoulder and it arrived into the outstretched arms of Miss Primm. She promptly fainted, to be recovered by brandy... and Iona, Mona and Shona sulked until teatime.

The meal was a triumph. Even strangers dined. Anything drinkable was swallowed, everything edible was consumed. Locusts couldn't have done better. Then the best man did his best. Banter was buttoned and cackle was cut and Richard began his speech.

He spoke about Walter being the unpaid factotum of Upsy-Daisy. He stated that Miriam was the most popular priest the Daisy District had ever had. He praised the bridesmaids and thanked 'Dreen' as maid of honour. Then he started on his jokes.

'I know a young lady who was about to get married and wanted to look her very best. So she went shopping for a new bra, a brassiere, something really tip-top. She went into the lingerie department of a posh store and made her requirement known to the sophisticated assistant.

"Well, modom, we have Roman Catholic bras, Salvation Army bras and Synod bras."

'The customer asked her to explain.

"Well, modom, the Roman Catholic bra holds masses. But the Salvation Army bra is most uplifting."

'The customer interrupted. "But what about me? What do you suggest for me?"

'The assistant looked at her from top to bottom, side to side and back to front.

"For modom I suggest the Synod bra, because the Synod bra can make mountains out of molehills."'

From then on, Richard's jokes became raunchier and bawdier, until Big Bill, sitting behind him, suggested that the band was ready to play and the guests were willing to dance. Daisy Hill Brass Band trooped on stage and played a slow, old-fashioned waltz: 'Now is the Hour (when we must say goodbye)'. And to tremendous applause, the bride and groom took to the floor and danced in the middle of the room. After the guests had jostled round the Co-op hall, the band had a break and Richard introduced a soloist, a singer with an excellent voice: Miriam's father, the cathedral chorister. He sang an old English ballad – 'Love Could I Only Tell Thee' – a superb song with fine lyrics and a tune most melodic.

'How old is your dad?' Wally asked.

'Fifty-nine.'

'He has a brilliant voice.'

'You have to have to sing a song of that quality.'

Miriam decided it was time to change into an informal dress, and with Dreen as her dresser, she changed and slipped into a skimmer dress. When they returned, Richard was on stage again.

'Ladies and gentlemen and others who probably shouldn't be here. The Daisy District has its own poet. And what do you reckon, we have him here tonight. Please welcome Dave with his ditty.'

Dave, of Dave and Dreen, walked casually on stage. 'Instead of writing about marriage, women or brainless bridegrooms, I decided to knock something together about this band who, for our benefit, have been blowing their brains out all night. It's called, *An Ode to a Brass Band*:

Although we meet, intending to play,
We'd rather have a good chat
About local gossip, and as bandsmen say:
Is it possible not to play flat?
We've twenty-four players blowing on brass,
With dunces banging the drums;
Some play by ear – alack and alas,
And leave sight reading for those who are good at sums.
Rehearsals start between seven and eight,
If enough players turn up.
If they don't, we'll drink tea and debate
Our chances of winning a challenge cup.
Watch our conductor, a right pantomime,
Is he beating three four or six eight?
He doesn't just stand there beating the time,
He also beats the date.
The bass trombone needs plenty puff
To produce a tone rich and deep;
But if you can't hear him doing his stuff
It's because the blighter's gone to sleep.
To play cornet well, they sup various ales,
Tipsy fingers twiddling fast;
Then they splutter their scales like force forty gales,

'Cause nobody wants to be last.
An audience helps – if you get one;
It's critics who give you a fright.
But it's obvious why this lot have come,
There's nowt on the telly tonight.
Players often match instruments down to a "T",
Tenor horns being usually thin;
And fat folk blow the double "B",
But they all contribute to the din.
Notation can be complicated,
You play, reading dots – then you rest.
A big blow and you're asphyxiated,
So rests are what we do best.
Competitions are fixed – we all know that,
Adjudicators prefer the banjo.
But a few gin and tonics, some boot-licking chat,
And you might have a trophy to show.
Trombone players slither and slip,
Push pulling their well-oiled slide,
They're often well oiled, having taken a nip,
It's a wonder they don't collide.
So, if to a brass band you now aspire,
Learn an instrument before you're dead,
But for ease of the bone – if you quickly tire,
Join a church choir instead.'

Then the cake was cut and everybody cheered. Those who could find some wine finished it off. It was now eight o'clock; the evening had drawn to a close. The taxi arrived; the happy couple stepped inside. A wide ribbon had been fastened to the back of the taxi which proclaimed the traditional announcement: Just married. The driver knew his destination and was experienced in conveying newly married couples, so he remained silent and almost invisible, especially as the partition was closed.

'The words of that song keep going through my head,' Wally admitted. 'What a beautiful ballad.' And he said to Miriam, '*Love could I only tell thee how dear thou art to me.*'

ABOUT THE AUTHOR

For 40 years, Jack – singer and composer – was an entertainer. Consequently, his debut novel is amusing.

He has written and composed musicals. *Down the Hatch* was made into a commercial record.

For three years – like the residents of *Upsy-Daisy* – he lived in a caravan. He was a coal minor.